"Yo

"I knew who you were

favor Glynis. She wa

"You knew who I was?" Callie gasped.

"Yep. Been waiting a lot of years to see that face, but when I finally got my chance, I guess I acted like a coward. I couldn't tell you who I was. Didn't think you really wanted to know, but I kept coming here just to get a glimpse of you."

Callie's hands trembled and tears stung the back of her eyes. "You're the reason I came to Homestead with the kids. Glynis said you were probably dead, but I had to know for sure."

"How is Glynis?" her father finally asked.

Obviously Wade wanted Callie to be the one to tell her father the truth. Telling another person could jeopardize their safety, but when Callie looked into her father's eyes, she knew she could trust him. So she told him their story.

Dear Reader,

Welcome to Homestead, Texas. Never heard of it? Well, you're in for a treat. This is the third book in a series called HOME TO LOVELESS COUNTY. The books, about a fictional town in the Texas Hill Country, are written by Roxanne Rustand, K.N. Casper, Roz Denny Fox, Lynnette Kent and me. I had a great time brainstorming with these wonderful authors. Please don't miss any of these exciting stories!

To save the dying town of Homestead, the mayor comes up with a land giveaway program. New residents arrive weekly in search of a new beginning, a new life.

Callie Lambert was born in Homestead, and when she needs a safe hiding place, she returns to her roots as an applicant for the Home Free Program. But Callie is a fugitive. She's kidnapped her brother and sisters from an abusive stepfather. Now all she has to do is stay hidden until her case can be heard.

To do that she has to avoid the handsome sheriff, Wade Montgomery. But he keeps checking on Callie and the kids, and against her better judgment she's drawn to the tall, lanky Texan. What will Wade do when he discovers her secret? Turn the page and find out!

I hope you enjoy your visit to Homestead, Texas.

Warmly,

Linda Warren

It's always a pleasure to hear from readers.
You can e-mail me at Lw1508@aol.com or write me at
P.O. Box 5182, Bryan, TX 77805 or visit my Web site at
www.lindawarren.net or www.superauthors.com.
Your letters will be answered.

ALL ROADS
LEAD TO TEXAS
Linda Warren

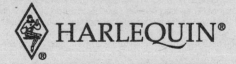

HARLEQUIN®

TORONTO • NEW YORK • LONDON
AMSTERDAM • PARIS • SYDNEY • HAMBURG
STOCKHOLM • ATHENS • TOKYO • MILAN • MADRID
PRAGUE • WARSAW • BUDAPEST • AUCKLAND

ISBN 0-373-71314-2

ALL ROADS LEAD TO TEXAS

www.eHarlequin.com

Printed in U.S.A.

Books by Linda Warren

HARLEQUIN SUPERROMANCE

To the other authors of the
HOME TO LOVELESS COUNTY series,
Roxanne Rustand, K.N. Casper, Roz Denny Fox
and Lynnette Kent. It was a privilege and a joy to work
with you, even during those times of panic. Thanks for
making the newbie feel right at home. And to our editors,
Paula Eykelhof, Laura Shin, Kathleen Scheibling and
Victoria Curran, for keeping us focused and on track.

ACKNOWLEDGMENTS

Mitch Siegert, executive chef, thanks for answering all my
questions so patiently. Wayne Landry, thanks for sharing your
colorful friends with me. Ladies in my aqua therapy group,
thanks for your encouragement and support on this book.

CHAPTER ONE

SHAFTS OF LIGHT pierced the darkness, illuminating a stretch of foggy grayness. Callie Lambert drove on and on, putting miles behind her. Up ahead loomed the unknown, the unfamiliar. Her hands clasped the steering wheel with a death-like grip and her stomach roiled with the enormity of her actions. She was on the run. A fugitive. She'd kidnapped her brother and sisters and could be arrested at any minute.

Those facts kept her focused, cautious and half-crazed with fear. What if she was caught? The kids would be returned to their abusive stepfather. And Callie would go to jail.

She wasn't worried about herself. It was the kids. She was their big sister and she'd do anything, go through anything, to protect them. But tangible fear throbbed at the back of her mind like a persistent toothache as she waited for the wail of a siren.

Raindrops splattered the windshield and she turned on the wipers. Their hypnotic action calmed her nerves and steadied her resolve. She thought of her mother and anger stirred in her breast. How could Glynis do this to them?

The past swept through her mind with each swish of the wipers. Glynis had left Callie's father when Callie was barely five and had become a waitress in a hotel restaurant in Houston. She'd struggled to make ends meet. Then Glynis met John Lambert, a wealthy stockbroker, and their lives changed for the better. John was twenty years older than Glynis, but

Callie liked him. When Callie was twelve, Glynis married John and they moved from Houston to New York City. John adopted Callie and life was better than she'd ever known.

She was always his oldest child. John never made a distinction between Callie and his own children and she loved him all the more for that. A year ago, he was diagnosed with colon cancer and it was a sad time for all of them. During the last month of his life, he had nurses around the clock, but Glynis only left his bedside to sleep.

After his death, Glynis decided to take a cruise for a much-needed rest and Callie gladly offered to care for her young siblings. It was a shock when Glynis returned home with a brand-new husband, Nigel Tremont, who was twelve years her junior. And it was an even greater shock when Glynis was killed in an auto accident three months later, leaving Nigel as sole guardian of the children and executor of her estate.

Despite the enveloping fog of grief and loss, Callie knew one thing for certain—Nigel was after her mother's money. He'd somehow convinced Glynis to change her will—whoever had custody of the children had control of the money. But how could she prove it?

Two months ago, Callie received a frantic call from her eleven-year-old half brother, Adam. He, nine-year-old Brittany and six-year-old Mary Beth were scared to death. Mary Beth had wet the bed and woken up crying, wanting Callie. Nigel had hit her with a belt and made her sleep in the soiled bed. When Nigel went to his room, Adam sneaked Mary Beth into his, then he called Callie from the den so Nigel wouldn't hear. She told him to lock Brit, Mary Beth and himself in the bathroom until she got there.

She met the police at her mother's home and to her horror, found they could do nothing. They said there was no evidence Nigel was abusing the kids and it was clear that the children needed time to adjust to their mother's death. The kids were so frightened they wouldn't say a word.

The police warned Nigel about hitting the children and said a complaint would be filed with Child Protective Services. This was standard procedure. Callie was asked to leave the house. She refused and was forcibly removed, even though Mary Beth was clinging to her. At that moment, she knew she'd have to fight to get them out of Nigel's clutches.

She'd immediately contacted an attorney and contested Glynis's will and guardianship of the children. The lawyer had said the procedure could take months, but Callie didn't have that much time. Each night, she got another desperate call. Nigel had slapped Adam. Brit was crying because Nigel had locked her in the closet for talking back. Mary Beth was wetting the bed and sleeping in it, afraid to say anything. Callie feared for their safety, for their peace of mind.

She had a friend from college, Miranda Wright, who was now mayor of Homestead, Texas, a dying small town in the Texas Hill Country. Miranda had told her that the city council had foreclosed on a large ranch and several old homes for unpaid back taxes. The land and homes were now being given away if applicants were approved by the Home Free Committee. The applicant had to live on the property for a year and make the necessary improvements and renovations, then it would be theirs. Families and children were encouraged to come to build the tax base—to save the schools and the town.

The plan intrigued Callie because she'd been born in Homestead, as had Glynis and Callie's father, Dale Collins. After her parent's divorce, Callie had never seen her father again. When she was older, she'd asked Glynis about him, and her mother had said that he'd probably died long ago since he was an alcoholic. Callie still wondered though. Maybe now she'd find out the truth about her father.

The town of Homestead had always held a mystique for her. She guessed it represented her childhood or safety, or life before things got complicated. She'd always wanted to go back. And now here she was at two in the morning headed toward Texas and hoping against everything that she wouldn't be caught.

She glanced back and saw Brit was asleep, her head sideways on a pillow—a purple pillow. Everything in Brit's life these days had to be purple. One hand clutched a cowboy hat. She was going to Texas to ride a horse and become a cowgirl. Callie was glad Brit saw this as an adventure.

Mary Beth was also asleep, leaning toward the window, her head on a Barbie pillow, her doll, Winifred, better known as Miss Winnie, held tight against her. This was hardest on Mary Beth. She wanted her mother and Callie's anger mounted at Glynis's insensitivity. How could she leave her precious children in the hands of a man like Nigel Tremont?

It was now her responsibility to do what was best for her brother and sisters. Callie could only pray and hope they'd find some peace while she waited for her case to be heard.

Callie had invented a new identity and had applied for one of the free homes in Homestead. When she'd been approved, she'd taken money out of her savings, money that John had left her in trust until her twenty-fifth birthday, and opened a new account in Philadelphia. There was no way Nigel could find out about the account, and she could wire for the money once she reached Texas.

She was staggered by how easy it was to change your identity. Someone in the restaurant where she worked knew a guy, who knew a guy and with the right amount of money she could be anybody she wanted. So they were the Austins and Callie was the young mother of three. At twenty-eight, she was hoping she could pull that off. She was sure she'd aged ten years in the past month and for once in her life she was hoping it showed.

She'd given up her job as executive chef in a New York restaurant, her dream ever since she could remember, and they were headed for a new life, a new beginning far away from New York City—in Homestead, Texas.

Adam stirred in the passenger seat. He'd been dozing for a while but Callie knew he slept lightly, so afraid that they were going to be taken back to Nigel.

"You okay?" she asked, turning off the wipers. The light shower had stopped, leaving a stretch of wet highway.

He rubbed his eyes, gazing into the watery beam of the headlights. "Yes. Where are we?"

"Somewhere in Pennsylvania."

He jerked up straight. "You do have a map and a route planned, don't you?"

"Not exactly." She'd been in too big of a hurry to leave New York. She planned to buy a map once they were on the way.

Nigel had gone out for the evening, like he usually did, leaving the kids by themselves. The children used to have a nanny, but Nigel had fired her, saying the kids were too old for one. Once Nigel had left, Adam had called Callie and turned off the security system. He'd done this several times before so Callie could get into the house and see the kids. Nigel had denied her any visitation and he'd warned Adam about calling her. Adam was told he'd be severely punished if he even thought of contacting his sister. The phone was only to be used for emergencies.

Minutes after she'd arrived at her mother's home, they'd been on the road. Nigel wouldn't check in on the children. Adam said he never did. It wasn't in his nature to be paternal, especially after a night of drinking and partying. Once he'd sent them to bed, he expected his orders to be obeyed.

Callie was hoping tonight would be no different, so they'd have a head start of several hours.

"Callie…"

She patted his shoulder. "Don't worry, little brother. All roads lead to Texas."

"They do not."

To her, they did. "Trust me on this one. I'll get us there."

"Just drive carefully so a cop won't stop us."

Poor Adam. He'd taken on the role of older brother and protector at too early of an age. "I always drive carefully."

"You do not. I was with you twice when you got tickets."

"But that was Callie Lambert. Callie Austin is a diligent, cautious driver."

He was silent for a moment then said, "Sorry about Fred, but Mary Beth wouldn't leave without him."

Fred was Mary Beth's goldfish, a must-have after watching the movie *Finding Nemo*. Callie looked down at the goldfish bowl she'd managed to wedge into the console. Fred was the last thing she'd planned to pack, but she didn't have the heart to tell Mary Beth. She'd lost two parents in six months and Callie couldn't take anything else away from her.

"It's okay. I guess Fred wanted to go to Texas, too."

THE DAYS THAT FOLLOWED were very stressful. The constant vigilance was getting to Callie. She kept waiting for the sound of a siren and when she heard one in Virginia, she almost lost the Big Mac she'd just eaten. But the trooper sailed right by her, stopping the car ahead of them. It took an hour for her nerves to settle down.

The kids were also nervous. As they passed the stopped car, Mary Beth asked, "Are those people running away, too?"

Adam quickly turned in his seat to look at Mary Beth. "You

can't say things like that, especially in front of other people. They'll take us back to Nigel and—"

Callie touched his arm, stopping him. "Adam is trying to say we need to be careful what we say."

"I will. I sorry. I don't want to go back."

"It's okay, sweetie," Callie tried to reassure her.

"I want to sit in the front with you, Callie."

"At the next stop you can change seats with Adam."

"'Kay."

Callie's heart broke at what this was doing to them. Mary Beth was scared all the time. Hyperactive Brit couldn't sit still and chatted nonstop. Adam, quiet and pale, just stared straight ahead at the road in front of them. And they were only half-way to Texas.

Then Callie had another problem—she noticed Fred float-ing face-up. Poking him with her finger, she found he was dead. She made a mad dash into a Wal-Mart with the bowl in her arms, leaving Adam in charge and telling Mary Beth that Fred needed fresh water. It took several minutes, but she bought a new Fred and they continued on their journey.

In Arkansas, Fred died again and Callie realized that gold-fish did not travel well. Another Wal-Mart. Another fish. Cal-lie prayed she could get this one to Homestead. She was tempted to tell Mary Beth that Fred had gone to heaven, but they'd had too many of those discussions lately. Callie wasn't ready for another one.

THE JOURNEY WAS LONG. From the metropolis of New York to the farmlands of Pennsylvania, through the tobacco farms and timberlands of West Virginia and Virginia, to the Smoky Mountains of Tennessee—sometimes it looked as if they were in a tunnel, with sixty-foot pines on each side of the road—then they reached the Ozarks of Arkansas and soon the rolling plains of Texas. They'd made it! The kids shouted with joy. Callie was happy, too. It had been three days and they hadn't been caught. And Fred was still alive. That was also reason to cheer.

She drove through the Dallas–Fort Worth area and took I-35 to Austin. She showed the kids the University of Texas where she'd gone to college. Somehow the beautiful hill country with its peaceful rolling hills, brilliant live oaks and craggy ledges made her feel at home. It was early June so the heat of the summer hadn't dulled the landscape. Even the air was invigorating.

"That's where I want to go to college," Brit stated.

"We're going to Harvard, just like Daddy planned," Adam was quick to correct her.

"Oh. I forgot."

John had started planning the children's futures as soon as they were born. They would attend the same private school in New York John had as a boy. The school was known for its academic excellence. Then they would apply to Harvard, as he had. He'd wanted them to have the best education possible.

On his deathbed, Callie had promised to do everything she could to see that his wishes were fulfilled. No matter what happened, she had to keep her word.

She headed toward San Antonio, turned off the interstate and took the state highway to Homestead. When they saw the city-limit sign, they cheered again. The sign read Population 2,504, but Miranda had told her that about fifteen hundred people now lived in the small town—the reason Miranda and the city council had come up with a plan to repopulate the area.

Callie went through a drill, making sure they knew their roles.

"What's our last name?"

Adam and Brit remained quiet, waiting for Mary Beth to

reply first. "Austin," she shouted. "My name is Mary Beth Austin and I'm from Chicago, Illinois, 'cause that's where my nana lived. I know that."

Callie had chosen Austin because it would be easy for them to remember—Callie had gone to school there. And Chicago because John's mother had lived there before she'd died two years ago.

"My name is Brittany Austin and I can't wait to ride a horse," Brit responded.

"Don't be stupid," Adam said. "We don't have a horse."

"Callie!" Brit wailed.

"We'll talk about the horse later. First we have to find our new home."

Callie knew it would be difficult for them to call her *mother* so they'd agreed they would just call her by her name. She would explain it the best way she could—being so young when Adam had been born, she'd allowed him to call her by her first name, and the other two children had followed his lead. Telling lies was becoming a habit.

There was a vegetable-and-fruit stand on the outskirts of town and a used car lot. It was time to stop for gas. Buddy's Gas and Auto Repair Shop was up ahead so she pulled in.

It was an old station, probably had been there for years, but the gas pumps were new. A wrecker parked to the side had Buddy's written across the door. An old wood fence separated the station from a junkyard. Through the broken and missing boards weeds grew wild and she could see rows of junked cars on the other side. A large building stood behind the station and Callie assumed this was the auto shop. Across from the pumps was a shiny Coke machine and a small office. Attached to the office was a double garage that had a car on a lift. A man was under it, looking up. To the right there was a small white frame house with a chain-link fence around it.

Callie got out and wrinkled her nose at the strong smell of gas, oil and rubber. The man walked toward her. He looked to be somewhere in his late forties or early fifties and he wore jeans, baseball cap and a chambray western shirt splattered with oil stains. He wiped his hands on a grease rag.

"Need help, ma'am?" His smile was friendly.

Callie was used to filling up her own car. She didn't think that kind of service was offered anymore.

"I just need some gas."

"Sure 'nuff." He jammed the rag in his back pocket and proceeded to remove the gas cap then stuck the nozzle into the tank.

"Can I get out, please?" Brit called.

"Yes," Callie said, thinking they probably needed to stretch their legs. They'd stayed at small motels and eaten take-out food in roadside parks so no one would recognize them. The rest of the time they'd been in the car.

They climbed out and stood by Callie. Brit plopped her hat on her head and tightened the string under her chin.

"You folks passin' through?" the man asked.

"No. We're here for the Home Free Program. I was approved for one of the houses."

"You don't say. Mighty good." He nodded. "We need more youngins in Homestead. I'm Buddy, by the way."

"I'm Callie Austin and these are my children, Adam, Brittany and Mary Beth." This was the first time she'd said those words out loud and she found it quite easy. "Nice to meet you, Buddy."

He looked at her blond hair pulled back in a ponytail with a colorful scrunchie and she could almost read his mind—too young to have three kids.

"Plumb nice to meet you, ma'am," he said, then glanced at the children. "Your youngins, too."

"Have you got a horse?" Brit asked, looking up at him, and Callie was relieved at the change of subject.

"Nope, little missy, but know lots of folk who do."

"I'm going to be a cowgirl."

"Mighty fine hat for a cowgirl."

The conversation stalled as a sheriff's car drove up to the station. Buddy withdrew the nozzle and replaced the cap. Callie's nerves tightened. She wanted to leave as fast as she could, but she had to pay for the gas. Glancing at the amount on the pump, she quickly dug in her purse.

"We better go," Adam whispered, nudging her.

Callie handed Buddy the money as a tall man got out of the car. He opened the back door of his vehicle and a black Lab bounded out and loped straight to Buddy.

Mary Beth, who was glued to Callie's side, came alive and moved in the direction of the dog. She loved animals.

"Buddy, I got a call from Mrs. Meyers. Rascal's chasing her chickens again."

Unable to resist, Callie glanced toward the strong, masculine voice. In khaki pants, a white shirt and cowboy boots, with a light-colored Stetson hat and a gun on his hip, the man in his mid-thirties moved with an easy swagger. She was sure she'd seen him in her dreams or fantasies at one time or another. He was like the Marlboro man and Brad Pitt rolled into a gorgeous package of Texas masculinity. She brought herself up short. She must be experiencing road lag. Or a mental block. The last thing she needed was to be attracted to the local sheriff. For that's what he was. It said so right there on his badge attached to the shirt that covered his very broad chest.

Buddy rubbed the dog's head. "He just likes to play, Wade."

"Try telling that to Mrs. Meyers. She said her chickens won't lay for a week now."

"I'll go over yonder and apologize."

"What's his name?" Mary Beth asked, patting the dog.

"Rascal," Buddy said. "Rascal's a bad dog."

"Better keep him penned up for a while or at least until Mrs. Meyers cools off."

"Sure 'nuff, Wade." He motioned toward Callie. "This is Callie Austin and her youngins. New arrivals for the Home Free Program."

"Howdy, ma'am. Wade Montgomery, sheriff of Loveless County." He tipped his hat and held out his hand. "Welcome to Homestead."

Callie had no choice. She took his hand—a hand that was strong and firm—probably like the man himself. Then she made the mistake of looking into his brown eyes and felt herself melting like butter on a hot grill. Heavens, he was handsome. And the sheriff. That little fact had her stepping back and taking control of her emotions.

"Thank you. We really have to go. It's been a long trip." She took Brit's arm, but Mary Beth was entranced with the dog and Callie knew it wasn't going to be easy to get her away from him.

"You have the Hellmuth house."

Callie glanced up. "Yes," she answered, wondering how he knew that.

As if he was clairvoyant, he added, "I'm on the Home Free Committee so I know about your situation."

Chills trickled down her spine and she resisted the urge to bite her nails. "My situation?"

"Yes. Your husband passing away and your desire for a fresh start in a small town to raise your children."

It took all of her effort not to show relief. Of course, he would have read her application—an application that was all lies. She had to concentrate on who she was supposed to be and not who she really was. And she definitely had to stop acting so guilty.

She put an arm around Brit and Adam. "We're looking forward to our new life."

He looked at her with a strange glint in his eyes. "I was surprised you applied for that house."

Did the man ever stop with the conversation? She wanted to leave, but she couldn't do that until the sheriff was satisfied. "Why?" she asked abruptly.

The good sheriff didn't seem to notice her annoyance. "Because it's very run-down and needs a lot of work. Miranda said she explained all that to you and you still wanted it."

"Yes." Her backbone stiffened. "I plan to fix it up."

"We had the gas, water and electricity turned on, but I'm not sure it's livable."

What business is it of yours? she wanted to ask, but bit her tongue. "We'll manage," she said instead.

"I'll just drive over there with you and make sure. Follow me."

"There's no…" Her words trailed away. The sheriff was already strolling to his car.

"Let's go," Callie said to the kids.

"Can we take Rascal?" Mary Beth asked, stroking the dog.

"Rascal belongs to Buddy," Callie reminded her.

"Oh." Mary Beth's bottom lip quivered.

"I'll bring him over to see you," Buddy said. "How's that?"

"'Kay." Mary Beth nodded and climbed into the Suburban. "Bye, Rascal. Bye, Buddy."

As they drove away, Adam whispered, "What are we going to do?" Fear was evident in his every word.

"For one thing, we're going to act normal and stop being so nervous and tensing at the sight of every police officer. We're here now and it's time to start our new life."

"But *he's* the sheriff," Adam stated, in case she wasn't aware of that.

"Relax, Adam. This is Homestead, Texas. No one has heard of us or even cares for that matter. We have a new beginning. Is everyone ready?" She held up her hand for a high five.

Reluctantly, Adam raised his hand and gave her a high five. "Ready," he said.

"Ready," Brit and Mary Beth chorused from the backseat.

"I want a horse," Brit said.

"I want a dog," Mary Beth added.

Adam turned to glare at his sisters. "Will you two grow up?"

"Shut up," Brit snapped back. "You're not our boss and I'm nine and I don't want to grow up just yet. So there, you big bully."

"You're stupid," Adam told her.

"You're stupider."

"Time out," Callie intervened. "Everybody quiet. Not one more word."

She didn't need them arguing right now. She had to keep her focus on the sheriff. As she took a ragged breath, she wondered if she was ever going to breathe normally again.

Following the sheriff's car toward the business district of Homestead, she hoped something would jog her memory from her childhood, but nothing looked familiar. The large yellow stone courthouse with granite columns was in the center of a town square shaded by big live oaks with drooping branches. Inviting benches were nestled beneath them. Several older men were sitting there chatting, whiling away the pleasant summer day.

Callie glanced up at the imposing clock tower and the scene triggered something in her mind, but for the life of her she didn't know what it was.

Soon her attention was diverted by the town itself. Many businesses were boarded up. The town had a deserted feel and she could see what Miranda was talking about. People were leaving, looking for better jobs, a better life. It was a sad scenario for a small town. Hence the Home Free Program—a way to bring people back.

Miranda knew that Callie didn't plan to stay forever, but she'd promised her a year and to fix up the house. Callie intended to do that. Her lawyer had told her it would probably take a year for her to gain custody of the children. At that time, a judge would decide if Callie would face any charges for abducting them. That part she didn't want to think about.

She turned from Main Street onto Bluebonnet and the feel of bygone days was very evident. There was no Gap or Starbucks, just a kolache shop, a hardware store, a general store called Tanner's and a dollar store that was the closest thing she saw to a clothing store. The storefronts looked old, but their bricks and mortar had stood the test of time. Their occupants had not.

A truck pulling a horse trailer was parked parallel at the hardware store, blocking traffic. The sheriff stopped to speak with the driver. A cowboy stepped out of the truck in worn boots and jeans.

"Look, Callie, there's a cowboy," Brit shouted. "Wow! He's got boots. I need boots. Can I get boots?"

"Me, too," Mary Beth chimed in.

"We'll see," Callie answered absently, her thoughts on other things.

She was glad when the sheriff got back in his car and continued on his way. When he stopped at the large three-story Victorian house, Callie caught her breath. It was exactly like she knew it would be. Of course, she'd seen a photo, but seeing it in person was so much better. The paint was peeling and a leaning pillar supported the first- and second-floor wraparound verandas. Some of the gingerbread trim was missing. The windows had cobwebs and weeds grew to the windowsills. The house was not in good shape. But she fell in love the moment she saw it.

Getting out, she waited as Wade strolled toward her, his badge glinting in the sunlight, reminding her of who he was. Her first thought was to run and to get as far away from Wade Montgomery as she could. He could end their new life as quickly as it had begun. She couldn't let that happen. No way was she letting the sheriff take her and the kids back.

She had to get rid of him.

CHAPTER TWO

WADE'S MIND KICKED into overdrive as he walked toward Callie Austin. She wasn't what he was expecting—something about her wasn't quite right. She was defensive, nervous and way too attractive, with blond flaxen hair, blue eyes and a nicely packaged body that had curves in all the right places. He was surprised he noticed that. After his son's death and his subsequent divorce, that part of his nature had taken a vacation. He wasn't sure whether to be happy or not that it was back.

Looking at Callie's blond beauty, he had a feeling she could be trouble— to his peace of mind. Something he'd fought very hard to achieve in the past four years.

"I called Miranda and she's on the way over," he told her as he reached her side. "The house is open so you can take a look around."

The kids tumbled out of the car.

"Thank you," she replied. "I'm sure you're a very busy man so I can handle it from here."

He lifted an eyebrow. "Are you trying to get rid of me?" God, she had the most beautiful eyes and he couldn't resist teasing her.

"Of course not. I just don't want to impose." He got a frosty reply for his efforts.

"Since I'm on the Home Free Committee, you're not imposing. Consider it part of my job."

"Okay, then." She gave in ungraciously and Wade wondered why she was so anxious for him to go. It was probably nothing—just his lawman's instincts. Callie was in a new town so she had a right to be apprehensive and cautious.

"It's gross," the boy remarked, staring at the house.

"Is it haunted?" the bigger girl with the cowboy hat asked in an eager voice.

"I want my mommy," the smaller girl cried, clutching a doll.

Callie pulled the child close to her side and he could see that all her defenses were out of love—like his had been for his son.

"Yes. The house needs work," Wade said, looking at the kids. They all had blue eyes and blond hair like their mother, except the younger girl's was a shade lighter. "And what are your names?"

Callie introduced them.

"Well, Brit, to my knowledge the house is not haunted."

"Oh." Her face fell in disappointment.

"But if you see a ghost, you call me and I'll come arrest him."

"Cool." She smiled, then quickly asked, "Do you have a horse?"

"Sure do. I live on a ranch with my dad and we have several horses."

"Do you let kids ride them?" She tapped her hat. "See, I got a hat."

"We better look at the house." Callie pulled Brit toward the walkway.

It didn't escape Wade's notice that Callie didn't want him talking to the children. That fueled his instincts further.

"We forgot Fred," Mary Beth cried and ran back to the car. Callie followed more slowly.

Wade was thinking dog. A goldfish was the last thing on his mind.

Callie carried a fishbowl in both arms.

Wade frowned. "You brought a goldfish from Chicago?"

"Yes," she answered in a clipped tone, almost daring him to ask anything else. She was the prickliest woman he'd ever met. And the most attractive. Not one more word was said about Fred.

They walked through the spot in the white picket fence where a gate used to be. Much of the fence now lay in the overgrown weeds, as did the gate. The walkway and steps to the house were made of brick. They stood on the veranda.

Two old rockers set there as if waiting for someone. Callie touched one, shifting the bowl in her arms. "These are beautiful."

"They've been here as long as I can remember," he said.

"I'm surprised someone hasn't stolen them."

"Try picking one up."

She handed the bowl to Adam and tried to lift a rocker. She staggered under the weight. "Oh, my goodness."

"Solid wood and steel. It would be hard for anyone to carry them away, but Homestead is a place where everybody knows everybody. If someone took them, I'd know in a matter of minutes where to go look. It's a close-knit town—not much crime here." He didn't tell her about some of the mischief the newcomers were experiencing. Little incidents that couldn't be explained.

"I'm glad they're here," she said, lovingly touching the rockers. "They go with the house." She had a faraway look in her eyes that Wade didn't understand, but he decided to let it go for now.

He pointed to the right. "Don't walk on that end of the porch. The pillar is rotted at the bottom and the floorboards are weak. And do not even think about going out onto the veranda upstairs." He looked at the kids. "Do you understand?"

"Yes, sir," Adam replied. "We won't go anywhere our mother tells us not to."

Wade took that as a backhanded reply. The boy was as defensive as his mother, and again his instincts told him something was wrong. He'd read through her application and everything checked out, but still…

He'd keep a close eye on the Austin family.

CALLIE COULD SENSE the sheriff's uncertainty, so she had to be very careful and not send up any red flags. How she wished Miranda had been here to meet them.

Wade opened the door and she noticed the beautiful beveled glass. "Is this the original door?"

"I believe it is. Frances Haase, the librarian and a member of the Home Free Committee, has all the information on the house. It was built in 1876 by Herman Hellmuth and it stayed in the Hellmuth family until about ten years ago. Agnes Hellmuth, a spinster, died and left it to the city and it's been sitting here in disrepair ever since. We put it in the Home Free Program hoping it would catch someone's eye."

He smiled a crooked smile and Callie felt her heart do a tap dance. "You found someone," she replied, and forced herself not to smile. "I love this old house."

"Then you're in for a treat. Some of the furniture is still inside. Miss Hellmuth gave away a lot of pieces to friends in her will, but a few items are still here."

As she stepped in, an eerie feeling came over her—the same feeling she'd had looking at the courthouse and touching the old rocker. It was as if she'd been here before…. It was possible she'd come here as a small child, but she didn't have time to ponder that thought as she took in the house.

The large entry had hardwood floors, as did the rest of the house. There were parlors to the left and right and a winding staircase curled to the top floors. The wood staircase showed off ornate craftsmanship and the mahogany crown molding around the ceilings reflected the same delicate work and was at least twelve inches wide. The woodwork alone was spectacular. She couldn't believe that no one wanted this piece of history.

Decorative inlaid tile made the fireplaces one-of-a-kind. The original brass wall sconces and chandeliers were still hanging. Two bedrooms were downstairs, as was a bath. The rooms contained beautiful beds with headboards that reached almost to the ceiling. Callie ran her hand over the exquisite wallpaper, a delicate pink floral print. It hadn't faded and she wondered how long it had been in the house.

"Is this the original wallpaper?" she asked.

"I suppose. The Hellmuths redid the house in the early fifties, installing plumbing and updating the wiring. I believe Frances said the paper was in such good shape that they kept it."

"It's absolutely beautiful."

In the dining room, one wall was decorated with a mural of a summer country scene, with oak trees, a pond, wildflowers and the Texas Hill Country in the distance.

"Oh, my." It was so beautiful she could only stare at it.

"That is gorgeous, isn't it?" Wade remarked. "That slight yellowing in spots is from eggs. Some teenagers broke in here and threw eggs around as a joke. You could paint over it if you wanted to."

She shook her head. "No way."

He smiled slightly, touching one of the dining room chairs. "This old set is still here. The chairs are wobbly and need some work, but they're usable."

The kitchen was a big mess. The cabinets were falling apart and all the appliances had been removed, leaving gaping holes. A large butcher block in the center of the room caught her eye. It was old and had been used a great deal, evident by the cuts in the wood.

Adam opened a cabinet door. "Look, Callie. What is this?"

As Adam said her name, a fleeting look of surprise crossed Wade's face. But he didn't question why her son had called her by her given name. A man of tact. She liked that. And against every sane thought in her head, she was beginning to like Wade Montgomery.

Focus. Focus. Focus.

She hurriedly inspected the cabinet. Inside was a tray and a rope that hung down.

"That's kind of like a dumbwaiter," Wade told them, standing close to her. Tangy aftershave wafted to her nostrils and she stepped back, feeling a little out of breath.

"The rope is on a pulley and when you pull the rope, it takes that tray to the second floor."

"Cool," Brit said. "Let's try it."

"I'm not sure it still works." Wade pulled the rope and the tray traveled upward. "Well, I'll be damned, it does."

"Let's go see where it went." Brit headed for the stairs with Adam behind her.

"Wait," Wade shouted. "Let me make sure those stairs are safe." He turned to Callie. "There's also a staircase off the kitchen."

The bare wood steps appeared rickety so they took the big staircase. Wade walked up first and they followed. Callie was glad for some distance. What was wrong with her? She was acting as if she'd never been around a man before. She worked with men and had had her share of dates, so what was making her so aware of this man? This Texas sheriff. That was it. Sheriff. Her sensory antenna should read: avoid at all costs. But the woman in her was getting another signal.

The kids darted off to find the tray and Callie took a moment to get her head straight and look around. Everything was coated with dust and there was a musty smell in the air. There were four bedrooms and another parlor that contained bits and pieces of old furniture. A magnificent claw-foot slipper tub occupied the bathroom. Grime and grit coated the surface. It would take a lot of scrubbing to remove, but it would be lovely to lie in and relax, and she intended to scrub until she had it sparkling. The third floor was an open attic cluttered with more old furniture and junk. They slowly made their way back to the main floor.

The house needed a lot of work, especially the kitchen, but Callie was optimistic about the project ahead of her. This was a good place to live.

A good place to hide.

Now it was time to get rid of the friendly sheriff. The signal this time was very clear.

Adam and Brit were trailing each other from room to room, but Mary Beth was attached to her side. They needed some privacy. She wrapped an arm around Mary Beth and looked at Wade.

"Thank you for showing us here. I really appreciate it, but..."

The phone on his belt rang and he reached for it saying, "Excuse me." Turning away, he spoke into the receiver. In a second, he turned back. "I've got to go. Miranda should be here any minute."

"Of course. Thank you."

Callie let out a long breath as he walked out of the house.

"I thought he'd never leave." Adam sighed.

"Is he gonna arrest us, Callie?" Mary Beth looked up at her.

Not if I can help it.

Callie stroked her hair. "No, baby. Now let's get settled into our new home."

"Fred doesn't like it here," Mary Beth said, leaning against her.

Adam had set the goldfish bowl on the floor and Fred

looked content. At least he was still swimming. Mary Beth always used Fred's name when she was upset.

"I don't like it either." Brit pulled off her hat. "It's spooky."

"And the house is dirty," Adam complained.

To Callie, the house was everything she'd been expecting. To the kids, it was just a strange place. They really wanted to be back in the brownstone with John and Glynis. She had to give them a sense of security. A sense of home.

"Time for a meeting." Callie sat on the floor and the kids flopped down beside her. "When we talked about this, I told you it would be a hardship. Did you not understand what that meant?"

Brit and Mary Beth had blank looks.

"I just didn't realize it would be like this." Adam scowled.

Callie decided to try from another angle. "Let's look at this like camping out. We've done that before."

"Yes," Adam mumbled.

"We have a roof over our heads, electricity and running water. There's two bedrooms downstairs with a bathroom. We can sleep there until I can get started on the renovations. And the beds are so beautiful. We'll feel like Cinderella sleeping in them."

"I want to be Cinderella." Mary Beth brightened.

"I don't," Brit said. "I want to be a cowgirl." She reached for her hat.

"You're so stupid," Adam taunted. "You're going to get us in trouble always asking about horses. We don't have a horse, stupid, so forget about being a cowgirl."

"You can't tell me what…"

All of a sudden everything came down on Callie. She buried her face in her hands and the room became very quiet. The kids were tense and fighting. The house needed so much work. Was she crazy for coming to Texas? There were so many other places she could have gone. Had she made the right choice?

"Callie," Adam whispered.

She raised her head.

"We're sorry." His face was lined with worry.

All three threw themselves at her and she held them tight. "I love you guys. That's why I'm doing this. I know this isn't the brownstone or the house in the Hamptons, but this is our home for now. So what's your decision? Stay or leave?" She was giving them a choice when there really wasn't one, but she could do no less. They had to be united or it wasn't going to work.

"I'm staying," Brit said.

"Me, too," Mary Beth added.

Adam looked around then stuck up his hand for a high five. "I'm in."

Callie gave him a high five as did Brit and Mary Beth.

"We're home."

"Anybody here?" a voice called from the front door.

They scrambled to their feet and met Miranda Wright, the mayor and the driving force behind the Home Free Program, at the door. She was tall and Callie always felt dwarfed by her height, but Miranda's warm, outgoing personality took away any awkwardness.

They'd met at the University of Texas, both business majors. The moment Miranda had said she was from Homestead, Callie had felt drawn to her, wanting to know all about the town she was born in. But most of all, she wanted to know about her father.

Not once, though, in all the times they'd talked, had Callie mentioned her father. She recognized that for what it was—a defense mechanism. Her father had signed over his rights to Glynis when Callie was five years old. As a child, she didn't quite understand what that meant, but as an adult she knew. Her father didn't want any connection to her. As a child that had hurt. As an adult it hurt even more.

She'd told Miranda that her family had moved away when she was five and Miranda hadn't pried into her family affairs.

So now here she was in Homestead and she could find out if her father was dead or alive. Callie had a lot of conflicting emotions about her father and it was time to sort through them. And she would not involve Miranda in that part of her life. Miranda had done enough for her.

Miranda and Callie hugged. "Glad you made it," Miranda said, looking at the children.

Callie introduced the kids again.

"And that's Fred," Mary Beth said, pointing to the fish.

"A very nice goldfish," Miranda commented.

"He wants to go home," Mary Beth whimpered.

Callie and Miranda exchanged glances.

Callie picked up Mary Beth, her heart breaking at the pain she was going through. "It's all right, sweetie. This is our home now."

"I know," Mary Beth mumbled into her shoulder. She rubbed her head against Callie and saw the dog squatted at Miranda's feet.

Mary Beth raised her head. "What's your dog's name?"

"Dusty." Miranda patted the yellow Lab mix.

"Can I pat her?"

"Sure."

Mary Beth slid to the floor, stroking Dusty, happy again.

"Has Wade given you a tour?" Miranda asked after a moment.

"Yes," Callie replied.

"I had Ethel Mae Stromiski clean out the two bedrooms and bath downstairs and they're livable until you decide about the renovations. Her son June Bug will be over to start work on the rotted column."

"June Bug?" Callie's eyebrow arched.

"Don't ask." Miranda smiled. "He's a very good carpenter and he'll be able to help with a lot of the work."

"Good."

"As we talked about, this is an old house and needs lots of work. Frances Haase, the librarian, has all the info on it if you're interested. I have all the paperwork at my office, so if you're ready we can go over there and you can sign all the necessary forms to become a part of the Home Free Program."

"Thank you, Miranda."

A message passed between them. Her secret was safe with Miranda. In return, Callie would live up to her end of the bargain.

But a lot could happen in a year and Callie fervently hoped that it was all for the best. She just had to stay hidden and keep from getting arrested.

That meant avoiding the local sheriff.

WADE WALKED INTO the Lone Wolf Bar and spotted his father, Jock Montgomery, immediately. He'd gotten a call that his father was causing trouble. Jock sat at a table with a bottle of scotch and an almost empty glass in front of him, hurling curse words at Herb, the bartender and owner. The bar was empty—evidently Jock had gotten rid of the rest of the customers.

"He came back here and got the bottle, Sheriff," Herb said. "I couldn't stop him."

Wade picked up the bottle and carried it to Herb. "I'll take care of this."

"Thanks, Sheriff."

Wade could see that Herb was nervous. He'd been here when Jock had been sheriff and knew that no one said no to

Jock Montgomery. His dad had done what he'd wanted in this small town. But not anymore.

"Let's go home, Pop."

Jock took the last swallow from the glass. "You call my son, Herb? You yellow-bellied bastard. In the old days that would have meant betrayal and I'd have thrown your ass in jail."

Herb didn't answer, just kept wiping the bar.

"Let's go home," Wade said again.

"I'm not ready. I want more whiskey." He slammed the glass several times against the table. "Herb, you sorry ass, bring me another drink."

Wade grabbed the glass out of his hand. "No more. You're drunk. Let's go."

"I can drive myself home," Jock scoffed, his words slurred.

"You're not driving drunk in my county."

"Hmmph. Used to be my county. I was sheriff here for over forty years—before you were born, so don't tell me what to do."

This was difficult for Wade, dealing with his father and his attitude. Rescuing him from drinking binges was becoming a common occurrence.

He caught Jock by the elbow and helped him to his feet. Jock tottered a bit, but he didn't resist or protest. Wade led him out the door.

"Thanks, Herb," he called over his shoulder.

"You bet."

He opened the door of his squad car and Jock got in without one word of complaint. His dad didn't have his cane so it must have been in his truck. Jock never used it when he was drinking. Taking the driver's side, Wade headed for Spring Creek Ranch.

"I'm not drunk," Jock said, staring at him through bloodshot eyes.

"I know, Pop." Wade didn't feel he needed to argue the point.

"All these new people in town make me mad as a fightin' rooster."

"I know." Wade knew that all too well and he didn't feel the need to argue that point either. They had many times to no avail. His dad was more stubborn than Mr. Worczak's mule.

Jock leaned his head back in his seat. "Had it all planned, son. Invest in the KC consortium and retire in luxury. With Zeb Ritter as foreman, what could go wrong?"

Whenever his father drank, he talked about the same thing. Jock and a few old rancher friends had formed a consortium and bought the old K Bar C Ranch when the owner had died and the heirs had run the ranch into bankruptcy. When the land came up for auction, Nate Cantrell had pulled together some of his friends, and with their life savings had bought the ranch. They'd made big plans, but those plans hadn't materialized and Jock had never gotten over it. Then Zeb had committed suicide and that was just another blow Jock couldn't handle without drinking. When Jock had been thrown from his horse and busted up his leg, he'd retired as sheriff. He'd gone downhill ever since. His father didn't care about life anymore.

"We didn't count on the drought and the bottom falling out of the cattle market. We didn't count on a lot of things." He rested his arm over his eyes. "Clint had a lot to do with everything in my opinion. He wanted that land, but we got it before he could and he made sure our venture didn't succeed. Can't prove it, but I know he's a yellow-livered snake and the reason the bank wouldn't renew our loan."

Clint Gallagher, a Texas senator, owned the big Four Aces ranch outside of Homestead. He'd been trying to buy the K Bar C for years. An aquifer that supplied a large percentage of water to the Four Aces ran beneath it. Clint wanted the water rights, but Jock and his friends bought the ranch before Clint found out about the auction. Clint was still angry over the deal. He and Jock had once been friends, but were now foes.

After the consortium had failed, Nate had gone to work for Clint and the rumor mill had had a field day. The investors suspected Nate had been in Clint's pocket the whole time and had sabotaged the consortium deal for Clint. The town had labeled him a two-timing, back-stabbing crook and had treated him as such. Then Nate had suddenly been killed in a freak auto accident and the townsfolk didn't lose any sleep over it. Small-town people with small-town minds.

When Nate's daughter, Kristin, had returned to Homestead on the Home Free Program, she'd kept searching and digging to clear her father's name. Her findings showed her father had gone to work for Clint because he'd needed a job. It was that simple. And the evidence proved Nate's accident wasn't an accident. He'd been murdered by Leland Haven, Clint's lawyer. Leland had been stealing from Clint for years and when Nate had found out, Leland had decided to get rid of him. Nate Cantrell's name had been cleared, but sometimes the old-timers, like his dad, seemed to forget that.

"Now Homestead is giving away the damn land. Never heard of such shenanigans. And a woman mayor. Never heard of that either—not in my kind of Texas."

"Miranda's doing a lot for Homestead," Wade felt a need to say.

"Hmmph."

"Take a look around you. Homestead was on the verge on becoming a ghost town. Now people are coming back. We have kids enrolling for school and that builds our tax base. That's good. Miranda had nothing to do with the failure of the consortium so cut her some slack."

"My grandson should be here," Jock muttered in a broken voice. "Our boy should be here." A tear rolled from his eye.

Wade's throat closed up and he didn't respond. He couldn't. It had happened four years ago but it felt like yesterday that he'd gotten a hysterical call from his wife, Kim, telling him their son had been rushed to the emergency room. But they'd been too late. Zach was dead.

At twelve, Zach had wanted to go to a party a friend from school was giving. Wade and Kim didn't know the boy all that well and they'd been hesitant. In the end, they had relented because Zach had wanted to go so badly. There had been drugs at the party and, after a lot of teasing and egging from the older boys, Zach had tried the stuff. He'd had an allergic reaction to the drug and had died thirty minutes later. Just like that, his young life was gone.

Wade and Kim had blamed each other, the boys at the party and the world in general. But placing blame didn't ease it or accomplish anything besides creating more guilt.

He and Kim had been high-school sweethearts and they'd become parents when they were seventeen. So young, but they'd thought their love would last forever. With their parent's help, they'd continued with their education and Kim had become a teacher and Wade a police detective in Houston. They'd been through so many trials, but they couldn't get through the death of their son. At least not together. Kim had moved to Phoenix to live with her sister and Wade had returned to Homestead.

His father had retired and Miranda had encouraged Wade to run for the job. He had and being here in the slow, easy pace of Homestead was helping the wounds to heal. Until his father said things like he just did. Then the blame and the guilt came back tenfold.

And the grief.

IN SILENCE, WADE CROSSED the cattle guard to Spring Creek Ranch. The property consisted of the house, the barns and five hundred acres. The rest of the land Jock had put into the consortium that had failed. The city now owned it and was giving away parcels to people willing to build on it and make their home in Homestead. That was a hard pill for Jock to swallow.

Board fences flanked the road that led to the three-bedroom brick house Jock had built for his wife, Lila. She'd died ten years ago and Jock's life had never been the same. He'd started to make bad decisions, bad choices.

As Wade drove to the back of the house, Poncho and Tex Alvarez came toward them, two Mexican brothers in their fifties who ran the ranch and watched out for Jock. They'd been here for thirty years and lived in the old home place below the hill. Tex's wife, Yolanda, helped out in the house.

"Wonder why he no come back from town," Tex said to Wade. Tex, a short, thin cowboy with a protruding beer belly, loved his beer and could ride a horse better than anyone Wade had ever seen. There wasn't anything he didn't know about cattle. Poncho, taller and heavier, had cowboying in his blood, too.

"He's had a little too much to drink at the Lone Wolf." Wade walked around to the passenger's side to help his father.

Jock stumbled out. "Don't need no damn help," he muttered.

Wade nodded to Poncho, who wrapped an arm around Jock's waist. "C'mon, Mr. Jock, that old sofa's just waitin' for ya."

They slowly made their way to the back door.

Yolanda held it open, frowning. Short and plump, she had a quick tongue and she and Jock often had days where they screamed at each other. Yo would swear she wasn't coming back, but in a couple of days she'd return to do the cleaning and cooking. "Lawdy, Mister Jock, ain't you got no sense?"

"Don't preach to me you sassy bitch."

Yo's black eyes flared. "You talk like that and I'll knock you out with a frying pan. It'll be swift and sure, not slow like that filthy stuff you drink."

"Yeah, yeah."

Yo grabbed his arm and Jock wobbled meekly into the den. Wade was grateful for small miracles, but when Jock was drunk he did more damage with his mouth than his fist. He'd have to do something about his father and soon. What? He wasn't quite sure.

"He went to town for a load of feed." Tex broke into his thoughts.

"His truck and the feed are at the Lone Wolf. You can ride with me and bring it back."

"Yes, sir."

"Pop, I'm going back to the office. Be back later." Wade knew that Tex and his family could handle Jock. He'd probably sleep until morning anyway, then they'd talk.

"Hmmph," was the only response he got.

Wade and Tex walked to his car. As Wade opened his door, he saw Lucky in the pasture, a buckskin mare that Jock had given to Zach on his tenth birthday. How Zack had loved to ride that horse. Wade felt a catch in his throat. No one had ridden her since his death. He thought of Brittany and her desire to ride a horse. Maybe it was time.

But could he stand to see another child on that horse?

CHAPTER THREE

CALLIE SIGNED THE NECESSARY papers and everything that had happened seemed real for the first time. She and the kids would be living in Homestead and hopefully Nigel would never find them, or at least not until her lawyer had procured a hearing.

Her main concern was sleeping arrangements for the night. Miranda wanted them to stay with her and her mom until the house was ready, but Callie couldn't intrude or involve Miranda any further in her situation. She had to make a home for the kids.

Miranda said the feed store carried sleeping bags, so after Callie unloaded the car she planned to go there. As she drove up to her house, she noticed an old tan truck parked in front. A rack was on the back with lumber. This had to be the carpenter—June Bug.

They got out and saw two men, somewhere in their thirties, inspecting the rotting column. One was tall and heavyset, the other short and wiry. The short one walked toward her with quick steps. He wore jeans, a T-shirt and a baseball cap that read Dallas Cowboys. As he reached her side, she realized he was shorter than her. He couldn't be more than five feet two inches tall.

"Howdy, ma'am. I'm June Bug Stromiski. Miss Miranda said you need some carpenter work done." He talked fast, not even taking a breath.

"Yes, I do. Thank you for coming." But for the life of her she couldn't figure out how this little man could repair her big house. He didn't seem to have enough strength to drive in a nail. But she shouldn't judge him. She needed his help and hopefully Miranda knew him well enough to be confident that he could do the job.

"This is my cousin, Bubba Joe Worczak. He's my helper."

Bubba looked like a lineman for the Dallas Cowboys and capable of doing anything. But after a bit of conversation, Callie realized that June Bug was the brains of the duo and Bubba Joe the brawn.

"Why they call you June Bug?" Brit asked.

June Bug shrugged. "That's a long story."

"'Cause he eats bugs, that's why," Bubba Joe spoke up.

"What!"

"That's right." Bubba Joe nodded.

"You do not," Adam said, always the skeptic.

Bubba Joe plucked a bug from the grass. "Show 'em, June Bug," he said.

June Bug popped it into his mouth and crunched away. Callie gasped and wanted to cover the kids eyes for some silly reason. They stood there with their mouths open, unable to speak.

"Tastes kind of like chicken," June Bug said in between munching. "If you have a real good imagination."

Callie found her voice. "Please don't do that in front of my children. Please don't do it at all. It's very unhealthy."

"Sorry, ma'am, I've been doing it since I was ten years old."

"Why?"

"I'm little. I've always been little and boys picked on me at school and I got beat up almost every day. They called me runt and things like that. Billy Clyde Hemphill was the worst. He'd hold my face down in the grass with his knee on the back of my neck until I couldn't breathe. He'd always say, 'Eat dirt, runt.' One day as he was coming toward me on the playground, I just got tired of it and knew I had to do something. I saw a june bug crawling on the playground equipment and I picked it up and put it in my mouth before I could think about it." He wheezed for a breath.

"Billy Clyde stopped in his tracks and the kids gathered round. I found another bug and ate it, then I handed one to Billy Clyde and told him it was his turn. He backed off saying I was crazy and the kids started calling him chicken. He ran away, but he never picked on me again. No one did. And that's the way I like it."

Callie just stared at him. "Why do you still eat them?"

Just then a truck drove by and someone hollered, "Hey, June Bug, what's for supper?"

"Anything flying," June Bug yelled back, and they heard laughter all the way to the stop sign.

Callie knew why he kept eating the bugs. It made him taller in his eyes, bigger and able to take on the town. But she refused to call him June Bug.

"What's your given name?"

"Odell, ma'am, youngest of ten kids and the only boy. I have nine sisters."

"I'll call you Odell."

"Only my mama and my sisters call me that."

"I'll still call you Odell." To her, calling him June Bug would be making fun of him and she couldn't do that.

"Yes, ma'am."

For the next thirty minutes he showed her what needed to be done to the column and veranda to secure it and she told him to go ahead with the work. They were unloading the car when an older lady jogged up in sweatpants, a T-shirt stretched over an ample bosom and sneakers. Her gray hair was curled in a tight perm.

"I'm Ethel Mae Stromiski," she introduced herself, wiping sweat from her forehead and gasping for air.

"Nice to meet you," Callie said, figuring this was Odell's mama.

"I cleaned up two bedrooms and the bath like Miranda asked me to." She talked fast just like her son, reminding Callie of the hum of a sewing machine. She listened close to catch each word.

"Thank you. I appreciate it."

"I'll be back tomorrow to do more cleaning."

"I —ah—"

"I got to jog this damn mile like the doctor told me to. He said if I want to keep living I need to exercise more. What I need is a damn cigarette. Odell, what time you coming home for supper?" She didn't even take a breath.

"I don't live with you anymore. I'll come home when I want to."

"Smart-ass," Ethel muttered to Callie and gulped a quick breath. "He built him a room in the back of my house and he calls that moving out. Kids always have to do somethin' different. What's wrong with living with your mama? You just better not be eating bugs again," she yelled to Odell. "Or I'll wash your mouth out with soap."

"Go home, Mama. I got work to do."

"Supper will be ready at six."

"I won't be there."

"Where you gonna eat?"

"Maybe I'll have a beer at the Lone Wolf. I don't know. It's my business."

"Kids—you give 'em your heart and they stomp on it. Now if he was meeting a woman at the Lone Wolf instead of Bubba Joe, I wouldn't mind. I gotta find that boy a woman." With that she jogged off down the street, panting.

"Is this a circus or what?" Adam asked.

"Be nice," Callie scolded, but she could feel herself wanting to laugh and she hadn't felt that way since her mother had died. She hadn't felt much of anything besides fear. Homestead was going to be good for them—a simple way of life with some interesting characters. Though she couldn't get too friendly with the townspeople. To guard their safety, she had to keep a low profile.

With all the luggage in the house, Callie decided that buying sleeping bags was the next order of business, but first she had to call her lawyer, Gail Baxter. She got her answering machine so she called her friend, Beth, in New York, for an update.

She'd bought the phone under the name of Amy Austin so if the FBI starting checking out her lawyer or her friend's phone, they couldn't trace it to Callie Lambert. She didn't want to use her first name—it might give her away. She'd had no problem getting the phone in that name.

Beth picked up on the second ring.

"Oh, Callie, I'm so glad you're okay. Just don't tell me where you are because I'm not good under pressure."

"Don't worry. I don't plan to. How are things there?"

"Not as much commotion as you'd think. The FBI is investigating and they questioned everyone here at the restaurant, but they were actually nice. I told them that if you took the kids then they were safe because Nigel was abusing them. They asked what kind of abuse and I told them all the things you'd told me and how worried you were."

"Did they believe you?"

"I suppose so because Nigel came into the restaurant and accused me of spreading lies about him. Someone called the police and they picked him up. One of the agents came in yesterday and said your lawyer had called and informed them that you had the kids and you weren't bringing them back until a hearing was set. He told me to call if I heard from you."

"I'm sorry you're caught in the middle of this."

"Don't worry. If I don't know anything, I can't tell them anything. Just take care of yourself and those kids."

Callie hung up hoping her lawyer could get something done. She could wait as long as the kids weren't with Nigel.

The kids were outside watching Odell and Bubba Joe work. She knew they were waiting for Odell to eat another bug. Oh yes, life was changing.

She grabbed her purse and saw the sheriff's car drive up. Wade got out and opened his trunk. Another officer was with him. Now what? She didn't need him showing up every few minutes. She laid down her purse and stormed outside. Wade strolled along the walkway with a sleeping bag in each hand. The other man also had two bags.

Wade set his on the porch. "Miranda said you planned to stay here so I thought you might need these."

"I was planning to buy them myself." She tried to quell her annoyance and couldn't. "I might look helpless, but I assure you, Sheriff, that I'm not. I can take care of my family."

Wade tipped back his hat. "No doubt in my mind about that, ma'am, but you're not in Chicago anymore. Around here we try to help each other, especially the newcomers. I'm sorry if you have a problem with that."

The kids came running, preventing her from further embarrassment. She was not only giving him a red flag, she was waving it in front of him. Why couldn't she keep her cool around him? And why did he have to be so damn handsome?

"Sleeping bags," Brit shouted. "Are they for us?"

Wade glanced at Callie for an answer.

She swallowed her pride. "Yes. The sheriff brought them for us."

"Cool," Brit said. "And look, there's a purple one. I get it."

The other man brought his bags forward and Wade introduced him. "This is Virgil Dunn, my deputy." Painfully thin, Virgil was average height and wore the same kind of clothes as Wade, except his were starched and ironed, noticeably so. And he wore a tie. It was obvious Virgil was proud of his job.

"Nice to meet you," Callie mumbled.

"Welcome to Homestead, ma'am." He nodded his head and laid the sleeping bags by the others with nervous, quick movements.

"Look, there's a Barbie one," Mary Beth cried. "I get it. I get it."

"Oh, yay. There's one with horses on it. I want it." Brit was changing her mind.

"You can't have two, stupid," Adam said with his usual scowl.

"You can have the purple one," Brit told him.

The scowl became fierce. "I'm not sleeping in a purple bag."

"I'll take the purple bag," Callie intervened. "Adam, you can take the nice green one."

"Okay, but she shouldn't get to change her mind. She's always doing that."

Brit stuck out her tongue at him.

"The kids are tired and out of sorts, so I better get their sleeping arrangements set up." Callie thought it was time to end this visit. "I do appreciate the sleeping bags. I'm sorry I was curt. I'm tired, too."

"No problem," Wade said and made to walk off, but he turned back. "Brit, if it's okay with your mom, I have a horse you can ride. She's quite tame and I'll teach you the basics."

"Oh, wow, that's totally cool." Brit looked at Callie. "Can I, please? Can I?"

"I—ah—"

Seeing Callie's difficulty, he added, "Think about it overnight and I'll see you tomorrow."

He walked down the steps, followed by the deputy, and they went to where Odell was working. Their voices floated over her head.

"Is it going to be much of a problem to fix?" That was Wade's masculine voice.

"No, Sheriff, just take a little time, but I'll make it rock solid."

"Thanks, June Bug."

"Bubba Joe, don't be climbing on that roof." That was the deputy. "You'll fall through and try to sue the city."

"Give it a rest, Virgil," Wade said. "Let's go."

Callie watched them leave feeling as if she were in a fish bowl with the people of Homestead looking in. And there wasn't any escape. But the thought did cross her mind that being trapped with Wade Montgomery wouldn't be too bad. That thought lasted a split second. The man probably labeled her a raving lunatic with her mood swings. She had to stay focused on her siblings' futures.

Picking up a bag, she followed the kids inside.

"THAT MRS. AUSTIN SURE IS touchy," Virgil said as they reached the sheriff's office. "Mighty pretty, too."

"I think she just wants her space, Virg." Wade had his own suspicions, but he wouldn't mention them to Virgil. Virgil's overactive imagination sometimes ran away with him and he didn't want to give him any ammunition.

Wade was just trying to help her. He'd found the horse sleeping bag and the green one at the feed store, but he'd had to search through Tanner's General Store, which had an assortment of anything imaginable, to find the purple and Barbie ones. And she'd bit his head off for no reason.

So he intended to back off and give Callie her space. The

incidents happening to the newcomers bothered him though. He didn't want anything to happen to those kids. Or Callie. The house wasn't that far from his office and he could keep an eye on things without her really knowing.

He cursed himself for mentioning the horse. Clearly Callie didn't want her daughter to ride. At least not with him. He'd have to rescind the invitation, but he hated to break the little girl's heart.

Before he could reach his office, Millicent Niebauer came through the door, a birdlike woman with a camera around her neck and a pencil behind her ear. Barbara Jean, his secretary, was gone for the day or he'd let her handle Millicent. She and her husband, Hiram, ran the local newspaper and Millie was always on the lookout for a story. Or more to the point, gossip.

"Sheriff, I heard we have newcomers in town over at the Hellmuth house."

"Yes, Millie. Mrs. Austin arrived today with her three kids."

"What's she like?"

"Touchy," Virgil spoke up.

"What do you mean?" Millicent turned to him and Wade sighed. Virgil was worse than any old woman gossip.

"Well, you see, the sheriff and me took sleeping bags over to—"

"Virg, aren't you supposed to answer that call we just got from the Tuttles' neighbor?" The only way to sidetrack Virgil was with police work.

"Ah, Sheriff, I hate going over there. Cora Lou shoots at Norris every time he comes home from one of his long-haul trips, accusing him of having an affair. I'm getting tired of having to break them up. I don't know how she misses him. His chest is as broad as a side of a barn." Virgil headed for the door, still grumbling. "I just might arrest Cora Lou and maybe she'd stop all this foolishness."

"Then do it," Wade said as the door closed.

"What's the scoop on the new lady, Sheriff?" Millie didn't skip a beat. "Virgil said she's touchy. Why do you think that is?"

Wade suppressed a groan. As always, Millie was searching for a story where there wasn't one. "There's no story, Millie. She's a single mom with three kids and wants to raise them in a small-town atmosphere."

"Single, hmm?" Millicent scribbled something on a pad. "That's going to get the young bucks in this town stirred up. Like when Kristin and Kayla came to town. They found husbands. You think Mrs. Austin's looking for a husband?"

"I got work to do." He walked into his office and closed the door.

A lot of things didn't add up with Callie Austin, her nervousness, her desire to be alone and her kids calling her by her name. That was odd. It had thrown him for a minute. He'd taken the high road, though, and hadn't asked. He'd learned that discretion worked best in his job. The details usually came out later, especially the ones people tried to keep hidden.

Sinking into his chair, he couldn't stop thinking about Callie. Millie thought she was looking for a husband. He didn't think so, but she was looking for something. What? He had no idea. Maybe it was peace and quiet and time to get over her husband's death.

Whatever it was, the town had to leave her alone.

And that included him.

CALLIE ARRANGED the sleeping bags in one of the bedrooms. She had to put hers in between Brit and Mary Beth because both wanted to sleep by her. Adam arranged his at their feet. They found a table for Fred and fed him. Then Callie opened the ice chest with their food stash. Since she didn't know the layout of the town, she thought it best if they just had a sandwich for tonight. Their diet had been atrocious lately, fast food and sandwiches. Until she got the kitchen fixed, she didn't know how much longer it would be before she could cook them a decent meal.

They gathered in the parlor around the ice chest, sitting on the floor. "I want peanut butter," Mary Beth said, Miss Winnie in her lap. "Peanut butter with bananas. You know how I like it, Callie."

"I sure do, sweetie."

"I want mine with grape jelly," Brit added.

Adam made a face. "'Cause it's purple."

Brit stuck out her tongue again.

"You're stupid," Adam told her.

"You're stupider."

Callie stopped in the process of opening the jar. The kids were acting so out of character and Callie suspected it had something to do with Nigel's abuse. They'd gotten along well until he'd come into their lives; now they were bickering and being rude. It had to stop.

"We have to talk. Adam, you will not call your sister stupid again. And Brit, you will stop sticking out your tongue."

"What if I forget?" Brit asked.

"Then you say I'm sorry."

"To him." She jabbed a thumb toward Adam. "No wa…" Her voice fluttered away when she saw the look on Callie's face. "Okay, but I think you need to punish him—make him sleep in the attic or something."

"No, Callie," Mary Beth cried. "Don't make Adam sleep in the attic."

The thought of any of them being punished again upset Mary Beth. "No one is sleeping in the attic." Callie rubbed

Mary Beth's arm to comfort her. "Let's eat dinner, then we'll take a bath and go to bed. We're all tired."

They ate their sandwiches in silence and Callie cut apples and oranges into slices. After eating, Callie gathered the remains and put them in a plastic bag. She noticed Mary Beth's eyelids drooping. It was time for bed.

Brit and Mary Beth took a bath first in the antique tub with claw feet. It was almost identical to the one upstairs, except it was clean thanks to Ethel Mae. For something so old, it was in very good shape. The toilet had a pull chain and it worked. Being in the house was like taking a step back in time.

She helped the girls into their pajamas while Adam took his bath. Snug in their bags, Callie hurriedly took a bath and slipped into pajama bottoms and a T-shirt. She left the bathroom light on so the house wouldn't be in total darkness.

Soon they were all comfy. Or so Callie thought. "Callie," Mary Beth whispered.

"What, sweetie?"

"What if I wet the bed?"

"Then I'll clean it up and we'll go back to sleep."

"But my sleeping bag'll be wet."

"Mary Beth, sweetie. Don't worry about it. I'll wash the bag tomorrow and you can slide in with me."

"'Kay." Mary Beth turned onto her side, Miss Winnie in her arms. "Night, Fred. Don't be afraid. Callie's here."

They went through this every night. Mary Beth just needed reassurance. Before Glynis's death, she'd never wet the bed or been afraid. Once their lives settled down, the bed-wetting would stop. Since they'd been on the run, Mary Beth had only wet the bed once—their first night in a motel. Callie was hoping that soon she wouldn't be wetting the bed at all and she wouldn't be so afraid.

Callie gazed into the semidarkness, listening to the occasional sound of a car and the creaks and noises of the old house. They were here. They were safe—for now. Just the thought of that relaxed her.

"I can't sleep," Brit complained.

"Me, neither," Mary Beth chimed in. "Tell us a story."

"Not the princess one again or I'll puke." Adam made his wishes known.

"There's a prince for every princess, right, Callie?"

"Right," she answered Brit's question, but she wasn't sure. She'd met a couple of horned toads in her day. And kissing didn't help.

"Daddy was Mommy's prince," Mary Beth said.

"Yes, he was," Callie agreed. There wasn't a better man than John Lambert.

"And Nigel's a frog." Brit giggled. "You know what? If he comes here maybe we can get June Bug to eat him."

"Maybe he'll eat you." Adam joined the conversation.

"Callie, he's being mean again." Brit wanted to make sure she knew that.

"Everyone go to sleep."

Silence for a moment, then Mary Beth's tiny voice asked, "Can Mommy see us?"

Callie swallowed. "Yes, she can."

"Daddy, too?"

"Yes, Daddy, too."

"Then that bad sheriff won't arrest us 'cause they'll take care of us."

How Callie wished that were true. And that Glynis had never met Nigel or that John hadn't died. Now she had to deal with the consequences.

Once she heard Brit and Mary Beth's steady breathing, she slipped from her bag. Adam's recent behavior was unacceptable and they had to discuss it. Lying on his back, he stared at the ceiling. She went down on her knees beside him.

"Can't sleep?"

"No."

"Why are you being so mean to your sister?"

He turned on his side to face her. "Because she's being silly and she's going to get us caught. Then they'll take us back to Nigel and put you in jail. I can't take that, Callie. I can't. And if you're in jail, I'll just die. I'm so scared."

"Oh, Adam." She gathered him in her arms, her heart breaking. "Please stop worrying so much. I'll take care of us. I promise."

"But the sheriff keeps coming here."

"He's just being nice." As she said the words, she knew they were true. Wade Montgomery was a nice man. "Listen to me. Worrying is my department and I will handle the sheriff. I want you to turn back into the sweet little boy you've always been. Okay?"

"Okay." He rubbed his face against her.

"Now go to sleep."

Callie walked out onto the front porch and sat in one of the rockers, her heart heavy. It was a beautiful moonlit night with a million stars twinkling through the live oaks. She drew her knees up and wrapped her arms around her legs, listening to the gentle serenade of the crickets. Everything was quiet. Peaceful. Except her thoughts.

How could her mother do this to them? she asked herself again. Put them in the position of fleeing from the law. So much anger churned inside her at the turmoil Adam was going through, and the grief and fear Mary Beth and Brit were experiencing. She tried not to be angry at Glynis, but she was. She'd been taken in by a con artist. Nigel had lavished her with attention and praise, something she'd needed after John's death. Still, it didn't give her the right to bring that awful man into their lives.

Glynis could be impulsive and selfish at times, but she'd never done anything like this. She and John had had a good marriage, a good life, so how could she fall for Nigel? Callie didn't understand that and every time she'd tried to talk to her mother, Glynis would say they'd talk later. But later never came. Instead, a nightmare had followed and she was still…

Her thoughts skidded to an abrupt stop as a car pulled up to the curb. Wade. *Again.* He unfolded his tall frame from the vehicle and started up the walk. It was late—too late for a friendly visit. What was he doing here? There could only be one reason. He knew her identity and had come to arrest her.

Her first reaction was to run inside, lock the front door and get the kids out the back. But her car was in front.

She was trapped.

And she didn't even hear a siren.

CHAPTER FOUR

AS THE SHERIFF STROLLED UP the steps, Callie held her breath until her chest burned. Why was he here?

"Mrs. Austin." Wade tipped his hat in welcome.

"Sheriff," she acknowledged in a hesitant voice, her heart ticking like a time bomb about to explode.

"I was making my last drive through town before heading home and I saw you sitting out here." He leaned a shoulder against a pillar.

Her lungs expanded with relief. He didn't know who she was—yet. She had more time. Tightening her arms around her legs, she said, "It's so relaxing and quiet. I can barely hear the traffic on the highway."

"Yep. Homestead's a peaceful place. Not much happens."

"I like that."

"That's why you came to Homestead, isn't it?"

Her eyes shot to his, trying to make out his expression in the moonlight. Was there something hidden in that remark? There seemed to be, but she really couldn't tell. Her perception wasn't all that good lately, and her nerves were a mangled mass of spaghetti.

"What do you mean?" she asked for good measure.

Wade walked over and sat in the other rocker. It squeaked against the floorboards from his weight. "A small quiet town to raise your children."

"Yes."

Away from Nigel Tremont and his sadistic behavior.

Wade clasped his hands between his knees. "I really came by to apologize."

"Oh?"

"I should have spoken to you first before offering Brit a chance to ride a horse. That put you in an awkward position."

Callie tucked her hair behind her ear, amazed at his sensitivity. "Since we started making plans to come to Texas, Brit has talked about being a cowgirl. She's never been near a horse so I'm not sure where the idea comes from. I feel once she gets near the big animal all that will change. Brit's very impulsive."

"And very charming. Like her mother."

His voice felt like a caress in the night, warming her skin and… Oh, this was getting too intimate—with the wrong man.

A tense pause followed, then he said, "I'm afraid I had personal reasons for making the offer."

"Personal reasons?"

"Yeah." He rubbed his hands together. "My son died four years ago and his horse hasn't been ridden since. I was hoping another child would…" He stopped for a moment. "My father is very protective of that horse and it probably wouldn't have worked anyway."

Callie's heart filled with compassion. "I'm so sorry about your son." She could only imagine the grief and the heartache of losing a child and she could hear it in every word he spoke.

"Thank you," he said and got to his feet with restless energy. It was clear that talking about his son wasn't easy and he quickly changed the subject. "I thought I better warn you, too, about the townsfolk. They'll be eager to help and I hope it's not going to offend you. People around here are just friendly."

She stood on her bare feet facing him. "I'll remember that

and I'm probably going to need a lot of help. The house—" she waved a hand toward the front door "—needs lots of work."

"June Bug is a good carpenter and he can fix just about anything."

"Odell's a very interesting person."

A dark eyebrow arched in amusement. "Yeah. I think he's been called that a time or two."

"I'm not calling him June Bug. I consider it an insult."

Wade studied her in the moonlight, which seemed to form a halo around the blond hair that hung loosely to her shoulders. Without her shoes, she barely came up to his shoulder, but despite her petite size he had a feeling Callie Austin was a very strong woman. She would be a pleasant surprise for the town of Homestead. That was his personal opinion. His train of thought seemed to be completely sidetracked since her arrival in town.

"I really hate to disappoint Brit."

"Don't worry about it. Brit forgets things easily, and frankly I need to spend all my time on the house."

And not getting involved with me. Where did that thought come from? He didn't even know the woman, but he liked her and…

He cleared his throat. "Are the kids comfortable for the night?"

"Yes. They're completely exhausted."

He nodded. "I'm sure you are, too, so I'll let you get to bed." He tipped his hat again. "Have a good night."

With that, Wade strolled down the step to his squad car. He'd vowed to stay away from Callie and give her some space, but when he'd glimpsed her sitting in the rocker he'd stopped without even thinking. The offer of Brit riding a horse bothered him. After he'd done it, he realized he shouldn't have, especially after Callie's reaction. And of course Jock would be against anyone riding Lucky. It was best to rectify things now, but he didn't feel good about hurting Brit. He wondered how Callie would explain it.

Before getting into his car, he glanced at the front porch. Callie had gone inside. He felt a moment of loneliness and he had no idea what that meant. He felt lonely all the time—nothing and no one could make that go away. Talking to her was almost surreal, like this was something he needed. And he'd told her about Zach. He never spoke to anyone about his son, except his friend Ethan Ritter. Ethan had lost a sister, so he knew about that kind of pain.

He got in his car and headed toward Spring Creek Ranch. And a confrontation with his father.

WHEN WADE WALKED into the kitchen, Jock was sitting at the table nursing a cup of coffee. The mug trembled in his hands.

"How you feeling, Pop?"

"Hummph."

Wade poured a cup and straddled a chair across from his father. He and Jock used to be the same height, but at sixty-nine Jock's height had diminished. His hair was silver-gray and his face leathery and wrinkled from years in the sun. A man who once walked with pride now found it a struggle to get through each day, and on days when he needed help, he depended on the bottle. There were too many of those days to Wade's way of thinking. They had to talk.

Where to start? Talking to his father had always been a hard thing to do. Wade had idolized Jock and wanted to be just like him. He'd been Wyatt Earp and John Wayne combined to a young Wade. Seeing him in this state of depression was even harder. Now Wade would have to be the strong one.

He gripped his cup. "Pop, this drinking has to stop."

Jock held his head with both hands. "My head's pounding, son, and if I get angry it might explode."

"Then stop drinking."

"What else have I got to do?"

"Work this ranch like you always have." He paused, using all the ammunition he had. "That's what Zach would want."

Jock gulped down a swallow of coffee. "I don't want to talk about Zach."

"We have to," Wade insisted, knowing they had to get to the root of Jock's problem. "You blame me. You haven't come out and said it, but I know you do."

Jock glared at him through bloodshot eyes. "Why did you let him go to that party? Why?"

It was the first time Jock had asked that question and it was long overdue. Wade removed his hat and slowly placed it on the table, that permanent knot in his stomach felt like a rope pulled taut. To avoid the pain, he could get up and walk away like he always did. But he couldn't do that anymore or soon that rope would choke him to death.

He swallowed to ease the knot. "Zach wanted to go and it was a party for twelve-year-olds. Kim and I thought it would be safe."

"But it wasn't, was it?"

Unable to sit any longer, he stood and jammed both hands through his hair, losing control. "No. I killed him because I didn't check out the situation. Does that make you feel better?"

Jock hung his head.

"I will feel the guilt of his death every day of my life, but I'm not going to sit by and watch you drink yourself to death. You and I are left to face this world so let's do it the best way we can. Without arguing—like Zach would want."

"Zach never liked it when you and I argued." Jock brushed hair out of his eyes.

"No," Wade agreed. "He loved us both."

"Yeah. He was a good kid. I just don't see why those boys didn't get jail time."

Wade took his seat again, suddenly feeling a relief to be able to talk about his son. "I tried everything I could, but they were twelve years old. They're on probation until they're twenty-one and their activities are monitored. That's all the court would do."

That still rankled Wade, but he'd learned to live with it the best way he could.

An awkward silence followed.

"Pop, there's a kid in town who wants to ride a horse. Lucky needs to be ridden and—"

Jock stumbled to his feet. "Nobody rides that horse. Nobody."

Jock hobbled away and Wade buried his face in his hands. Was life always going to be like this? He'd had just about his limit. From out of nowhere, Callie Austin's face appeared in his mind and he wondered why he could see it so clearly.

THE NEXT MORNING, Callie woke up to noise and she scrambled from her bag into her clothes. She heard the pounding of a hammer, the whiz of a saw, the buzz of a mower and voices—several voices.

"What's that?" Adam asked, sitting up and rubbing his eyes.

"I'll check. Stay with your sisters."

Callie opened her front door and stopped short. People were everywhere and she didn't know any of them. Two men were working on the picket fence, another was mowing the grass. Several men were working on the roof and the column. Odell stepped up on the porch with a tool belt that looked bigger than him around his waist.

"Odell, what's going on?"

"You told me to fix up the place and that's what I'm doing."

"I'm paying for all these people?"

"No, ma'am. The guy mowing is Walter and he's retired and just likes to mow. He helps out the new residents—sort of makes them feel welcome. That's Delbert and his son, Little Del, working on the fence. They help out when they can and they owe me a favor. And the men working on the house I hired so I can do the job as quickly as possible. That's what you wanted, right?"

"Yes," she answered absently, realizing for the first time that no one ever said their last name. Everybody knew everybody, Wade had said, so she supposed there was no need, except she didn't know anyone. It would help to know a last name, especially if it was Collins.

"We'll have the column and porches secured by the end of the day then I can start on the inside."

"Thank you, Odell," she said, feeling as if she were in a trance as she went back into the house. Wade had said the people were friendly and he was right. Maybe a little too friendly. No one did anything for free, did they? She was budgeting her money and she had to be careful so that it lasted a year.

THE DAYS THAT FOLLOWED were busy and hectic and she became more familiar with the town and its people. The kids absolutely loved Tanner's General Store, where anything from beef jerky to toys to large jars of assorted hard candies could be found. Then there were barrels stuffed with gourmet treats. Adam went for the pickle jar while the girls debated over the candy. Callie favored the food area where the meat and produce were fresh and the best she'd ever seen. She missed cooking, but knew it would be awhile before her kitchen was ready. They were making do with a hot plate and that limited what they could eat.

She found there were very few good places to eat in Homestead. There was a kolache shop, a Dairy Queen and the Lone

Wolf Bar. She was told that no self-respecting woman would be caught dead in there. Then there was a barbecue place and small diner that looked as bad as the Lone Wolf. That's when the idea had come to Callie. She couldn't take a whole year without cooking, so she decided to open a café.

At first the idea seemed crazy since she wasn't planning on staying in Homestead. But repairing the house was going to take a lot of money and she needed a way to earn an income. She didn't want her savings to dwindle down to nothing. And cooking was what she did.

A decent place to eat would be good for the town and it would keep her busy, keep her from constantly worrying. The right side of the house would work for the café. Frances Haase had explained that in the old days, the Victorian house had been built to accommodate the entertainment of men and women. There hadn't been much to do besides go to a local bar and the upstanding citizens hadn't done that—or if they had, no one had ever spoken of it. Instead, they'd entertained in their homes.

The right parlor was where the men had gathered with their cronies to play poker or cards and to smoke cigars and indulge in their drink of choice. In the left parlor, the women had had their side to gather with friends to knit, crochet or quilt and to imbibe a drink if they so chose without their husband's permission. Large sliding doors were in a pocket of the wall on each side of the entry and could easily be pulled for privacy.

Each area had access to the kitchen, which made Callie's idea perfect. With the bedrooms upstairs and the parlors and dining room downstairs, the left side would be their home. Callie became excited with her plans for the kitchen and the café. She talked with Odell and he seemed to be able to do everything she wanted. For once, something else occupied her mind besides fear.

The kids were helping with the cleanup and they were

more energetic. Odell had redone the staircase to make sure it was safe and the kids had chosen their rooms upstairs. Although, Callie suspected Mary Beth and Brit wouldn't sleep in their own room for a while—even Adam, for that fact. But it was okay. They were safe for now.

Buddy and Rascal were regular visitors and while Mary Beth played with Rascal, Buddy helped on the house. One day she made fresh lemonade for all the workers. Del sat in one of the rockers taking a break.

"Mighty good lemonade," he said.

"Thank you." Callie thought for a minute then asked, "I don't believe I caught your last name?"

"My last name?" Del sat rigidly straight and Callie knew she'd made a big mistake. Del was offended.

"I'm sorry, but I'm new in town and I don't know anyone and no one says their last name."

He carefully placed his glass on a small table. "There's a reason for that. Around here we all know and trust each other." He rose to his full height, his chest puffed out. "But if it'll ease your mind, my name is Delbert Brockmoor."

"Thank you, Del."

Del went back to work and Callie felt as if she'd committed a faux pas. Buddy walked onto the porch for a glass of lemonade. "Somethin' wrong?"

"I think I hurt Del's feelings."

"How'd you do that?"

"By asking his last name."

"Oh."

She turned to Buddy, needing an answer once and for all. "Do you know any Collinses that live here?"

Buddy took a long drink of the lemonade. "Nope, can't say that I do."

Callie's heart sank. But she'd keep asking until she found

someone who knew her father or her grandparents. She'd definitely use more discretion, though.

"I noticed the tires on your Suburban and it's time to replace 'em. If it's okay, I'll order 'em and put 'em on. Oil probably needs checking, too. Women tend to forget that."

She smiled at Buddy. "Go ahead. I haven't even thought about the tires or oil."

"Consider it done."

Wade was right. The people were helpful and friendly. It reaffirmed her decision to come to Texas.

CALLIE HAD CLEANED THE TUB upstairs and was happy that under all the grime the porcelain was still in good shape. Next were the filthy windows. She was busy cleaning them in a parlor when someone knocked on the door. The kids were wiping dust from the baseboards.

"I'll get it," she said, thinking it was Ethel, but Ethel never knocked. She just came in, usually with a cigarette in her mouth. From day one, Callie had made it clear that smoking was not acceptable in the house or around the children. Ethel was a good sport about extinguishing the cigarette.

Opening the door, she found an attractive couple with a boy who looked to be around eight or nine. He had bright auburn hair and a big smile.

"Hi," the woman said. "I'm Kristin Gallagher and this is my husband, Ryan." She stroked the boy's head. "And this is my son, Cody."

"Nice to meet you." Callie shook their hands.

"I'm the physician's assistant at the small health clinic. With three kids, I thought you might like to know that."

"Yes. Thank you."

"My mom said you got kids I can play with," Cody spoke up.

Brit walked up before Callie could answer.

"She's a girl," Cody said to his mother.

"Cody…"

"You're a boy," Brit answered before the adults could intervene.

"I don't like girls."

"Well, I'm not crazy about boys, either." Brit put her hands on her hips for effect.

Adam joined the group. After being introduced he asked, "Want to go outside and play? And don't worry about Brit. She's almost like a boy."

Brit's face creased into one big frown. "I am not. I'm going to be a cowgirl—not a cowboy."

"Cool," Cody beamed. "I like horses, too. Can I stay?" Cody glanced at his mother.

"No. I have to go to the clinic." Kristin smoothed his hair. "Maybe another day."

"Ah, Mom. Hayden and Sara are on vacation and—"

Ryan came to the rescue. "I have some errands to run in town. I can pick Cody up in about an hour if that's okay with Callie."

"Sure. The kids need a break."

"Are you sure?" Kristin asked. "You're so busy with the house and I must say it's looking very nice."

"Thank you. You're the first person to say that. Everyone else thinks I'm a lunatic for taking on this big house."

"But I love it."

"I do, too." In that moment, Callie knew she'd found a friend. "And no, it's no problem for Cody to stay. The kids are bored with all the cleaning."

"Okay." Before the word left Kristin's mouth, Cody darted into the house and stood between Adam and Brit.

"I'll be back in a little while," Ryan called as the couple walked off.

The kids played outside for a while, then they played games in the dining room. Mary Beth was feeling left out and trailed behind Callie. Callie told her to show Cody her fish and that did the trick. They lay on the floor watching Fred swim around, talking about fish. She could hear some big tales being told.

There was another knock at the door and Callie put her rag down and went to see who it was. A tall, blond, good-looking man in boots stood there.

He held out his hand with a smile. "Mrs. Austin, I'm Father Noah Kelley from St. Mark's Episcopal Church."

She blinked in confusion. "Excuse me?" He didn't look like any priest she'd ever seen and he didn't wear a collar.

"I'm Father Noah Kelley." His smile broadened. "My dad is the rector at St. Mark's. He had a stroke and I'm filling in." Shaking her hand, he added, "Please call me Noah. I came by to invite you and your children to Sunday services, and of course, the children are always welcome to join our Sunday school classes."

"Oh. Thank you. But as you can see—" her hand swept around the place "—I have so much to do."

"There's always time for God, Mrs. Austin."

Callie was duly chastised and felt color tinge her cheeks. "Please call me Callie, and I will try to make time."

The children's laughter echoed from the parlor.

"Do you mind if I speak with the children?" Noah asked.

"Ah…no." Stepping aside, she watched as he walked into the parlor and sat on the floor with the kids. She could see that he had a way with children. They were laughing and talking as if he were one of them.

When Noah left, he called, "See you Sunday, Mrs.…Callie."

"Bye, Fath…Noah." It would take a while before she was comfortable with calling a priest by his first name. But then, she had a feeling Noah was going to be easy to know. The kids missed going to church, so she just might take him up on his offer. Staying out of the limelight didn't seem to be an option here in Homestead.

Ethel arrived and Callie continued with the cleaning. It seemed like no time at all had passed by the time Ryan came back. Cody wasn't ready to leave, but he went meekly, promising to return soon.

At the door, Ryan paused, "My father is Clint Gallagher, a state senator, and he's not real pleased with the Home Free Program. So if he gives you any flak, don't pay him any attention. His bark is worse than his bite."

"Thanks for the warning. I'd heard there were some disgruntled people in town."

"For the record, I'm for the program. It brought Kristin back into my life."

"Oh?"

He grinned, looking a little embarrassed. "It's a long story and Kristin'll probably tell you."

Ryan was obviously a man who didn't like to talk, especially about intimate things. But he couldn't hide the love in his eyes and Callie knew a lot of good was coming from the land giveaway. The last thing she needed, though, was a state senator breathing down her neck. She'd have to be very careful.

Callie went back to work thinking love was a wonderful thing. Catching sight of Brit, she stopped. Her sister was staring out the window at the street. Callie knew who she was looking for. Wade.

Wade had stayed away and Brit had asked about him every day. He'd promised her a ride on a horse and she wasn't forgetting that, as Callie had thought she would. Seeing Brit so disappointed was disheartening. Soon she'd have to do something, but making friends with Wade was not a great idea. And she didn't know why she thought about him constantly.

She remembered the love and the hurt in his voice when he'd talked about his son. Wade had an inner compassion that was hard to resist. Her instincts were telling her to stay away from the sheriff. Her heart was telling her something entirely different. But then, what did her heart know? It had taken so many knocks lately that she was sure it was malfunctioning.

Ethel was cleaning the woodwork and Callie went to find her, leaving Brit to her own devices. She'd find a way to make her dream come true.

"Odell says you're going to open a café here," Ethel said, straightening from her stooped position over the baseboards.

"Yes, I am."

Ethel frowned. "Do you know how to cook?"

Callie paused in her sweep across a window. "Yes. Actually I went to school to learn."

"Went to school?" Ethel's voice rose. "Well, don't that take the biscuit. Never heard of such a thing. I learned to cook as soon as I could hold a spoon in my hand and stir. My daughters learned the same way. All nine of 'em, Edith Mae, Etta Mae, Erma Mae, Emma Mae, Earla Mae, Eva Mae, Ella Mae, Essie Mae and Eloise Mae."

Callie gaped at her. "Your girls have the same middle name and their first names start with an *E?*"

"Sure do. Easier to remember 'em that way."

"But isn't it confusing?"

"Sometimes, but when they're all home I just shout Mae and they all come running."

A smile tugged at Callie's mouth. She could imagine that. When Ethel hollered in high-throttle sewing-machine mode, everyone had a tendency to run—in the opposite direction.

Callie rinsed a rag in warm water. "Please tell me Odell's middle name is not Mae.

"Of course not. He's named after his father, Odell Willard—everyone called him Willie. I went through ten births to give that man a son and what does he do? Up and dies on me. No warning, no nothing." She snapped her fingers. "Just like that, he's gone and I'm left to raise ten kids alone."

"That had to have been hard."

"Wasn't easy, but my girls started working as soon as they could and they're all married and have good jobs, except none of them live here. Got a couple in San Antonio, but it's just me and Odell now." Ethel surveyed the cobwebs on the ceiling. "We'll need a ladder to get up there."

"Yeah." Callie followed her gaze. "I'll borrow one from Odell."

"Why did you have to go to school to learn to cook?" Ethel returned to their former conversation. "Didn't you have a mother?"

Callie inhaled deeply. "Yes, I had a mother and I learned to cook at an early age, too. It's something I've always loved to do and I had a neighbor who taught me a lot. But I went to culinary school so I could learn the skills of being an executive chef in a fine restaurant."

Ethel had a bandanna tied around her hair and she pushed it back slightly. "You mean you're one of those fancy know-it-alls I see on the tube?"

"Something like that."

"Well, swat me with a fly swatter. Ain't that somethin'. Wait until I tell my cousin Bertha. She thinks she's the best cook in the county 'cause people come from all over to eat her kolaches, which I make most of the time and she gets all the credit." She thought for a minute. "I might just come to work for you. What are you gonna pay?"

"What do you think you're worth?"

An eyebrow darted up. "A lot more than you can pay."

Callie laughed out loud and it felt good. It also felt good to be in Homestead and to meet so many heartwarming people.

THE NEXT MORNING, Callie drove to San Antonio to purchase appliances, mattresses, bedding, dishes, pots and pans and other things they needed for the house. She was able to bring some of the items back with her, but the rest would be delivered later. A computer was a must for Adam and she managed to get it in the Suburban. The phone and Internet services were being installed today and everything was falling into place. With a little more work, their home would be livable.

As they drove by the courthouse to Bluebonnet Street, Brit asked, "Can we stop by the sheriff's office?" Her face was glued to the window.

"No, sweetie, we can't."

"Why not? He said he'd take me riding and he hasn't and I want to ask why."

Callie bit her lip, needing to tell Brit the truth. "Because I asked him not to."

"Why'd you do that?" Tears choked her voice.

"I don't want us getting involved with the sheriff."

"Use your head, Brit," Adam said. "We have to stay away from the sheriff or he'll figure out who we are and take us back to Nigel and Callie will go to jail. Is that what you want?"

"No. I want to ride a horse."

"You're—"

"Adam," Callie stopped him. "I'll find a way for you to ride a horse, Brit. I promise."

"Daddy's kind of promise?"

Callie chewed on her lip until she tasted blood. Another

difficult decision that required an answer. God, she wished she had a book for these things. But she didn't. All she had to go on was a sister's love. And when it came to her siblings, she was a softy. "Yes." She kissed the palm of one hand, curled it into a fist and carried it to her heart. That was John's way of making a promise to them—a message kept in the heart never to be forgotten.

Now she had to keep the promise. There was no way she'd break it.

LATER THE KIDS PLAYED OUTSIDE with Buddy and Rascal. Callie stared at her new phone and debated her choices. She'd met a lot of friendly people and she could ask them about Brit riding a horse. But then that action might make the sheriff suspicious and she didn't want to slight him or give him a reason to check into her background more thoroughly.

The sensible solution would be to call Wade, but she hadn't been sensible in weeks. Yet it seemed right. Brit could ride a horse and it wouldn't hurt to make friends with the sheriff. If the FBI found them, she would need all the allies she could get.

That wasn't her only reason. She wanted to call Wade. There was something building between them. It couldn't be seen or touched, but she felt it deep in her heart. She picked up the phone before she could change her mind. Another decision made in haste and she hoped she didn't live to regret it.

Wade was out and she was surprised at her disappointment. The woman took her name and number and said Wade would be in touch as soon as possible. She added that he had a cell phone if it was an emergency. It wasn't, so Callie didn't take the number. She just had a little girl with a broken heart.

She fixed supper and put the kids to bed. Brit pulled on pajamas then slipped into her boots they'd found at Tanner's.

Callie frowned. "Brit, why are you putting on your boots?"

"'Cause I'm sleeping in them until I ride a horse."

"Sweetie, it will be very uncomfortable. You can put them on first thing in the morning." Callie tried to reason with her.

Brit's eyes narrowed. "Are you gonna make me?"

"Yes," Adam answered before Callie could make a decision, "because your feet will fall off if you sleep in them."

"Adam…"

"You're a big fat liar," Brit snapped back.

"Okay." Callie intervened before they got into a shouting match. "You can sleep in them." That seemed easier than upsetting her further.

The kids asleep, Callie got up and went outside to the rocker, her favorite place. The nights were getting warmer, but she didn't mind. The wind picked up and blew her hair across her face. A mosquito bit her arm and she swatted it. Life was different here and she was beginning to enjoy just the simplest things like a starlit night, fresh air and a friendly smile.

Drawing her knees up, she wondered why Wade had ignored her phone call. She thought for sure he would arrive within a matter of minutes, but it had been hours. Where was he?

Tomorrow she'd make other arrangements for Brit to ride a horse even if she had to take the day off. And she had so much to do to the house. Mainly, she had to go over her budget to make sure she hadn't overextended herself with all the purchases she'd made today. They needed everything, though, especially the mattresses. Sleeping on the floor was getting old and uncomfortable. The appliances were expensive, yet necessary for the type of kitchen she was planning. By the time she was finished with the house, her savings would be gone and she'd have to depend on her skills as a chef to make a living.

But then she might also be in jail. The truth of that paralyzed her for a moment, then she shook it away. The future was so uncertain and... Headlights beamed across her yard from Main Street and a car pulled up to the curb. Her pulse quickened.

Wade.

CHAPTER FIVE

WADE STROLLED UP THE STEPS and tipped his hat. "Evening, ma'am."

"Sheriff." Her voice was cool.

"Sorry I'm so late, but I was involved in a family dispute and I didn't get your message until a few minutes ago."

"Is everything okay?"

Relief tinged her words. Relief that she couldn't hide. Did she think he was deliberately ignoring her? "Not really." He took a seat in the other rocker, needing to explain. "Norris is a trucker who's gone for weeks at a time and his wife, Cora Lou, is very jealous. Every time he comes home, it's fight after fight and I don't mean fists. She gets the rifle out and tries to kill him. Virgil broke them up a few days ago and he was called back over there again today. When he tried to arrest Cora Lou, she hit him with the rifle and gave him a black eye and a concussion. I locked up Cora Lou and Norris, and Kristin is attending to Virgil. Virg doesn't take pain well so Kristin will probably be holding his hand until the morning, then Ryan will be calling me."

From the porch light, he saw her white teeth nipping her bottom lip. "You're wanting to laugh. I can see you're holding back."

"How long have you been sheriff?" she asked, and he knew she was stifling a chuckle.

"Almost four years. My dad was sheriff for over forty and I ran for the office when he retired."

"After your son died?"

Wade didn't shut down like he usually did when someone mentioned Zach. "Yeah. My wife and I had been drifting apart for years and we never realized it until after Zach's death. He was keeping us together. We couldn't find our way back to what we once had. We tried, but we both knew our marriage was over. She moved to Phoenix to be near her sister and I came home."

"To grieve."

He stared at her, realizing she probably understood since she'd lost her husband. It felt strange talking to her about such a personal thing, but it felt right, too. And he didn't understand that. He barely knew her. She was easy to talk to though—when her guard was down and she wasn't so prickly.

"Yeah. But the colorful people of Homestead keep me balanced." He glanced at the clean, mowed yard and the straight column. "The house is taking shape. June Bug is doing a good job."

"Odell."

"What?"

"Call him Odell—that's his name."

There was a short noticeable pause.

"Now you're wanting to laugh. Don't you dare," she told him.

"Okay." He couldn't stop a grin, suddenly loving that teasing quality in her voice. "What did you call about?"

"I have a broken-hearted little girl who wants to ride a horse."

"Damn. I knew it. Why didn't you call me sooner?"

"I thought she'd forget about it."

And you didn't want me around. What had changed her mind? Because now it didn't seem to matter. They were talking like old friends and he had a difficult time reminding himself that they weren't.

"Well, tomorrow I'll take y'all out to the ranch and Brit can get an up-close-and-personal view of a horse."

"Please don't use your son's horse if it's going to cause problems."

He clasped his hands together. "We have several horses, so don't worry about it. I have a gentle bay mare she can ride."

"Thank you. I'd appreciate it."

His eyes caught hers and he saw the blue flame—like the heat of a match before it ignites a fire. He felt it in parts of his body that reminded him that he was a man. A man who liked women. As a teenager, he'd dated a lot of girls, but once he'd met Kim, she'd been the only woman in his life. He'd been faithful to her and a small part of him would probably always love her. But now he needed more and looking at Callie Austin more seemed within his reach.

The door opened and Brit came out in purple pajamas and cowboy boots. She didn't even notice Wade sitting in the other rocker as she crawled into Callie's lap like a two-year-old.

"Why'd you tell him not to come back?" she murmured against Callie.

Without anyone telling him, Wade knew Brit was talking about him and it was clear Callie had told Brit that she'd asked Wade not to take Brit riding. She'd taken all the blame, which wasn't fair. He was the one who'd made the offer without asking Callie first. Here was his chance to make it right. He never wanted to hurt a child and that's exactly what he'd done. But he was going to change that.

"I am back."

Brit whirled around to face him. "Mr. Sheriff, you're here."

"Sure am."

Brit scrambled off Callie's lap to stand in front of him and pointed to her feet. "See. I got boots—real cowboy boots. That's what Mr. Tanner said."

"Then you're ready to ride a real horse."

"Yeah." Suddenly awake, she was breathless with excitement.

"Then tomorrow afternoon I'll pick everyone up and we'll go to my ranch and you can ride a real horse."

"Oh boy." Brit turned to Callie. "Did you hear?"

"Yes. I heard."

"Then we can go?"

"We can go."

Brit pinned Wade with a serious gaze. "Are you a good sheriff?"

Wade was taken aback for a second. "I like to think of myself as a good guy."

"Then you don't arrest kids."

Wade pushed to his feet and ruffled her hair. "No. I don't arrest kids."

"And you won't arrest Callie?"

Wade was puzzled, but answered honestly. "Not unless she's broken the law, and I can't imagine your mother doing that."

Callie stood and wrapped her arms around Brit's neck and pulled her close to her. "Brit, sweetie, it's time to get you in bed."

"Callie wouldn't break the law unless she had a good reason," Brit told him.

Wade glanced at Callie and even in the moonlight he could see her hands were shaking. He had that feeling again—something wasn't right. What was she hiding?

"I'm glad you're a good sheriff," Brit added.

"I'll be back tomorrow about five. Is that okay?"

"Yes," Callie answered.

"You won't forget, will you?"

"No, Brit," Wade replied. "I'll be here tomorrow."

His eyes held Callie's for a moment. "Good night."

"Good night," he heard as he strolled to his car. That soft voice stayed with him all the way to Spring Creek as he tried to sort through the child's innocent words. Was Callie trying to hide something? He had read over her application personally and checked out the facts. Could the facts be false? Of course, there was always a way to falsify records. But why would Callie do that?

He couldn't let his overactive lawman's instincts take over. He liked Callie and her kids and, until he had some concrete evidence, he wasn't going to think about it anymore.

But he knew he wouldn't stop thinking about Callie—in a more intimate way. And that shocked him more than the other thoughts in his head.

AFTER ALMOST SUFFERING a heart attack last night because of Brit's too-direct questions, Callie put the incident out of her mind and hoped Wade would too. She couldn't worry about every little thing or she'd go crazy.

Odell always came to work at sunup and stayed until he couldn't see anymore. Callie had never met a more hardworking person. And he was very talented. He even made the missing parts of gingerbread trim in his workshop. He not only did the carpentry work, he did the electrical and plumbing, too. She didn't think there was anything he couldn't do. Except get a date.

She'd heard that story from Ethel on more than one occasion. Girls didn't want to go out with a man who ate bugs. Callie could empathize with that thought. But there had to be a girl in Homestead for Odell.

Odell knocked at the door as he did every morning to go over the day's work. They were in the kitchen going over the installation of the appliances that were supposed to arrive the next day.

"I wish I had more room in here," Callie said, not sure if

the commercial stove and refrigerator she'd ordered were going to fit.

Odell tapped a wall that separated the kitchen from an eating area. "I could take this wall out and make it one big room."

"Oh, that would be wonderful." Callie walked to the middle of the kitchen. "But I want to keep this butcher block. It gives me more counter space and maybe you can install a rack above to hang pots and pans."

Odell removed his baseball cap and scratched his head. "I don't know what kind of rack you're talking about."

"Adam has a computer, so I'll order one from the Internet."

"Good, then I can sure put it up." He took a measuring tape off his belt. "I'll measure the block so you'll know the size." He took the length and width and gave it to her, also scribbling it on a notepad he kept in his pocket. Attaching the tape to his belt, he asked, "Have you thought about how you're going to heat and cool this place?"

"No," she admitted. "I'm getting a little overwhelmed with everything that needs to be done."

"If it was me, I'd go with central air and heat. It might be more expensive to install, but it'll be cheaper in the long run and I can install it at a low rate."

Without thinking, Callie hugged him. "You're just wonderful, Odell."

Too late, Callie realized her mistake. Odell's eyes were so big they were about to pop out of his head.

"No girl's ever hugged me before, except my mama and my sisters."

"If you'd stop eating bugs, there would be a lot of girls who would want to hug you."

"You think so?" His voice was hopeful.

"Sure." And she meant it. "Promise me you'll stop eating bugs."

His face crinkled. "Don't know, ma'am. Been doing that a lot of years."

"Girls don't go for guys who eat bugs."

His eyes brightened as he gazed at her and she realized again that she might be giving him the wrong impression. She had to make one thing clear. "You and I are just friends, Odell. You understand that, don't you?"

"Yes, ma'am. You're about the nicest person I've ever met."

"Thank you. I have three kids to raise and this house to fix up and I appreciate all your help."

"I'll be here until it's done." He scribbled something on his notepad. "When do you think you'll get the paint for the outside?"

"In a couple of days. I'll make a trip to the hardware store and see how much white they have. To paint this house, they may have to order more."

"Yeah. I'll have the rotten boards replaced on the outside by then and I'll have some figures on the central unit, too. I'll leave early today to see what I can come up with. My sister Etta's in town and she's a whiz on the computer, so I'll get her to do some looking for me."

"Thank you, Odell."

As Odell went outside, the kids came running in. Brit was dressed in her jeans, a western shirt, hat and boots.

Adam pointed to Brit. "She says she's going riding."

"She is. We're going to the sheriff's ranch so Brit can ride."

"Callie…" Adam's voice wavered with worry.

Brit picked up on it immediately. "Don't worry, Adam. Mr. Sheriff is a good sheriff and he's not going to arrest us."

"How do you know that?"

"Because I asked him." Saying that, Brit sauntered into the dining room with Mary Beth trailing behind her.

"She did *what?*"

Callie put her arm around Adam's thin shoulders. "Stop worrying. This afternoon we're going to Wade's ranch and we're going to enjoy ourselves."

"I'm not going. I don't like him and I'd rather stay here and play on my computer."

Callie let out a long breath and decided not to pressure him. She just made it very plain that if he didn't go, that no one would. It was called subtle pressure—something Glynis had used on her many times.

At five o'clock, they were all sitting on the front porch waiting. Even though Adam and Brit argued, Callie knew that he wouldn't disappoint her. Callie was watching for the patrol car, but a white truck drove up. Wade got out dressed in jeans and boots, no badge or gun. He seemed like an ordinary cowboy, except Wade was not ordinary. He was about the best-looking thing she'd ever seen. A real Texan. A real cowboy.

Brit ran to meet him, asking questions faster than Wade could answer them. The others followed more slowly. Wade waved to Odell and Bubba Joe and they climbed into the truck.

It was a four-door truck and Callie sat in the front, the kids in the back. Adam slumped in a corner, clearly determined not to enjoy this.

"Can Fred come, Mr. Sheriff?" Mary Beth asked, Miss Winnie held tight in one arm.

Wade looked at Callie and she noticed his eyes were dark and warm. It was like seeing into the darkness and feeling the warmth and not being afraid. At that moment, she realized she wasn't afraid of Wade. He stimulated her senses and…

She blinked, bringing herself back to the conversation. "No, sweetie. Fred has to stay in his bowl."

"I don't think Fred likes horses," Mary Beth said, and Callie knew she was nervous and scared.

She smiled at her. "It's okay, sweetie. We're just going to watch. Buckle up."

Wade started the truck and they drove off. "You're just going to watch, huh?"

"Yes."

"Have you ever ridden?"

"Yes. In college."

"Good, then you'll enjoy it again."

"This is Brit's day and I'll be happy to watch."

A crooked smile curved his lips and she couldn't help but smile back. She was at ease and happy and hoped this day turned out as good as she felt.

Brit sat by the window and pointed out horses and cows as they rode, as if they couldn't see them. It was the first time they'd been on this road and Callie soaked up the view. Barbed-wire fences enclosed ranches and farms and the scene was spectacular with its rolling hills dotted with magnificent oaks and foliage. It was all wrapped in a serene, peaceful package of wide-open spaces and incredible vistas.

"What's that?" Brit asked pointing at a field.

"It's a goat, stupid," Adam said.

"Callie, he said it again. You have to punish him or he has to say he's sorry."

Callie closed her eyes briefly, not wanting to have this conversation in front of Wade.

"No, Callie," Mary Beth cried. "Don't punish him. He's sorry, aren't you, Adam?"

"Yeah," Adam mumbled, and Callie was grateful Mary Beth had taken it out of her hands. Being a parent wasn't easy even if it was fictional.

"How's your deputy?" she asked to change the subject.

"I gave him the day off to recuperate and my secretary's husband, who works part-time, is on duty."

"Are you on call twenty-four hours a day?"

"Just about."

It was probably the way he wanted it. If he was busy, he couldn't think about his son. After John's and Glynis's deaths, she just wanted to be with the children—that was the only thing that gave her any peace. But she supposed Wade didn't have anyone. That made her very sad.

They crossed a cattle guard and saw a wrought-iron sign that read Spring Creek Ranch. White-faced red and black cattle grazed contentedly beneath oaks trees on both sides.

"We run a cow-and-calf operation here," Wade said.

"What does that mean?"

"We buy quality bulls, some Angus, Brangus or Herefords. We breed them to a herd that is also a mixture. When the calves are weaned, they go to the auction barn. A good cow produces a calf every year. Some heifers we save to replace the older cows."

"So this is a working ranch?"

"Yep."

"Is this it, Mr. Sheriff?" Brit asked.

"Yes, Brit. This is the ranch, and you can call me Wade if it's okay with your mom." He glanced at Calhe.

"Sure," she answered.

"Where's the horses?" Brit wanted to know.

"At the barn. Be patient."

"I don't think I can."

Wade stopped the truck and a Mexican rode up on a horse. They climbed out. Brit stared up at the horse with her mouth open. The Mexican dismounted and handed the reins to Wade.

Wade rubbed the horse's face. "Brit, this is Fancy. See? She has a white mane and three stocking feet—that's why we call her that. She's very pretty and gentle." He held out his hand to Brit. "Come and meet her."

Brit seemed turned to stone and Callie put her arm around her. "Have you changed you mind?" Brit had a habit of doing that.

Brit shook her head, the hat bobbing on her head.

"Are you sure?" Callie tightened the string under her chin. Brit nodded.

Wade led the horse forward and stopped a few inches from Brit. "Touch her. She loves to be rubbed."

The Mexican came forward and handed Wade some carrots.

"This is Poncho," Wade introduced him. "He takes care of the horses and horses love carrots, don't they, Poncho?"

"*Sí,* Mr. Wade."

Wade broke a piece off and gave it to Fancy. She munched away. Then Wade placed a small carrot in Brit's hand. "Feed her. It's easy."

Brit held out the carrot and Fancy took it. Brit turned to Callie, her eyes shining like headlights. "Fancy ate it."

"Yes, she did." Callie was excited, too. She didn't think Brit was ever going to make a move toward the horse.

Within minutes, Wade had her petting the animal and then he placed her in the saddle and swung up behind her. He slowly guided the horse around the pasture and soon Brit was reining the horse herself. If Brit's eyes got any brighter, there would be no need for stars tonight.

Two men rode up to the barn. The older man dismounted and walked over to Wade. Callie noticed that he limped.

"What are these people doing here? And what's that kid doing on that horse?"

"I'm letting her ride, so be nice, Pop."

"This ain't no damn riding farm. They can go over to the Ritters' for that. I want them off this property."

Callie knew this had to be Wade's father and she also knew it was time to leave.

She hurried Adam and Mary Beth to the truck and went to get Brit, who came running toward her. Wade and his father were having words and Callie got into the truck with Brit, not wanting to hear their conversation.

Wade soon joined her and they drove away in silence.

IT TOOK A MOMENT for Wade to calm down. He'd had many arguments with Jock but this one was uncalled for. It was the last straw.

"I'm sorry," he said. "My dad's going through a rough time. He's more angry at me than you." That didn't explain a whole lot, but he hoped Callie understood. Hell, he didn't understand how one man could have so much bitterness inside him.

"He's a mean old man," Mary Beth said.

"Did you see me ride, Callie?" Brit broke the tension and her busy chatter filled the cab.

As Brit relayed how well she could ride to Adam and Mary Beth, Wade whispered in a low voice to Callie. "I really am sorry. My dad's never gotten over the death of my son or the failure of the consortium where he lost all his life savings."

"I heard about that in town and it seems there are a lot of people who are against all the newcomers. Ryan told me about his father, the senator."

"There's been a lot of heartache in Homestead and the old-timers can't get past all the broken friendships and back-room deals."

"Being on the Home Free Committee pits you against your father."

"Yeah. My father's used to being a powerful man. In the old days, he and Clint controlled this town. But things have changed and now they're adversaries."

"How sad."

He was impressed with her insight. She understood what he couldn't even put into words.

"Please understand that my father's attitude has nothing to do with you personally."

"He just hates everybody."

He nodded. "But there's nice people here, too." He pointed at a nearby ranch. "That's Ethan Ritter's place. He and his wife, Kayla, run a therapeutic riding school. Kayla is also one of the new landowners. She's started a vineyard and it's doing very well. She has a daughter and they've adopted two more children. They're about Brit's age."

"I'd like to meet them one day."

"I'm sure you will."

As they drove up to Callie's house, she stared in horror. Her new picket fence was again lying on the grass and all the windows on the left side were broken. When the truck stopped, she jumped out and ran to the house.

"Callie," Wade shouted. "Come back here."

But she kept running. She paused as she reached the front door. Someone had sprayed red paint across the outer wall as a welcome message.

Wade grabbed her before she could go in. "Stay here until I check this out." In a minute, he was back and his face was angry. "Someone's trashed the house."

"Who? Who would do this?" Her hands trembled and the fear she'd managed to dampen was now returning full force. Had Nigel found them? Had he done this?

Wade took her in his arms. "I don't know, but I'll find out."

Callie leaned against him, feeling his strength, his warmth and it was good to lean on someone else for a change. She breathed in his masculine scent and it bolstered her, sustained her to face what lay ahead. Suddenly she wanted to tell him who she was.

He stroked her hair and she closed her eyes, getting lost in the feeling of his gentle touch.

"Ready to see the inside?"

"Where are the kids?" She drew back and wiped away an errant tear.

"I told them to stay in the truck. Do you want them to get out?"

"Yes. They're probably scared."

"I'll sort this out." He softly kissed her and the fear in her disappeared for that brief moment. She let herself feel the joy of his caress, an intimate brush of his masculine lips against hers with a hint of pleasures yet to come.

But worries hammered away at her. What if Nigel had done this? No, that was insane. He would have called the FBI and had her arrested. There was no need to do anything else to get what he wanted—the kids. With all of the doubts that plagued her, she desperately needed a friend—a friend she could trust.

She looked into Wade's eyes and saw his concern and compassion, reaffirming her belief that he was a man she could trust. Figuring out men had never been one of her strong suits, though, so she had to go solely on a gut feeling and the way her heart raced when he looked at her.

Callie took a deep breath and braced herself. "I have to tell you something."

CHAPTER SIX

"Callie."

She turned to see her brother and sisters standing behind her, fear on their faces. They bolted for her and she picked up Mary Beth and held her tight. Brit and Adam clung to her waist.

"What happened?" Adam mumbled into her blouse.

"Someone has vandalized the place," Wade answered.

"Is he here, Callie?" Mary Beth cried into her shoulder. "Is he?"

Callie stroked her hair, feeling her insides quiver. Mary Beth was talking about Nigel—they were all thinking about Nigel. Callie had to reassure them. "No, sweetie. No one's here."

They walked inside and Callie inhaled sharply. Their things were thrown all over the place and their sleeping bags had been sprayed with the same red paint as the front of the house. Jagged pieces of glass from the windows littered the bedroom floors.

Callie gasped at the sight and set Mary Beth on her feet. Clearly someone did not want them here. But who?

Mary Beth ran to the goldfish bowl that miraculously had not been turned over. "Fred's okay. He didn't hurt him."

Suddenly Callie felt drained. All the hard work they'd done had now been undone. She'd never felt more alone than she did at that moment. How could she keep this up? Everything was going against her.

Adam slipped his hand into hers. "We'll fix it up again."

That tiny voice of hope, and the faith they had in her, gave her strength, then she glanced into Wade's worried eyes and the despair quickly vanished. He cared about them. He would help.

"You can't stay here, so gather some clothes and let's go. You're staying at my place."

"We can't do that," Callie said. "Your father doesn't want us there. I noticed a motel on the outskirts of town and we'll stay there."

"You're not staying in that crappy place. There's plenty of room at the ranch and I'll handle my dad."

"Wade…"

"Get your clothes." His voice was firm and Callie gave in because she didn't really have another option. She didn't want to bother Miranda.

"While you're getting your clothes, I'll call June Bug and get him over here to board up everything until I find out who did this."

Callie didn't argue. She grabbed their clothes and threw them into a suitcase, then they loaded up again in the truck—this time they took Fred. Wade went by his office to talk to the deputy on duty and soon they were headed back to Spring Creek Ranch.

On the ride, no one said much and Callie was numb, wondering what she was going to do. She'd signed a contract to stay here and she'd keep her word. She wouldn't run, but so many emotions were urging her to do just that. Especially her fear. But her top priority was the kids and their safety. That's why she was going back to face Jock Montgomery—something that wasn't on her to-do list. But she trusted Wade.

She hadn't had a chance to tell him. Now it was only a matter of time. He had to know the truth about her. She was a wanted criminal. What would he do? Oddly, she didn't have any fears about that and she knew something good was happening between them.

DRIVING UP TO THE DOUBLE-CAR garage, Wade said, "Wait here. I have to talk to my father first."

"Wade…"

"Just wait."

With that, he hurried into the house. Jock was bent over his plate at the kitchen table, nibbling on the supper Yolanda had left him.

"You get rid of those freeloaders?"

Wade clamped his jaw tight and placed his hands flat on the table, knowing there was only one way to deal with Jock—to be as hard-hearted as he was. "Pop, listen to me. Mrs. Austin's house was vandalized and she has no place to stay. I told her she and the kids could stay here."

Jock's fork fell onto his plate with a clatter. "Over my dead body."

Wade straightened. "Okay, Pop. You're forcing my hand. This is my house, my land and I say they stay."

"You gonna throw that in my face, are you?"

"I don't want to, but nothing else gets through to you." The five hundred acres was his mother's inheritance from her family and she'd put it in Wade's name before Jock had had all his financial problems. Everything Jock had owned had gone into the consortium.

"Fine, I'll leave then." Jock got to his feet.

"Suit yourself, but I'm only doing what you've taught me all my life. You taught me to care for people, to help them in times of need. There are three kids outside who need a place to sleep. I'm not turning them away, because I had a father who believed that every child should be cared for and loved."

"That father died four years ago." Jock hobbled past him, and down the hall to his bedroom. The door slammed.

Wade waited, expecting Jock to come out with a bag and leave. But the door stayed close. He finally walked to the door and knocked.

"Pop, all I'm asking is for you to be civil."

No response. Wade didn't know exactly what he was expecting, but his father was never going to change. He'd been hurt too deeply.

He thought of calling Miranda. He knew she'd be glad to have them, and he could call Buddy. He had room, too. Buddy was known for taking anyone in who needed help. It would make things a lot easier on Wade, but for some reason he didn't make the calls. He drew a deep breath and went to get Callie and the kids.

WADE SHOWED THEM to the guest bedroom. "It's a queen-size bed and should be big enough for you and the girls," he said. "There's a sofa bed in the den that Adam can use."

"I'm not leaving my sisters." His chin jutted out with stubborn pride.

"Okay," Wade said. "There's a cot out in the garage. I'll bring it in and you can sleep in here, too."

"Thank you," Callie replied.

They were busy the next hour getting sleeping arrangements ready. Wade made sandwiches for supper and they ate without a word. Callie helped the girls with their bath then gave Adam the bathroom. Tucking the girls in, she wondered where Wade's father was. Tomorrow she would have to make other arrangements.

Soon the lights were out and they settled in for the night.

"I'm scared, Callie," Mary Beth whispered. "What if I wet the bed?"

"Then I'll clean it up and put on fresh sheets."

"But that mean old man lives here." Mary Beth wasn't convinced.

Callie pulled her a little closer. "It's okay, sweetie. I'm right here."

"'Kay." Mary Beth snuggled against her, Miss Winnie tight in one arm.

"Do you think Nigel found us?" Adam asked into the silence.

"No," Callie answered. "If he knew where we were, I'd be in jail. We're safe here, so go to sleep."

"But that mean old man lives here," Mary Beth pointed out again.

"I don't think he's so mean." Callie was trying to alleviate their fears when in reality she knew nothing about Jock Montgomery. "He just needs a little company."

"And maybe Wade'll let me ride Fancy again," Brit said eagerly.

"We won't be here long so let's be on our best behavior while we are."

"I'm always good," Brit pointed out. "Adam's the troublemaker."

"And you're st—"

"Adam." Callie's voice cut him off before he could finish the word.

"Sorry," he mumbled.

"Tell us a story," Mary Beth begged.

Her mind was a maze of worry and fairy tales eluded her. She didn't feel much happiness, except… "Once upon a time there was a sheriff who owned a beautiful horse that needed to be ridden."

"That's Fancy, right?" Brit joined the story.

"Then a little city girl came to town who wanted to be a cowgirl and the sheriff thought she was perfect to ride his horse."

"Is the sheriff a prince? Mary Beth wanted to know.

"No. He's a flame-eating dragon." Adam rose from his cot with his arms outstretched and jumped onto the bed. The girls screeched and dove beneath the covers. Adam bounced around and hissed and poked at them. They giggled and wiggled until Callie called a halt. Adam flopped down by Mary Beth and the room became quiet, but the tension was gone. Laughter was the best medicine and she knew they were going to be fine.

After Adam was back in his bed and the girls asleep, Callie crawled out of the bed and went to find Wade. She had to talk to him. She found him in the kitchen at a table, staring at a piece of paper. When he saw her, he turned the paper over.

"Do you need something?" he asked, a weary look on his face.

"No." She tucked her hair behind her ears.

"I heard the kids laughing. I'm glad they're okay."

"I hope we didn't disturb your father."

"Everything disturbs my father, but he's barracked in his room so don't worry about it."

"I'm sorry. We'll leave first thing in the morning."

"You'll stay as long as you need to," he said. "It's time my dad dealt with life again and three kids in the house is just the way to start."

"Still, we have to go back to our house." She took the seat next to him and tightened the belt of her lightweight robe. "Do you have any idea who would do such a thing?"

He raked a hand through his hair and she noticed his dark hair had a slight curl and a few strands of gray, making him that much more appealing.

"I have to be honest with you. As I told you, a lot of people are not happy with the newcomers in town. I've had several incidents that I can't explain, except for just plain meanness and mischief making."

"So you think someone was trying to scare me out of town?"

"Or to make the Home Free Program look bad."

"I see." She twisted her hands in her lap. She had to tell him the truth about herself, but doubts inundated her. Was she crazy? What purpose would it serve? He could arrest her and put her in jail, then what would happen to the kids?

She glanced around at the country kitchen with its cream tiled floor, oak cabinets and table, white appliances and sunflower curtains. It had a very warm, very friendly atmosphere— just like Wade. In that moment, she knew her earlier decision was the right one and she prayed she didn't live to regret it.

"I need to tell you something."

"You said that at your house."

"Yes." She locked her fingers together. "I'm not sure where to start."

He turned the paper over and pushed it in front of her. "Will this help?"

She stared down at her face. At the top in bold letters was written Wanted. At the bottom For Kidnapping. Her name, Callandra (Callie) Lambert, was under her photo and the kids photos were at the very bottom with their names. Wade knew. He knew who she really was. Her stomach rolled with a sick feeling.

She licked suddenly dry lips. "How long have you known?"

"It came through on the wire service when I was at the office. I took it before Virg or Ray could see it."

"Why?" She swallowed convulsively, waiting to see if her instincts about him were right or wrong.

"Brit said you wouldn't do anything bad unless you had a good reason. I suppose I wanted to hear that reason."

He was giving her a chance to explain. Air gushed into her lungs—her instincts were right. She gripped her fingers until they were numb. How could she convince him to help her? Feminine wiles, she'd heard her friends say, worked on men.

Bat her eyes, show some leg, a little more cleavage. What was she thinking? Wade was not that type of man. She'd definitely watched too many movies and listened to too many crazy friends. She had to be honest because if she had to depend on her feminine wiles she'd be in jail for the rest of her life.

"I didn't have time to get all the details, but why would you kidnap your own children?"

She exhaled deeply, glad for the opening. "They're not my children."

His eyes narrowed and she rushed into speech. "They're my half siblings." From there it was easy and the whole story spilled out.

"So everything on the application was false?"

"Yes. I never realized it was so easy to get fake IDs."

He leaned back in his chair and folded his arms across his chest. "Tell me about your relationship with your mother."

"My mother was fickle, impulsive and wanted a better way of life for both of us—that's why she left my father." She didn't mention her father being from Homestead. Like always, she pushed it to the back of her mind. "He was an alcoholic and couldn't hold down a decent job. We lived in a one-room apartment in Houston and it was depressing. Glynis went through a string of men and I spent a lot of time with our elderly neighbor, Mrs. Heinbacker. She taught me how to cook and I basically took care of Glynis and myself. I did the cooking and cleaning because Glynis didn't care about any of those things. She kept telling me she was going to find us a rich daddy.

"She didn't love John when she married him, but as the years went by she grew to love him. John was a good, decent man. He adopted me and we moved to New York and we became a family. John wanted more children but it took five years for that to happen. I've always been there for the kids. Glynis was busy with social functions and I kept them when John and Glynis went on vacations or out for the evening. The only time I was away from them was when I was in college, but then John would send tickets for me to come home every other weekend. I still miss him." She forced back tears. "When he was dying, I promised to help Glynis with the children. Mom had a habit of getting stressed out and making bad decisions. John had the kids' futures planned from the day they were born. Education was his top priority, and he wanted the children to attend the same private school that he did. From there they will apply to Harvard as he did. Their education is paid for and I gave my word to see that his wishes were carried out, but Mom knew his plans and the kids wanted to be just like their father and I never thought there'd be a problem. That was before Mom met Nigel."

There was a long pause before Wade spoke. "Did you ever ask your mother why she married him?"

"Yes, and she got angry and said I didn't understand what she was feeling. So I stayed out of the picture. She called me the week before she died and said that she and Nigel were arguing. He wanted to send the kids to boarding school. That was something John had never considered and he would have been fervently against it. He wanted the kids at home with family. Glynis said she didn't know what to do."

"What did you tell her?"

"I reminded her of what John had wanted and she told me again that I didn't understand." Callie smoothed the fabric of her robe. "The night she died, she called me at the restaurant and said she needed to talk to me. I told her I didn't get off until twelve. She said she'd made a big mistake and didn't know what to do and that she had to see me. I told her to come to the restaurant and she agreed. I waited and waited but..."

"She was killed before she could reach the restaurant," Wade finished for her.

"Yes." This time a tear escaped and she blinked it away. "I guess she was going to tell me she'd changed her will." She raised her eyes to his. "Are you going to arrest me?"

"I should. That's my job."

Callie waited, her breath wedged in her throat like pine needles. As the silence grew, she plunged into speech. "They'll give the kids back to Nigel and they're deathly afraid of him. Please don't do that."

Wade ran both hands over his face. "You're asking me to break the law."

She watched the turmoil on his face. "You knew who I was when we stopped at your office. Why didn't you arrest me then instead of bringing us out here—to your home?"

He sighed. "Because I guess I knew then that I was going to break the law."

Her eyes held his. "You're not going to arrest me?"

"It would be best if you go back and face this situation. Fight it in the courts."

"I tried that. The courts take time and no one seemed to care that Nigel was hitting them and making Mary Beth sleep in a bed of urine. And he leaves them alone at night with no one else in the house. I also tried to get Child Protective Services to remove them from the home until my case was heard, but they refused. I didn't have any options left but to abduct them and run."

"That's makes you the criminal."

"Yes. It wasn't easy to make that decision. I'd be taking them away from the environment John had planned for them. But I knew in my heart that he wouldn't want them being afraid or hit. I did the only thing I could under the circumstances. I hired a lawyer and as soon as she can get a judge to hear my side, I will take them back. Until then I will stay on the run unless…" She gnawed on her lip. "What are you going to do?"

The silence grew and she resisted the urge to bite her nails. Suddenly he looked at her, his expression unreadable.

"I think I'll check out Nigel Tremont."

Callie jumped up and threw her arms around his neck. "Thank you. Thank you." She kissed the side of his face, knowing she was right on target about this man.

He stilled. "I don't want that kind of thanks. And don't read anything into my offer. I'm only trying to get to the truth."

"I'm sorry." She immediately pulled away, feeling as if he were putting handcuffs on her—handcuffs on her heart.

He rose to his feet. "Callie, I'm looking for answers and it's not going to help if you and I get involved. You've falsified an application and done a lot things I shouldn't be turning a blind eye to. I'm taking a big risk, but you're safe here until I get those answers."

She brushed her hair back with a nervous hand. "Okay."

"No more lies and no more running."

She hesitated. "I can't really promise about the running. I'll do everything I can to keep those kids away from Nigel."

"Give me some time."

She nodded and walked to her room.

"Callie."

She looked back. "I'm leaving early in the morning so just ignore my father and don't take his attitude too seriously."

"The kids and I will go with you. I have to start repairing the damage to our house."

"Not tomorrow. I don't want anything touched until I've caught the culprit."

"Oh."

"Just enjoy the ranch. I'll have Poncho saddle up Fancy

again for Brit and he'll help her learn to ride. He's very good with horses. I'll be back before you know it. "

"I don't guess I have much of a choice."

"No."

WADE WATCHED HER WALK into the bedroom with an ache in his gut. From the start, he knew she was hiding something. From the start, he knew she was trouble. And from the start, he knew he'd be powerless to change the way she made him feel. He touched the side of his face where her lips had kissed his skin, still feeling her softness and that stir of desire in his lower abdomen. But he had to stay focused. He could lose his job over this. His job kept him sane, kept him going. Without that, he'd become a bitter old man like his father.

Why was he risking everything for a woman?

CHAPTER SEVEN

WADE WAS UP EARLY and in town before the sun rose. In all good conscience, he couldn't arrest Callie or notify the FBI. He didn't doubt for one minute that she was telling him the truth. The kids were tense and afraid and clung to Callie, clearly a sign of trauma. He'd noticed that from the start, but wasn't sure of the cause, thinking it had something to do with their father's death. Now he knew the real reason and there was no way he'd send those kids back into that situation. He saw how much they loved Callie and how much she loved them. Until he got some answers about Nigel Tremont, he'd protect them.

Her best recourse was to go back and face the music—that was the legal way. He'd been a lawman long enough to know the legal way wasn't always right and he couldn't force her to do that. She'd have to spend some time in jail and he wanted to make sure those kids were well taken care of before that happened. And hopefully, he could find something on Nigel so Callie wouldn't have to go through that. He'd work tirelessly to keep her safe.

He didn't question his motives. He already knew his heart was involved, even though there wasn't any future for them. That was the way it had to be. Seemed as if the two of them were tortured souls looking for a safe place to hide. He'd found his, but Callie's place wasn't in Homestead. She'd leave as soon as her life was sorted out. And the future would be the same for him—just another day to get through.

He hated leaving her to face his father, but he had a feeling Callie could handle anything.

His first stop was the office. He had to make sure no other bulletins had come in on Callie and he needed to call a detective he knew in New Jersey. Simon Marchant had been a detective with Wade in Houston, but after being injured on the job, he'd resigned and moved to New Jersey where his wife's family lived. He was now a private investigator and if anyone could find dirt on Nigel, Simon could.

He then spoke to Ray about Tolliver Craddock, who'd been arrested for poisoning Kayla Ritter's vineyard and was out on bail thanks to a fancy lawyer from Austin. Wade's deputies were keeping a close eye on him, though. Ray said Craddock had gone to San Antonio to visit his sister and hadn't returned. That meant Craddock wasn't in Homestead at the time of the vandalism and was therefore not involved. Or so it seemed.

Later, Wade drove to Callie's house to check things out. He frowned as he stopped at the curb. June Bug was asleep in a rocker on the porch with a shotgun across his lap.

As Wade hurried up the steps, June Bug jumped to his feet with the gun in his hands.

"Oh, it's you, Sheriff." His voice was sleepy.

"June Bug, put that gun down. What are you doing?"

He propped the gun against the house. "Making sure nobody does anything else to this house."

"Have you been here all night?"

"Yes, sir. We got a yellow-bellied coward in this town and if he comes here again, he's gonna get a load of buckshot. No one's hurting Mrs. Austin as long as I'm around."

Wade sensed that June Bug had a big crush on Callie. Hell, he did, too. "Go home and let me do my job."

"I'm not leaving until I get the house fixed up for Mrs. Austin."

It was useless to argue with him. Wade was familiar with the Stromiski stubbornness. "Just don't touch anything until I'm through here."

"Yes, sir."

Wade went inside to look around. Everything was thrown around, but the biggest damage was the spray paint and broken windows. Glass was everywhere. With his handkerchief, he picked up several rocks and placed them in a bag. In the kitchen, he squatted to study the floor. Nothing gave him a clue, then he spotted a gum wrapper by the back door. He added it to the bag. It probably belonged to one of the kids, but he'd still check it out.

As he stood, Virgil came charging into the kitchen, the left side of his face slightly blue.

"How's the head, Virg?"

"Fine. I'm back on duty. Ray said there was some vandalism here last night and I guess he was right."

"Yeah." He handed him the bag. "Lock this in the safe. I'll be over at the office later."

"Okay. What do you want me to do with Cora Lou and Norris? Cora Lou apologized for hitting me, but Norris is getting angry, saying he's going to sue the sheriff's department."

"I'll take care of Norris when I get to the office."

Virgil looked around. "Who'd do this?"

"Not sure yet."

Virg leaned over and whispered, "June Bug has a gun."

"I know."

"Want me to take it away from him?"

"No." The last thing he needed was for Virgil to get into another altercation. "I need you on duty today."

"Come on, Wade. It wasn't my fault. Cora Lou's a mean bitch, but I'm still not hittin' her."

"Virg." Wade sighed. "I've got a lot to do today and I need you to take care of the office."

"I'm on my way." Virg headed for the door.

"And lock that bag in the safe."

"Got it."

Virgil was sometimes a little overeager, but he was a good officer. People didn't take him seriously, which was where the problems started. In a town this size, they were lucky to have him.

Wade walked outside to question June Bug.

He took out his pen and pad. "What time did you leave last night?"

"I left about five-thirty. I told Mrs. Austin I was because I wanted to check on some prices for a central air and heat unit. I called several places and my sister Etta was at my place and did some checking on the computer for me. Etta fixed supper. She can't cook like Mama, but—"

Wade cut in, not wanting to hear the whole Stromiski story. "Was anyone around here when you left?"

"No. Bubba Joe and me finished replacing those boards and left." June Bug pointed to the right.

"You didn't see anybody on the street?"

"No, oh, wait a minute. Buddy came by with Rascal. He was driving that old Model T of his."

"What did he want?"

"Said he brought Rascal over to visit with the kids."

"Who left first?"

"Buddy, and we followed him to Main Street."

"Okay." Wade put his pen and pad back in his pocket. "If you think of anything, give me a call."

"Yes, sir. Can I start work on the house?"

"No. I'm not through."

June Bug took his seat in the rocker, with the shotgun across his lap.

"If you fire that gun, I'm going to arrest you."

"That's okay. Sometimes a man has to do what he has to do."

And when the man is June Bug's size sometimes he needs a little help. Wade walked off, letting him keep his gun. Dignity came to men in different ways. For June Bug, protecting Callie was making him six feet tall. He guessed that was a hell of a lot better than eating bugs.

Wade took a couple of steps and saw Senator Gallagher and Ryan coming up the walk.

"What's going on here, Wade?" the senator demanded. Wade knew Clint had been diagnosed with macular degeneration and it seemed to make his attitude as bad as Jock's.

"Vandalism." Wade didn't see any reason to sugarcoat it.

"That's what happens when you get riffraff in town. I tried to tell the city council that, but no one was listening to me. Everyone was gung ho on this home-free nonsense and look how it's turning out."

"That's your personal opinion, sir, and you're welcome to it. Now I've got a crime to solve." He tipped his hat. "Senator. Ryan."

Ryan caught up with him. "I'm sorry, Wade. He clings to the old ways and he's never going to be a fan of the Home Free Program."

"I know. I've got one at home just like him."

Ryan nodded. "Yep, you do." He glanced at the house. "How's Callie and the kids?"

"They're fine." Wade's eyes narrowed. "How did you find out about this so fast?"

"We stopped in at Bertha's Kolache Shop this morning and it's the talk over coffee. Dad insisted on checking it out. I think he's gathering stones to throw at the city council."

Edith Mae worked at the shop, so June Bug had to have told her. Now it would be all over town in a matter of minutes.

"Good to see you, Ryan. I've got to run."

Before he could get into his vehicle, Miranda and Arlen Enfield, a member of the Home Free Committee, drove up right behind him. The grapevine was faster than he thought.

Miranda reached him first. "It's true," she said, staring at the house. "Where's Callie and the kids?"

"They're safe."

Arlen walked up, looking like something out of a magazine in his tailored jeans and jacket and groomed silver hair and dapper mustache. As a local real-estate agent, he dressed the part. He'd been mayor before Miranda had beaten him. She'd run on the platform of restoring Homestead and won, to Arlen's shock. After Arlen had gotten over his defeat, he'd backed the Home Free Program and had been appointed to the committee.

"This doesn't look good. What are you doing about it, Wade?"

"Standing around talking when I've got work to do." He looked at Miranda. "I'll talk to you later."

CALLIE GOT UP AND WOKE the kids. They dressed as quietly as possible, then made their way to the kitchen for breakfast. The light was on and the smell of coffee lingered in the air so that meant Jock was up, but the house was silent.

"What are we having?" Brit asked, her long hair hanging partially in her face and down her back. Callie dashed back to the bedroom and found the brush and hair bands and fixed Brit and Mary Beth's hair in ponytails. She didn't like it in their faces.

Opening the refrigerator, she saw milk and orange juice. She was hesitant about eating the food, but she would reimburse Mr. Montgomery for everything they used. It was nice to be in a kitchen again and the stove was gas, like she preferred.

She felt like a kid in a candy store and she couldn't stop herself. She had to cook. When she'd been in her teens, her friends had called her weird because she'd enjoyed cooking and trying new recipes. In college it had been the same, but her room had always been full of kids eager to taste her treats. Glynis had teased her about being from another era. But her mother and John had supported her in everything she'd wanted to do. They'd given her a summer in Paris as a graduation gift and being at the Cordon Bleu had instilled an even deeper desire to be a chef.

Pouring juice for Adam and milk for the girls, she realized she'd had a very good life. Now she had to make sure the kids had the life they deserved. Although she wondered how Wade was faring in his investigation, she threw herself into preparing breakfast. There were plenty of eggs and even buttermilk, so she decided to make omelets and homemade biscuits.

She cut fresh butter into flour until it was crumbly and added buttermilk, baking powder, baking soda and salt. As she was kneading the dough, Adam asked. "Why don't we just leave, Callie? No one wants us here."

Finding a baking sheet for the biscuits, she replied, "That's not true. We've met some nice people and I've signed a contract. I'm not breaking my word. That's what Dad taught us, right?" She couldn't tell him that Wade already knew who they were. It would worry him too much.

"Yeah," Brit said. "Daddy said you're as good as your

word and I'm real good and so is Callie. Besides Sheriff Wade said he wouldn't arrest us and I believe him."

"And you're an id—"

Callie held up a finger covered with flour to stop him. Before she could reprimand Adam, the back door opened and Jock walked into the kitchen.

The air became thick with tension. Callie could see that Wade looked a lot like his father; it was definitely where he got those dark eyes, but Jock's face was hard and his eyes cold. No warmth in sight.

"Why don't you make yourself at home in my kitchen," Jock snapped.

"I just wanted to fix the kids some breakfast and I'll repay you for all the food I use."

"I'll get my coffee and be outta here." Jock reached for a mug.

"We're having omelets and biscuits and you're welcome to join us." Callie put the biscuits in the oven, trying to be as civil as she could.

"Out of a can?"

"No. I made them from scratch."

"Callie makes everything that way and it's good " Brit took a swallow of milk.

"And I'm having a banana on my omelet," Mary Beth piped up.

"Those are my bananas, kid, so stay out of them."

Callie waited for the pouting lip, but to her surprise Mary Beth retorted, "You have to share. Callie says we have to share."

Jock filled his cup. "Callie can go to hell. Stay out of my bananas."

"You're a mean old man and you use bad words."

"Remember that, kid."

Jock stormed out the door, but Callie could see him standing on the long porch that ran across the back of the house, sipping on his coffee.

The aroma of baking biscuits permeated the room and Callie opened the door a crack so the smell could waft outside. A little trickery might work. They said the way to a man's heart was through his stomach. She just wasn't sure Jock Montgomery still had a heart.

She continued with the breakfast, breaking eggs and cutting up ham and cheese while keeping an eye on the porch. Taking the biscuits out of the oven, she placed them on the stove.

Turning, she saw Jock standing inside the door. "If you're gonna eat my bananas, I'm gonna eat your biscuits."

"'Kay," Mary Beth said. "That's sharing, Mr. Sheriff's Daddy."

Jock eyed her strangely. "My name is Jock." He removed his worn hat and took a seat.

Callie hurriedly put the biscuits in a bowl and placed them on the table with a dish towel over them. Then she slid the omelets onto plates, cutting one in half for Brit and Mary Beth, and carried them to the table with butter and honey, and took her seat.

Mary Beth looked at her omelet. "I want a banana on it."

Callie was hoping she'd forget about that. She looked at Jock.

"A deal's a deal." He spread a big dollop of butter onto a biscuit.

"Thank you."

Mary Beth frowned at Jock eating a biscuit. "We didn't say grace."

Jock paused with his mouth full.

"Go ahead, sweetie."

Mary Beth folded her hands. "Thank you God for keeping us safe. Thank you for this food and for Callie."

Jock swallowed. "Why do you call your mother Callie?"

Mary Beth squirmed in her chair. No one had asked that question, not even Wade. She'd noticed a few sharp glances, but no one had enough nerve to ask. Until Mr. Montgomery.

"They just do," Callie answered, not feeling a need to explain or lie. They ate in silence and Callie thought that was best.

Finally, Jock laid down his fork, looking at Adam. "What's your name, boy?"

"Adam."

"Do you ride?"

"No, sir."

"Why not?"

Adam glanced at Callie.

"Don't look at your mother," Jock shouted. "Answer me."

"Because we lived in the city and we didn't have a horse and I don't want to ride your old horses anyway."

"Don't talk back, boy." Jock shoved back in his chair and reached for his hat. There was a cane on the hat rack but he didn't take it.

He turned to face Callie. "How long you stayin'?"

Not more one second than I have to. "I'll be gone as soon as I can get back into my house."

Jock slapped his hat onto his head. "People always want somethin' for free, but gal, there ain't nothin' free on this earth—not even freedom. It all comes with a price."

Having had his say, he stomped away and slammed the door.

Callie felt like doing the same to his ornery head.

WADE DROVE OVER to Buddy's. He was underneath a car and Wade tapped on the hood. "Hey, Buddy. I need to talk to you."

Buddy pushed out and got to his feet. He was the best mechanic in town and working on old cars was his hobby. The Model T, a 1958 Corvette and a 1966 Mustang were his pride and joy and he kept them running like new. He didn't have any family left. In his younger days, he'd been a rabble-rouser and spent a lot of time in Jock's jail. He'd finally left town for a better life and had come back about twelve years ago when his mom had been dying. He'd stayed and opened up the old gas station. Today, he was a model citizen and Wade considered him a friend.

"What's up, Wade?" Buddy wiped his hands on a rag. "Squad car need servicing?"

"No. Had a bit of a problem over at Callie's house. Did you see anyone over there yesterday afternoon?"

"Problem?" He stuffed the rag in his back pocket, his eyes worried. "What happened?

"Someone trashed the house. Did you see anything?"

"No. Everything was quiet, even Mrs. Smythe, her neighbor, wasn't home. She said her car was running funny and I was going to take it for a spin. Are Callie and the youngins okay?"

"Yeah. I'm just trying to find out who did it."

Buddy's eyes narrowed in thought. "I waved to Mrs. Miller across the street. She was leaving, then I stopped at the Smythe house. When she wasn't home, I drove on to Callie's and met June Bug and Bubba Joe. They said Callie had gone to your ranch and I followed 'em to the square. I stopped at the hardware store to get a bolt and I talked to Myron for a bit. When I came out, the Harvey boys almost run over me with their bicycles. They sure were in a hurry headed down Bluebonnet Street. I was steamed because I thought one of them scratched my Model T as he tried to miss me. But he just kissed it with his wheel."

"Did you talk to them?"

"No. But I yelled a few words at 'em."

"Did you notice anything else?"

"No. I came home and checked over my car."

"If you remember anything, give me a call."

"Sure thing. You sure they're okay?"

"Yeah. They're at the ranch if you want to call them."

On a hunch, Wade headed over to Tanner's to speak with Ed. The Harvey boys were constantly in trouble and a step away from juvenile hall. Their father, Howard, didn't help matters. He was one of those people who'd been fervently against the land giveaway. But after it had been implemented, he'd applied for a parcel of land and had been rejected. That had made him angry. When the program had been launched, the Home Free Committee had set up guidelines and among them were no criminal history and no debt. Howard failed on those counts. He had two DUIs against him and he'd been locked up for hitting Melba Sue, his wife. Creditors were continually hounding him and he lived paycheck to paycheck. He worked for Rudy Satterwhite, a local fence builder and a member of the city council. Rudy had been peeved when Howard's application had been denied. Now Wade was wondering if Howard had influenced his boys with his hatred. It was a long shot, but still he'd check it out.

The bell jingled as Wade went inside the colorful establishment, which had been here as long as Wade could remember and run by the same family. Ed was in his early thirties and had taken over from LeRoy, his dad.

"Hey, Wade. What can I do for you?" Ed asked, counting change for a customer.

"Could I talk to you for a minute, please?"

"Sure." Ed called to another clerk to take care of the cash register and met Wade some distance away so they could talk in private.

"Were the Harvey boys in here yesterday?"

"Yep."

"Can you remember what they bought?"

"Sure. Bubble gum."

"That's it?"

"Yep. I watch those boys closely when they're in here. Caught 'em shoplifting a couple of times and I'm just real glad to see the backs of 'em."

"Did you hear them talking about anything?"

"The younger one, Cliff, kept saying they had to hurry."

"Where were they going?"

"Don't know, and didn't really care."

"Thanks, Ed." Wade walked out, thinking about that piece of information. They were in a hurry—same thing Buddy had said. Why? Were they in a hurry to get to Callie's house while she was out? The hardware store caught his eye. On another hunch, he headed there.

Wade walked in and an old, musty smell greeted him. The store was cluttered with all the paraphernalia a person could use from nuts and bolts to small kitchen appliances. And most of the items had probably been there for a long time, gathering dust.

"Hey, Sheriff," Myron said, getting to his feet from a chair behind the counter. Myron Guthrie owned the store and was also a lifetime resident of Homestead. There was only one word to describe him—*round*. He was a short, portly man who actually waddled when he walked. He'd been that way ever since Wade had known him. Myron had a full white beard and sideburns, but his head was as smooth as a bowling ball and just as big.

He looked at Wade over his skinny half-rimmed glasses. "What can I do for you?"

"Were the Harvey boys in here yesterday afternoon?"

"Sure were."

"Did they buy anything?"

"Is this police business?" Myron's eyes widened at the possible hint of gossip.

"Yes, and I'd appreciate an answer. Did they buy anything?"

"Yeah. A can of red spray paint."

God, this was too easy. Could those boys be that stupid?

"I asked what they were going to do with it," Myron was saying.

"Did they tell you?"

"They said they were going to paint their bicycles."

Wade didn't think so. They'd vandalized Callie's house and now he had to prove it.

"Thanks, Myron."

"Anytime, Sheriff."

WADE HURRIED TO HIS OFFICE to release Cora Lou and Norris. Norris had his chest stuck out, ready to vent his feelings but Wade wasn't in the mood to listen.

"I'm letting you go today hoping a night in jail will teach you a lesson. But if I get one more call about a disturbance at your house, I'm locking you both up and you'll do some serious jail time. You might want to think about those four kids you have at home."

"I'm sorry, Sheriff," Cora Lou apologized. "I didn't mean to hit Virgil. He just got in the way."

"Just make sure there's not a next time."

"Yes, Sheriff. Right now I just want to go home and see my babies."

"Sorry, Sheriff," Norris muttered as they went out the door.

Through the open door, Wade caught a glimpse of Millie coming up the sidewalk. He turned to Barbara Jean. "Take care of Millie. There's no news on who trashed Mrs. Austin's house."

"Sure, Wade."

"Any calls from Simon Marchant?"

"No. I'll let you know as soon as he does."

"Thanks, Barbara Jean." He slipped down the hall and out the back way before Millicent saw him.

Wade wondered how Callie was faring with his dad. Suddenly he had to know.

Callie answered the phone. "Montgomery residence." At her soft voice, the tension in him eased.

"Hi. It's Wade. How's it going?"

She told him about the morning and he laughed. "He actually ate?"

"Yes. He's outside now and I'm not sure what he'll do next, but I'm positive we'll all be entertained."

"I'm glad you have a sense of humor."

"I have to laugh to keep from crying." She paused. "Have you found out anything?"

"I'm following a lead. I'll tell you about it when I get home."

"Okay."

"And Callie…"

"What?"

He had no idea what he was going to say, but words were there at the back of his throat—words he wasn't ready to acknowledge or accept.

"Try not to worry."

"I won't. Just come home soon."

Home.

Why did that sound so right?

CHAPTER EIGHT

CALLIE HUNG UP, FEELING Wade's voice soothe her like a glass of her mom's best brandy. She had put her trust in the right man and now she had to depend on him to do the right thing. He wouldn't let her down.

Turning, she froze. In the doorway stood a well-rounded Mexican woman with a dead chicken in her hand, which had been plucked and gutted.

"Who are ya?" the woman asked.

"I'm Callie Austin and these are my children, Adam, Brit and Mary Beth. We're staying here for a while." The kids crowded behind her as if they might need some protection.

"With that old *bastardo?*" She carried the chicken to the sink and began to wash it. Without waiting for a reply, she continued, "Killed this young pullet because the old *bastardo*'s always complaining that all I cook is chili, beans and tacos. Hate frying chicken. Takes too much time."

"I'll fry it," Callie offered. "I don't believe I caught your name."

"Yolanda—everybody calls me Yo." She glanced over her shoulder at Callie. "Ya can cook?"

Why did everyone doubt her ability? "Yes. I can cook."

Yolanda grabbed a towel and wiped her hands. "Well, *niña,* have at it."

"Are there any vegetables?"

"It's June. My garden's bursting with vegetables. What do ya want?"

Callie loved fresh produce—that's what she loved about Tanner's. One day, she planned to have her own garden. "Potatoes, green beans or anything you feel Mr. Montgomery would like."

"Arsenic comes to mind, but I'll go gather up a few things." Yolanda looked at the kids. "Wanna come? Could use some help."

The kids didn't budge.

"They're not used to being away from me."

"Ya don't want to raise no sissies, now do ya?" Yolanda waved a hand. "Come, *niños.* Yo'll show you some of the ranch. We got cows, horses, dogs, cats, a couple of goats and—"

"You got dogs?" Mary Beth asked, her eyes bright.

"Sure 'nuff do."

"I want to go."

Callie was torn. The kids hadn't been out of her sight for days and she had to stay here to prepare the chicken.

"I'll go," Adam said, as if he were reading her mind.

"I'll go, too," Brit said. "I want to see the horses."

"Well, let's load up, *niños.*"

Protests hovered on Callie's lips, but Yolanda had them out the door before she could voice them. She was letting them go with a stranger. Running to the door, she grabbed the handle then reminded herself that Yo worked for the sheriff. She wouldn't hurt the kids and maybe it was good for them to be away from her for a little bit.

Callie busied herself in the kitchen and decided to make more biscuits to go with the fried chicken and gravy. She didn't have time to make rolls. She was just excited to be cooking again. When she heard the kids laughing, she was surprised they'd been gone over an hour.

"Look what we brought," Brit exclaimed, holding a bucket of green beans. Yo had a bucket of new potatoes and onions and Adam carried tomatoes and squash. Mary Beth held a large zucchini.

"Oh, my goodness, " Callie laughed. "I don't know if I can cook all this."

"We washed everything with a garden hose at Yo's house," Adam said. "To get the dirt off."

"Thank you very much."

Mary Beth handed her the zucchini. "I'm gonna go play with Peanut and Chester. That's Yo's dog and potbellied pig. He's so cute. We brought them back with us."

A pig? Was that safe? She glanced out the window to see a small pig with a big belly. Mary Beth was on the grass hugging it and the pig seemed gentle enough.

"Chester's a pet," Yo said, sensing Callie's worry. Opening the refrigerator, Yo saw the cut up chicken. "Lawdy. Ya do good for a city *niña.*"

"How do you know I'm a city girl?"

Yo sat down and began to snap the beans. "It shows."

Callie only smiled. Maybe it did. She wondered what Yo would say if she told her she'd been born in Homestead. Not time for that little secret. She had to tell Wade first.

As she worked, she thought about her father. After the debacle with Del, she hadn't felt comfortable asking anyone else their family name. And Buddy had said he didn't know any Collinses. With everything that was going on, she hadn't had time to investigate further. But she would. One way or the other, she had to know.

Yolanda chatted on while Callie worked. "Never saw anyone make potatoes like that."

"With milk gravy? It's a Southern recipe and delicious with new potatoes." Callie poured fresh milk over the scraped, cooked potatoes. She added several large blobs of butter and returned the pot to the heat.

"Did you make the butter that's in the refrigerator?" Callie asked, knowing the butter was homemade.

"Sure did. Can't eat that stuff in the stores. My family always makes it in Mexico and I make it here. My husband, Tex, milks the cow, though."

"It's wonderful—so creamy." Callie mixed flour with a little milk and stirred it into the potatoes until it thickened, then she added black pepper.

"Mr. Jock gonna think he's died and gone to heaven, and believe me, it'll be a new experience for him. Now I have to get home and fix a bite for my men."

Callie turned from the stove. "You're not staying?"

"I never stay, *niña*. The company's a little too—" she closed one eye and thought for a minute "—it's really the company. I'd rather spend time with a rattlesnake."

Callie didn't say much. She knew the feeling. Jock Montgomery was not an easy person to be around. "Thanks for the vegetables," Callie called as Yolanda left.

Callie was taking the biscuits out of the oven when Jock ambled in. The kids were sitting quietly at the table like little angels.

"Lunch is ready, Mr. Montgomery, if you're hungry."

Jock hung his hat on the rack, limped to the table and eased into a chair. "What's all this?" he asked, staring at the fried chicken, cream gravy, new potatoes, green beans and sliced tomatoes.

She set the biscuits in front of him. "Lunch."

"I'm not blind," he snapped. "I usually eat what Yo leaves in the refrigerator."

"I can get you something else."

"Nu-uh," he said, stopping her.

Callie blinked. "What does *nu-uh* mean?"

"It means *no*. Don't you know how to talk Texan, gal?"

"Guess not." She did notice certain words and phrases. Just talking to Ethel was a whole new language. But she'd never heard anyone say "nu-uh."

He reached for a wing. "Chicken's fine."

"Callie…" Mary Beth called. "We didn't say a payer."

Callie took the wing out of Jock's hand and placed it on his plate. She received a cold stare for that. "Okay, sweetie."

They bowed their heads. "Please God bless this food and everyone here, especially Mr. Sheriff Wade and Mr. Sheriff's Daddy. Amen."

Callie picked up the potatoes and handed them to Jock. He glared at her, but took them.

"You got a boo-boo, Mr. Sheriff's Daddy?" Mary Beth asked, munching on a chicken leg, obviously noticing his limp.

"I told you my name is Jock."

"You got a boo-boo, Mr. Jock?"

"Yeah, and I'm sitting across from it."

Reaching the end of her patience, Callie calmly laid her napkin on the table. "I've taught the kids to treat people with respect, and I'd appreciate it if you'd treat them the same."

"Are you telling me how to act in my own home?" His eyes were as black as soot.

"Yes," she replied without batting an eye.

"Hmmph." He spooned potatoes onto his plate and the meal continued in silence.

Callie smiled inwardly, suspecting Jock had a soft side. But years of grieving and bitterness had severely damaged that part of him.

Suddenly Jock said, "My mom used to fix potatoes like this. Haven't had them in years. Good, very good. Chicken not bad either. And biscuits and gravy—I could eat 'em all day long."

Callie drew back in surprise. Was that a compliment? She'd take it as one. Jock had two helpings of everything and three biscuits. Finally, he pushed his plate back and reached for his cane.

"Now I'm going into the den to take a short nap and I want complete quiet. Do you kids know what that means?"

Three heads nodded. "Good, and this afternoon, boy, you're gonna ride a horse."

"Yes, sir," Adam said, surprising Callie even more. She thought he would refuse.

"Me, too," Brit said. "I rode yesterday."

"Girls need to stay in the house."

"No, they don't." Brit's chin stuck out. "I'm going to be a cowgirl." Her blue eyes narrowed. "What do cowgirls do, Mr. Jock?"

"Annoy the hell out of cowboys," was his quick response.

Callie cleared her throat.

"Yeah, you can ride." Jock changed his mind and Callie tried not to smile. He really was a very lonely and hurt man.

"Fred doesn't like horses," Mary Beth put in her two cents.

"Who the hell is Fred? Is there another kid around here?" Jock's gaze swept over the room.

"Fred is her goldfish," Callie explained.

"Now that makes no sense at all."

"Kids rarely make sense, Mr. Montgomery."

"Yeah." His eyes became distant. "I remember." He trudged into the den without another word, leaning heavily on his cane.

WADE DROVE UP to the run-down Harvey house on one of the back streets. Three wrecked vehicles were in the front yard and weeds grew around them, as they did all over the yard. With tires and junk tossed everywhere among kids' toys, there was no way to mow the yard. The paint on the house was peeling and some screens had been broken and lay in the grass. A pit bull chained to one of the wrecked cars barked aggressively at Wade.

A shiny Chevy Z71 truck was parked out in front of the house. A man wearing a black hat hurried out the door and jumped into the vehicle and sped away. Wade had never seen the man or the vehicle in Homestead before and he wondered what business he had with Howard.

He knocked on the door and noticed two bicycles propped against the house, both rusty. Melba Sue opened the door with a one-year-old in her arms. In her early thirties she looked fifty, with a drawn face and thin features. The bruise under her left eye didn't escape his notice. Howard's old truck was in the yard so that meant he wasn't at work again. He must have tied one on last night and Melba Sue always received the brunt of his drinking bouts. Wade had tried to get her to press charges, but she'd refused on several occasions.

"Sheriff," she said in surprise.

"Could I speak with Howard, please?"

A look of fright came over her face and she hesitated.

"Who the hell's at the door?" Howard yelled from inside the house.

Wade walked past Melba Sue, through the living room to the kitchen where Howard sat at a table drinking coffee. There was so much stuff in the house that he basically followed a trail cleared through the junk. Two girls and a small boy sat watching TV in the living room. Melba Sue handed the older girl the baby and quickly followed.

"Howdy, Howard," Wade said, taking a chair across from him.

Howard was a big man with greasy brown hair and a

surly disposition. "What d'ya want?" Howard asked in a belligerent tone.

"The Austin house was vandalized yesterday."

"So what? Those people get everything for free and when I applied for ten acres, I was turned down."

"Still angry about that?"

"Damn right I am. I was born in Homestead and I should have been given first choice."

"For one thing, everything is not free. People who get the land have to build on it and the ones getting the homes have to repair them. It takes work and money, and from the looks of this place, you're not willing to do any work. And your criminal history was a big mark against you. We told you that at the time."

"Yeah, yeah. I done heard it all."

"Why aren't you at work today?"

"Rudy gave me the day off and it's none of your damn business."

Wade let that slide. "Where's Howie and Cliff?"

Howard's eyes narrowed. "What d'ya want them for?"

"They're in the backyard," Melba Sue said. "I'll get them."

"Shut up your damn mouth," Howard shouted at her and she cowered away.

Wade stood, resisting the urge to knock Howard out of his chair. "Howard, if I were you, I'd watch your mouth because I'd just as soon take you down to the jail as not."

The two men eyed each other and Howard could see that Wade was serious. "Get the boys," he said to Melba Sue.

She opened the door and hollered at them. In a second, they came inside grumbling.

"Why we gotta come in? I ain't babysitting." That was Howie, the older at thirteen. Cliff was twelve and they both had a skinny build with stringy blond hair. They looked like twins and a lot of people thought they were.

"What d'ya want?" Cliff asked. "We're playing and…" His voice trailed off as he saw Wade.

"Sheriff," slipped by Howie's lips.

Wade pulled out two chairs at the table and pointed. "Sit, boys."

They scurried into the chairs. "We didn't do nuthin', Sheriff," Howie said.

"I didn't say you did."

"Ask them what you want," Howard snarled, "then get the hell out of my house."

"You boys purchased a can of spray paint at the hardware store yesterday."

"Yep." Howie nodded. "We gonna paint our bicycles."

"I'd like to see the can."

Howie and Cliff shared a glance.

"Show him the damn can," Howard yelled.

Howie and Cliff hung their heads.

"You don't have the can anymore, do you?" Wade asked. "You threw it away after trashing Callie Austin's house yesterday."

"What the—" Wade raised a hand and cut off Howard.

"No, we didn't," Howie said quickly.

"Well, boys, I found some rocks and a bubble-gum wrapper inside. Now I can send them to San Antonio for finger prints or you can save the taxpayers some money and tell me the truth." He had no intention of doing any such thing, but they didn't know that.

"Did you do it, boys?" Howard asked with a touch of pride in his voice.

The boys immediately picked up on it and nodded. "We done it for you, Dad," Howie said. "That woman got everything free and we didn't get nuthin'. You said they should be run out of town and we—"

"You stupid bastards." Howard raised his hand to hit Howie and Wade grabbed it.

"Don't make me arrest you."

Howard's eyes blazed with rage and Wade had a feeling it wasn't because they'd trashed the house. It was because they'd been caught.

Howard jerked his arm away.

"Are you going to arrest them?" Melba Sue asked in a quiet voice.

"Yes, ma'am. Vandalism is a crime. These boys have heard so much hatred that they're starting to believe it."

"Is that a dig at me?" Howard scowled.

"Sure is. Get your act together and show the people of this town that you're sincere about turning your life around. Maybe something good will come of it."

"Go to hell." Howard spat out the words.

"You're responsible for the damage done to the house and I expect you and Melba Sue along with the boys in my office first thing Monday morning. If Mrs. Austin presses charges, you boys are looking at some time in juvenile hall."

"Oh, no," Melba Sue cried.

Wade inclined his head. "Let's go, boys."

"Where you taking them?" Melba Sue asked.

"They're going to clean up the mess they made." He motioned to the boys. "C'mon. June Bug can get you started."

"I'm not working for him," Howie exclaimed.

Wade put his hands on his hips. "You'll work with June Bug or go to jail. Your choice."

"The damn idiot eats bugs," Howard said. "I don't want my boys working with him."

"He doesn't eat bugs anymore. He's changed—you could learn from him. His name is Odell and that's what you'll call him."

"Dad," Howie wailed as Wade led them to the door. "We did what you wanted us to."

Howard didn't respond and Wade put them in the back seat and drove to Callie's house. Odell wasn't thrilled about the idea either. He'd rather they went to jail. But he cooperated, as Wade knew he would. He'd do anything for Callie.

Wade called Virgil to keep an eye on things in case the situation got out of hand.

HIS PHONE BUZZED and Wade headed to the city offices that were located on the first floor of the courthouse. Miranda and the Home Free Committee wanted to meet. They met in the law library. All the members were there, Miranda; Arlen Enfield, the Realtor. Frances Haase, the librarian; and Ruth Kelley, the wife of Father Holden Kelley.

They took seats around the table. "What do you have, Wade?" Miranda asked.

He told them everything he'd learned.

"So they trashed the house to please their father," Frances stated in disbelief.

"Yes," Wade replied.

"This is awful," Ruth exclaimed. "And it has to stop. Holden was upset by my vote to buy the K Bar C property and he's not happy with the Home Free Program either. I should have listened to my husband. Now our decision is causing crime."

Ruth Kelley was the perfect obedient wife and she never went against her husband's wishes. Voting to buy the K Bar C for back taxes was the first decision she'd ever voted for because she personally thought it was right for the town. And she'd received a lot of flak from her husband.

"Ruth, you did the right thing," Miranda told her. "And Wade will sort this out." She looked at Wade. "You said the boys are cleaning up the mess?"

"Yes."

"Howard works for Rudy." Arlen twisted a pencil. "I'll have a talk with him and see if he can have any influence over Howard. We don't need that kind of anger in town."

"No, we don't," Frances added. "I was hoping all these bad feelings would go away after the residents saw how good it was for the town."

Arlen threw the pencil on the table. "There are some people who are never going to see any good in the Home Free Program—Clint Gallagher for one."

Wade pushed to his feet. "Clint's not happy with the program, but he's not going to do anything to hurt it, though. I believe he wants the best for Homestead like we all do. We just differ in our viewpoints." He turned toward the door. "I'll be in touch."

"Wade." Miranda stopped him. "Tell Callie she's welcome to stay with Mom and me until her house is livable again."

"I'll let her know, but she's comfortable at the ranch and I don't see any reason to move her and the kids."

He tipped his hat and walked into the hall. That probably opened a can of worms, but he knew Miranda would squelch the gossip. If not, he didn't care. He wanted Callie close. They had a lot to talk about, especially Nigel Tremont. The board didn't need to know about that just yet.

He hurried to his office, hoping Simon had called. He'd left a message and Wade immediately called him back.

"Hey, Simon, you find anything?"

"Not yet. This is going to take a while. How big a hurry are you in?"

"Big, Simon. I need this bad and it's all confidential."

"Okay. I'm on it. There isn't anything I wouldn't do for you."

"C'mon, Simon, pulling you from a burning building doesn't mean you're indebted to me for life."

When he and Simon had been street cops, they'd cornered two drug suspects in a warehouse. Shots had been fired and Simon had been hit. The shots had ignited an oil drum and the place had gone up quickly. In the fresh air, Wade had realized that Simon wasn't with him. Without thinking, he'd run back in and dragged him out. It was all in the line of duty, but Simon never quite saw it that way.

"Ah, buddy, to me it does. I'll find everything I can on Nigel Tremont."

"Thanks, Simon. Call me when you have something."

Wade leaned back in his chair. He had to find a way to set Callie free.

Free to leave Homestead. And him.

Suddenly that didn't feel very good.

CHAPTER NINE

BUDDY CALLED AND CALLIE assured him they were all okay, then Ethel called and she told her the same thing. She spoke with Odell because he had some questions about the kitchen. Her hand on the phone, she realized she was forming bonds in Homestead, something she hadn't planned to do.

Shaking the thought off, she concentrated on the afternoon. She didn't want Adam to ride if he didn't want to and she certainly wasn't going to have Jock force him.

Jock had left some time ago and Adam was in the bedroom getting ready. The girls played with Peanut, who had found his way back from Yolanda's. A small brown-and-white terrier, Peanut clearly loved children. Mary Beth and Brit were throwing a stick and Peanut would quickly bring it back to them.

Adam came out of the bedroom and Callie stared at him. He had jeans and sneakers on instead of shorts and flip-flops.

"Adam, you don't have to ride if you don't want to." She wanted to make sure he understood that.

"I know." He looked down at his sneakers. "Wish I had some boots."

Callie did a double take. Adam had never shown any interest in horses or riding. So what had made him change his mind?

"I'm sure we can find some at the feed store."

"I want some like the sheriff wears."

"What kind is that?" She had seen Wade's boots, but she hadn't looked all that closely. Her interest wasn't in his feet.

"Cowboy boots. Real cowboy boots."

Callie put the back of her fingers to his forehead.

"What are you doing?"

"Seeing if you have a fever."

He grinned shyly. "Let's go. Mr. Jock might be waiting."

She caught his arm. "Wait a minute. Why the change of heart?"

He shifted from one foot to the other. "The sheriff's son died and after that Yo said Mr. Jock became meaner than a rattlesnake. But he's not mean, Callie. He's just angry and sad."

"How do you know that?" But she knew the answer.

"Well." He stared down at his sneakers. "When Daddy died, I was angry and sad, too. Then Mom married *him* and died and I was angry and afraid all the time. I know I'm mean to Brit, but she's always so happy and she shouldn't be because our parents are…"

"Oh, Adam." Callie wrapped her arms around him. Adam felt things deeply and once again she thought he was too young to deal with so much trauma.

He pulled back. "So you see, Mr. Jock doesn't want to be mean. He just can't help it."

"And what about the sheriff? I thought you didn't like him."

Adam shrugged. "He let us stay here, so he has to be nice and cares what happens to us. When I'm not angry, I can see that."

Callie cupped his face in her hands and kissed his cheek. "My Adam is back."

"Yeah." He grinned. "We better go."

"Okay."

They hurried out the door to join the girls. The late June afternoon was warm and there was a gentle breeze stirring up a faint smell of some sort of grass—probably what the cows were munching in the pasture. The house and barns had been built on a hill under tall oak trees and the green valley below was dotted with cattle. Everything was peacefully quiet, a horse neighed and a cow bellowed in the distance. For a brief moment, Callie felt safe, as if the outside world didn't exist—how safe would depend on Wade and his investigation. She wished he'd hurry home.

When they reached the pipe corral, not a soul was in sight.

Brit climbed onto the fence. "Where is everybody?"

"I don't know," Callie said, looking around. In the distance, dust swirled and three riders came into view, a single cow in front of them.

Adam saw them at the same time. "There they are," he shouted, pointing and climbing up beside Brit. "They're herding a cow?" He frowned. "Aren't they supposed to herd lots of cows?"

Mary Beth was holding Peanut and she put him down to join her siblings. They all watched as the group drew closer. They herded the cow toward an alley that came straight into a chute attached to the corral. Tex waved a rope above his head and yelled something in Spanish. When the cow almost reached the chute, she stopped, sensing a trap.

Tex came up behind her on the horse and shouted more Spanish and the cow shot into the chute. Quickly dismounting, Tex shoved a pipe through the fence behind the cow's legs so she couldn't back out.

Callie immediately saw there was a problem. The cow's udder was enormous and her teats were swollen. She was either fixing to give birth or already had. That thought was answered as Poncho rode into the corral with a small red-and-white calf across his saddle. He dismounted and lifted the calf to the ground, as if it weighed no more than a feather. It lay lifeless, making a guttural noise.

At the sound, the cow thrashed around, trying to get to her baby, but the pipe enclosure held her tight. Callie was so absorbed watching the distressed cow that she didn't notice Mary Beth crawling through the fence. When she looked up, Mary Beth was almost to the calf.

Her heart jumped into her throat. "Mary Beth," she screamed and was over the fence in an instant.

Peanut barked and Tex shouted, "Casa, dog." Peanut darted under the fence, down the hill to Yolanda and safety.

When Callie reached Mary Beth, she was kneeling in the dirt, patting the calf. Brit and Adam were right behind her. Callie didn't want Mary Beth doing that because she didn't know if the calf was sick or not and she'd heard of people getting diseases from cows.

"Has it got a boo-boo?" Mary Beth asked.

"Nah," Poncho replied. "Just hungry. Can't suck her mama 'cause her teats are too big."

"Poor baby," Mary Beth cooed, stroking the animal. Brit joined her in consoling the calf.

"Fix her up in no time," Poncho assured them.

Callie turned to see Wade driving up to the corral. Her heart skipped a beat. He opened a gate and strolled to where they were standing. She wanted to throw her arms around him in welcome and ask a million questions, but she didn't do either. That would have to wait until later.

He squatted by the girls. "A calf that can't suck?"

"Sí," Poncho replied. "Tex fixing to milk her mama and get some milk into the little one's belly."

Jock dismounted outside the corral and came through from the barn. "Get those kids out of here. This ain't no place for kids."

Wade rose to face his father. "Pop…"

The cow thrashed about wildly, banging against the pipe fence. Wade walked over to her, instead, putting his hand through the fence to stroke the cow. "Settle down, girl. No one's going to hurt you or your baby."

The cow paused in her struggle, as if she sensed a friend was near. Wade had that special touch just like she knew he had—someone to trust.

Adam moved to stand by Wade. "Can I pat her?" he asked, to Callie's astonishment.

Wade looked at Callie. She nodded. "Sure. She just needs to know that we're not going to hurt her."

Adam stuck his hand in and patted the cow. "What's her name?"

"Cow's don't have names, boy," Jock said with a touch of indignation. "See that tag in her ear. It says 842. That's her name and soon we'll have an identifying tag in the calf's ear to match her mother. That's how we keep track of 'em."

"Oh," Adam said.

Tex brought a small bucket. "Okay, let's see if she has any milk." He squatted and shoved the bucket under the bottom pipe, which had a larger space from the ground. The cow immediately kicked and squirmed.

"Talk to her," Wade said Adam.

"It's okay." Adam quickly did as he was asked. "They're not going to hurt you, but they need some milk for your baby. There, there, it's okay." Adam kept talking and the cow settled down. Callie just watched, amazed at this change in Adam.

Tex squeezed a teat and milk squirted into the bucket like the sound of rain on a tin roof. "Got milk. *Mucho* good."

Adam continued to pat the cow. "Mr. Sheriff?"

Wade turned to him. "Yes."

"Can I give the cow a name?"

"Sure." Wade didn't even glance at his father.

"I'll call her Sadie."

"Okay. We'll call her Sadie."

"Hummph," was Jock's opinion.

Tex pulled the full bucket through the fence and handed it to Poncho, who poured the milk into a large plastic bottle and attached a nipple. He then shoved the bottle toward Wade.

"Sheriff, do the honors."

Wade lifted an eyebrow in amusement. "You boys are gettin' lazy." But he took the bottle and walked to where Mary Beth and Brit were still cooing to the calf.

Kneeling in the dirt, he lifted the small calf's head. "Now let's see if we can get you to suck."

"Her name is Babe," Brit told him.

"Yeah," Mary Beth added. "We named her Babe."

Wade glanced at Callie and she felt a glow all the way to her toes. He was wonderful with kids and animals. To her, he was just wonderful.

He squirted milk onto Babe's nose and she sniffed, but she made no move to take the nipple. Opening her mouth, he gently pushed the nipple in and squeezed. Milk ran out the sides of her mouth and the guttural sounds became louder.

"C'mon, Babe." Brit rubbed the calf's back. "Suck the nipple. It's yummy and you need it."

Mary Beth joined in. "Take it, Babe. It's from your mommy."

Wade let them talk to her for a minute then he put the nipple in the calf's mouth and placed his hand over her nose and jaw and worked it with an up-and-down motion. The grunting grew intense as the calf tasted the milk. Suddenly, she lifted up her head, searching for the nipple. Wade quickly gave it to her and she sucked on her own.

"Look, Callie. Look," Brit shouted. "She's sucking."

"I see."

"Slow down, girl," Wade instructed as the calf sucked greedily.

"Her name is Babe," Mary Beth reminded him.

"Sorry. Forgot that."

"That's okay," Mary Beth said.

Wade removed the bottle and Babe jerked her head around searching for more. "Time to see if you'll suck your mama."

Tex finished milking all four teats into a larger bucket. He'd saved some in the smaller one. "There's some left for the calf. I got 'em down enough so she can get 'em in her mouth."

Tex carried the milk to three cow dogs waiting outside the fence. The dogs drank thirstily. Mary Beth was looking at them out of the corner of her eye.

"Are those your dogs, Mr. Sheriff?" she asked, as Callie knew she would.

"That's Tex and Poncho's cow dogs, Butch, Buster and Booger."

"What does that mean, cow dogs?" Brit was now taking an interest in the dogs.

"They help work the cattle."

"Why do you make them work?" Mary Beth had more questions.

"Because this is a ranch and that's what everyone does here, including the dogs." Jock's words were short and impatient.

Wade sighed. "Let's get out of the corral so Babe can meet her mama."

"But she'll miss us," Mary Beth protested.

Wade gave Poncho the bottle and picked up Mary Beth. "C'mon, little bit, you can visit with Babe later."

"'Kay." Mary Beth gave in without a whimper.

They all went through the gate to stand outside the corral. Jock stood silently by them. Tex removed the pipe and Poncho shouted to the cow and she backed out of the chute. Then Tex opened a gate into the corral and she charged in, sniffing and licking her baby.

The cow made sounds like Callie had never heard before

and she knew this was the cow's way of saying she was glad to see her offspring. The calf struggled to its front knees, then stood shakily on all fours. Babe immediately butted her head against the cow's stomach, searching for more food.

"It's in the back," Brit shouted. "That funny-looking thing."

Wade smiled. "It's called an udder."

"Why isn't it called a breast?" Brit wanted to know.

"That's just what it's called in a cow."

"Oh."

Finally Babe found it and latched on, sucking. Her tail wagged with pleasure and the kids clapped.

"Thank you, Mr. Sheriff Wade," Mary Beth said, hugging his neck. "You helped Babe."

As her little arms enclosed his neck, something inside Wade cracked and he knew what it was—the vault he'd built around his heart that had been sealed shut. He was feeling again and, gazing into Callie's eyes, the pain wasn't so strong either. A few weeks and this woman and the kids had totally taken over his life.

And he wished it could last forever.

"Can I ride now, Mr. Sheriff?" Brit broke through his thoughts.

He set Mary Beth on her feet. "Okay, let's see if we can find Fancy."

"There she is." Brit pointed to several horses in the pasture.

"Let's give Tex and Poncho time to get Sadie and Babe into another pen, then I'll call her up."

"Okay."

Tex herded the cow and calf into a pen on the other side of the chute because Wade said they'd have to keep an eye on her until the calf was sucking properly. Wade went into the barn to get a bridle. Going to the fence, he whistled, and Fancy reared her head and trotted over. He slipped the bridle on and led her into the barn where Callie and the kids were waiting.

"If you're going to ride, you have to learn how to take care of your horse."

"Is that what cowgirls do, Mr—"

Wade held up his hand, stopping her. "Remember, just call me Wade."

Brit looked at Callie and she nodded.

"Okay," Brit said.

"Talk to Fancy and get acquainted."

Brit rubbed the horse's nose and Fancy moved her head in a lazy fashion. "She remembers me."

"Yep, seems like she does. Now we put on a saddle blanket." He straightened the blanket across the horse's back. "Then the saddle." He reached for a regular saddle on the saddle rack and saw the smaller one that used to be Zach's. When Jock had bought him Lucky, he'd also bought a new saddle and Zach had never used the small one again.

Without thinking about it, he swung the saddle onto Fancy's back. It was time was all that he would let himself think. "See." He pointed out the straps attached to the saddle. "These hold the saddle on the horse. You cinch them tight." As he talked he worked. "You'll need help for a while then you'll learn it."

"Can I ride by myself, Mr.…Wade?"

"You think you're ready?"

Brit shrugged. "I want to."

Wade glanced at Callie and she nodded again and he felt strengthened by her faith in him. He lifted Brit into the saddle and handed her the reins. "These are the reins. Hold them in your right hand like I showed you the other day. The reins are kind of like a steering wheel. They guide the horse where you want her to go. To go right, you pull to the right. To go left, you pull to the left. To stop, pull up or toward you. Do you understand?"

"I think."

"Don't get discouraged. It takes practice. Put your feet into the stirrups."

Brit looked down and moved her feet until she found the stirrups. "They're just right," she exclaimed.

"Now, riding is about balance and it's something you'll learn as the horse moves. Use your legs to grip Fancy. Use your feet, too, try to keep your heels down. Fancy pretty much knows what to do. Are you ready?"

Brit nodded, her hat bouncing on her head.

"Let's go for a walk in the corral," Wade said, catching Fancy's bridle and leading her into the pen. Once inside, he let go and Fancy walked along the pipe fence with Wade walking beside them. When Fancy came to a corner, she stopped.

"How do you make her go left?" Wade asked.

"Like this." Brit pulled the reins left and Fancy continued walking until she reached another corner. Without Wade telling her, Brit pulled the reins again and Wade knew she was going to be fine. She liked horses and she wasn't afraid. He had a feeling she wasn't going to have a problem with balance either.

Jock stormed into the pen. "Get that saddle off that horse," he shouted.

Wade turned to his father, reaching for Fancy's bridle so she wouldn't move. "Pop, Brit needs a smaller saddle so her legs will reach the stirrups."

"That's Zach's saddle. No one uses it."

Wade felt that old familiar knot in his stomach. "Zach would want other kids to use it."

"Take it off, Wade."

Wade stuck to his decision. "No, and that's the way it's going to be."

Jock hurried back into the barn, stumbled and almost fell, but he grabbed the barn door and went in.

"Do you want me to get off?" Brit asked.

Wade focused on her shining face and not the pain in his chest. "No, let's keep walking so you can become familiar with the movement of the horse."

CALLIE WAS HOLDING HER BREATH and she released it with a whoosh. Since Wade didn't take Brit off the horse, she didn't insist that he do so either, figuring he knew what he was doing. She tightened her arm around Mary Beth and noticed that Adam wasn't beside them. Jock had said that Adam was going riding today, but nothing had been mentioned about it so far. He was so excited and she didn't want him disappointed. Taking Mary Beth's hand, she moved to the barn door. Adam was sitting by Jock on a bale of hay and she could hear their voices clearly.

"When my daddy died, I was angry, too," Adam was saying.

"Go away, kid," Jock responded.

"Where would you like me to go?"

"Anywhere but in my face."

"I can't because we don't have anywhere to go."

Silence, then Adam said, "I'm sorry about your grandson."

"You know nothing about my grandson."

"I know what it's like to lose someone you love more than anything. I promised my daddy I wouldn't be sad, but I couldn't keep that promise. I'm sad a lot."

Callie swallowed, realizing Adam needed a man to talk to. She wouldn't have chosen Jock Montgomery, but Adam seemed drawn to him. Maybe because he was close to John's age.

"Do you hate everybody?" Jock asked in a hoarse voice.

"Sometimes."

"Me, too."

There was silence again.

"You said I was going to ride a horse today," Adam reminded him. "Did you change your mind?"

Jock didn't get a chance to answer as Wade led Fancy and Brit into the barn.

"Callie, did you see me?" Brit asked, getting off the horse. "I could turn her and everything."

"Yes, I saw you." Callie gave her a hug.

Jock lumbered toward Fancy. "You want to ride, boy. This is your chance." He lengthened the stirrups. "Put your left foot here and swing up."

Adam did so effortlessly.

"Do you remember what I told Brit?" Wade took over.

"Yes, sir."

"Listen to Wade," Jock said. "I taught him everything he knows."

As Adam rode in the corral, even Callie could see he had a natural ability. He seemed to know what to do before Jock or Wade told him. And by the smile on his face, he was obviously enjoying himself.

Wade stood by Callie. "This is good to see. Pop taking an interest in something."

"Adam misses his father and for some reason he's formed a connection to Jock."

A horse trotted to the corral and neighed. Wade's face turned a pasty white. "Is that Zach's horse?" she asked, already knowing the answer.

"Yeah." The word came out broken. Wade swallowed. "Lucky probably thinks Zach is back. He and Adam are about the same size."

Callie placed her hand on his arm and felt his tense muscles. "Are you okay?"

Wade didn't answer for a moment, just kept his eyes on Lucky, who kept neighing and shaking her head.

"Yes," he finally said, and he looked into her eyes. "Has it been a rough day?"

She shrugged. "Not too bad. Did you find out anything?" She'd been dying to ask that for the last hour.

"Yeah, and I asked a friend to do some checking on your stepfather."

"And?"

"We'll talk later."

She didn't know if she had enough patience to wait until later. But she didn't have much of a choice.

CHAPTER TEN

HORSES WERE UNSADDLED and fed. After their gear was put away, Tex and Poncho went home. Wade saved Fancy for last so Brit and Adam would learn how to care for the horse. They unsaddled her, rubbed her down and fed her, then led her back to the pasture with the other horses.

"Where does she sleep?" Brit asked.

"In the pasture."

"Even in winter?" Adam was as curious as Brit.

"Yep, even in winter," Wade told them. "If it's really cold, we leave the corral open so they can get in the barn, but they rarely do. They're used to the outdoors, just like the cattle."

The kids waved bye to Fancy and as they walked back into the barn, Jock said to Callie, "What's for supper?"

"Pop!"

Jock shrugged. "Well, since she fixed breakfast and dinner, I just assumed she'd be fixing supper—paying for her keep."

"Pop…"

"It's all right, Wade." Callie put a hand on his arm. "I don't mind fixing supper. I just don't know what to cook."

"There's a freezer full of Texas beef. Take your pick, but I'd like chicken fried steak."

"It will take time to thaw out," Callie pointed out.

"Then I'll mosey to the house and get started on that." Jock headed out of the barn.

"I'll go with you, Mr. Jock." Adam fell into step beside him.

"Me, too," Brit shouted and dashed after them.

"Wait for me," Mary Beth called.

Callie was on the verge of calling them back when Wade said, "They'll be fine and we'll be right behind them in the car."

GETTING INTO WADE'S CAR, Callie was greeted by the aroma of coffee. Wade loved coffee—one of the little things she was learning about him. Besides a police radio, a large mug, a pair of sunglasses, handcuffs, several pens and a notepad rested in the console. This was the first time she'd been in a police vehicle and she fervently hoped it would be her last...unless Wade was at the wheel.

Callie turned to him. "Did you find out who trashed my house?"

He told her about the Harvey boys.

"They did it out of spite because they didn't get a parcel of land?"

"Yes. Their father is very bitter and kids soak up that kind of stuff."

"Why would he want to teach his kids to hate?" The whole thing appalled Callie.

"As I told you, there are a lot of people here who are against the Home Free Program, but I didn't realize their attitudes were being passed down to their children. We all thought they would eventually come around. People like my dad, though, cling to the bitterness."

"And Senator Gallagher."

Wade stopped at the house and ran his hands over the steering wheel. "This all started long ago when the owner of the K Bar C died and the heirs ran the operation into bankruptcy. My dad, Zeb Ritter, Nate Cantrell, Jase Farley, Holden Kelley, Robert Bell and Nan Wright joined forces and bought the property at auction. They formed a consortium with Zeb as the foreman and Nate putting in a lot of hours to get the ranch into shape. It was a surefire thing. No one thought it would ever fail."

"What happened?"

"They borrowed money to increase the herds, drilled more water wells, built new fences, new corrals and barns and hired more cowboys to work the cattle. Then the drought hit and they had to start buying hay and feed. The bank refused to extend their loan so they decided to start selling off the cattle, but mad cow disease was sweeping the country and the bottom fell out of the cattle prices, especially in foreign markets where they shipped a lot of cattle."

"So the KC consortium went under?"

"Yeah, the county was getting ready to take the land for back taxes, then Miranda came up with her idea and basically sold it all over town. People thought she was crazy but Homestead was becoming a ghost town and I, for one, supported her. Our tax base was eroding as families and kids moved away. When she ran against Arlen Enfield for mayor, no one thought she'd win. It was a narrow margin, but she won and set her plan in motion as quickly as she could. Arlen's always been in Clint's pocket, but lately they've been on the outs."

He took a breath. "It had to be one of those quick deals because everyone knew Clint wanted that land. It would make him the biggest rancher around here. But he was busy in Austin and his boys, Trevor and Garrett, didn't care about expanding the Four Aces and Ryan wasn't here. When Clint returned, the city owned the K Bar C and he's been steamed ever since."

"So much resentment and heartache," she commented.

His hands tightened on the wheel. "All this doesn't feel right to me. I don't know what it is because I know for certain the Harvey boys trashed your house. I'm just not clear about the motive."

"You think it was more than trying to impress their father?"

"Maybe."

Silence filled the car. She could see how distressed he was over the whole vandalism ordeal and her heart went out to him. But something else was on her mind and she had to bring it up.

"Has your friend found out anything?"

"Not yet. It's going to take some time, but if there's any dirt on Nigel, Simon can find it."

She licked her lips and he watched the action. "So you're not turning us in to the FBI?" He'd said that he'd needed answers, but she needed to know for sure what he was going to do.

"No. I couldn't live with myself if I did that."

"Oh, Wade." She threw herself across the seat at him. "Thank you. Thank you." She kissed the side of his face, his forehead, his nose and, in the process, knocked off his hat.

He caught it before it fell into the back seat. "I thought we weren't going to do this."

"I didn't agree to that." She smiled and touched his lips gently.

He took her mouth with a fierce hunger and hers opened under his, giving herself up to this moment and Wade. Nothing was said for some time as they tasted and discovered each other.

Finally Wade rested his forehead against hers, just feeling, not thinking and letting himself enjoy the touch and feel of her. It had been a long time since he'd felt like this and he wanted to hold on and never let her go. But first they had to get her life sorted out.

"We better go in," he whispered.

"You really are a chef, hmm?" he asked, as they walked toward the back door.

"Yes. I'm really a chef. I didn't lie about that. Why else would I be opening a café?"

"I heard around town you were planning to do that."

"I have to start earning an income. The house is taking so much money to repair."

He wondered if she even realized she was putting down roots, settling in and making Homestead her home. Or was he dreaming? Yep, probably was. He knew Callie's situation, but it didn't keep a man from hoping.

"After graduating from college, I attended the Culinary Institute of America in New York," she was saying. "When I got my degree, I worked in a large hotel then on a cruise ship. I was excited to land the executive chef job at a fine restaurant in New York, something I'd been working very hard to accomplish."

He opened the door, hearing the pride in her voice. "You gave it all up for the kids?"

Her expression changed dramatically. "Yes. I just couldn't bear the thought of them suffering, but I've wondered so many times if I've done the right thing. John wanted them in New York and I've taken them hundreds of miles away. I keep telling myself that soon I'll be able to take them back to the life he'd planned for them."

"You loved John a great deal."

"Oh, yes, and I will keep my promise."

That promise meant that Callie and the kids would only stay in Homestead a short time, then they'd return to their lives. So much for hoping. He had to be happy about that. It might take some work, though.

"You'll let me know when you hear anything about Nigel?"

His eyes centered on her troubled face. "Oh, yeah, you'll be the first I tell."

"What if you can't find anything on him? Will you…"

He touched her cheek, unable to bear that sadness in her voice. "Let's take one day at a time." He would protect her and those kids with everything in him. No one was arresting Callie or taking the kids back to an abusive stepfather—not as long as he was the law in Loveless County.

SUPPER WAS A FAMILY AFFAIR. Everyone helped but Jock. He stayed in the den watching television. Callie fried the steaks like she'd done the chicken earlier—by dipping them in flour then in milk and egg. She did more milk-gravy potatoes and there were green beans and biscuits left from lunch. While she sliced tomatoes, the kids ran to wash their hands.

Seated at the table, Jock paused before reaching for the platter of steaks. "Who's saying the prayer? I'm so hungry I could eat a saddle blanket."

"Me, too," Adam said.

Brit giggled, then replied, "I'm saying the prayer." Everyone bowed their heads. "Thank you God for bringing us here to Wade and Mr. Jock. Please keep us safe and thank you for this food…and Callie. Amen."

Nothing was said as the food was passed around. "This is good—no, this is great." Wade took a swallow of tea, realizing he hadn't eaten a thing all day and the food was the best he'd ever put in his mouth.

"Callie's the best cook," Adam told him.

Wade knew that. Just watching her was a pleasure. She cut, diced and served with an expertise of someone who knew their craft.

"Pretty damn good," Jock agreed, pushing away from the table. "Now I'm going to watch my TV shows."

Wade leaned back. "You could offer to help with the dishes."

"Don't think so, son." Jock reached for his cane and limped into the den.

Callie carried dishes to the sink. "He's probably never washed a dish in his life."

"Oh, yes, he has. Yolanda refuses to come over here with a sink full of dirty dishes waiting for her. If dishes are in the sink, she goes back home and doesn't cook. They had that tug of war for a long time, but Pop's finally realized if he doesn't put his dishes in the dishwasher, there'll be no food the next day."

Wade handed her dishes as she loaded the dishwasher. "Yo's a colorful character." She paused in thought. "I've met a lot of colorful characters since I've been here."

"Yep. Homestead is down-home country folk."

They smiled at each other and suddenly there was just the two of them, getting lost in each other.

"Callie. Callie…"

She realized someone was calling her name and she turned to Mary Beth. "What is it, sweetie?"

"Look at my knees. They changed color."

Callie stared at her brown knees. Mary Beth had on shorts and had been kneeling in the dirt in the corral and Callie suspected it was more than dirt.

"Time to get you in a bath."

"Go ahead," Wade said. "I'll finish the dishes."

"Are you sure? There's pots to wash yet."

"I can wash pots," he assured her.

"I like a man who can wash pots." Her eyes met the laughter in his, which suddenly changed to a simmering heat.

She backed away, but still felt his warmth. "Ah…girls, bath time."

"I'll watch TV with Mr. Jock until it's my time," Adam said.

"Or you can use the bath in the utility room," Wade offered.

"No, thank you. I'll just wait."

"Okay." Wade put soap in the dishwasher, wondering how Jock was going to take someone watching TV with him. He had his sports, crime shows and westerns that he never missed and he insisted on complete quiet.

Wade turned on the dishwasher and started to scrub a pot. Zach used to watch westerns with Jock. He was the only person who could tolerate TV with Jock longer than thirty minutes because Jock tended to scream loudly at the people on the screen.

Peering around the corner, he saw Adam lying on the floor in front of the set watching a baseball game. Jock lay in his chair not saying a word, but that wouldn't last.

CALLIE QUICKLY HAD THE GIRLS bathed and in their night-clothes. Brit chatted nonstop as usual. "Adam and I rode real good, didn't we, Callie?"

"Yes, you did." Callie took the bands out of Brit's pony-tail, so grateful that she wasn't jealous that Adam had ridden her horse. Their normal personalities were surfacing again in the peace and quiet of the ranch. John had taught them to share and to respect and love each other. In the past few weeks, Callie hadn't seen much of that. Fear had turned them into angry children and Callie hesitated to discipline them.

The future loomed with uncertainty, but now Callie didn't feel so alone. She had Wade to help her. Her fingers touched her lips, remembering his kiss. She didn't want him to get in trouble because of them. Before she'd let that happen, she'd take the kids and leave.

The thought tore at her heart.

THE KIDS SOUND ASLEEP, Callie went in search of Wade. He was at the kitchen table reading the *Homestead Herald*. She sat down and he turned the paper so she could see the head-line—Vandals Hit Mrs. Austin's Home.

Callie read the article. "Millie doesn't miss a thing does she?"

"Not much in this town." His eyes caught hers. "Do you want to press charges against the boys?"

"They're so young." She hesitated. "But I don't want them doing this kind of thing again."

"I dropped them off at your house to start the cleanup and I'm sure June…Odell still has them working. He was very upset about the whole thing. I believe Odell has a crush on you."

"Maybe a little, but I talked to him about it and he understands there can never be anything between us. I just feel for the awful childhood he had—people teasing him because of his size. Thank you for calling him Odell."

He grinned. "Caught myself just in time there."

Callie clasped her hands in her lap. She had to tell him everything. "I need to tell you something else."

Wade shifted in his chair. "What?"

"I…ah…I met Miranda in college."

His eyes narrowed. "So Miranda knows who you are?"

"Yes. I was always intrigued when she talked about Homestead and I'd heard about her plans for the town. When I knew I had to take the kids out of that situation, Homestead seemed like the perfect place to hide. After I got all the false IDs, I sent the application in to the Home Free Committee. I didn't tell Miranda who I really was until after I was approved. She was very sympathetic to my situation and I agreed to stay a year and fix up the Hellmuth house so Homestead would be able to find a buyer for it. In its present condition it was almost worthless."

"So that's why you took the Hellmuth house?"

"Yes. And this was all my doing—not Miranda's."

He frowned. "You don't have to take up for Miranda. She can take care of herself."

"I know, but I don't want her blamed for this…and there's something else."

"There's more?"

"Yes. I had a reason for being intrigued with Homestead." She chewed on the inside of her mouth for a moment. "I was born here."

His frown deepened. "What?"

"My mother divorced my father when I was five and we moved to Houston. I never saw him after that. He signed away all his rights to me, and I've wondered over the years if he was still alive. My mom said he was an alcoholic and probably died long ago. Somehow I need to know."

"You said your stepfather adopted you, so what was your biological name?"

"Collins. My father was Dale Collins. I've listened for names since I've been here, but no one seems to have the name Collins."

"Have you asked?"

"Yes. I asked Del and he bit my head off because I wasn't too tactful, and I asked Buddy."

"What did Buddy say?"

"That he didn't know any Collinses." She linked her fingers together. "My dad gave up all rights to me and may not want to meet me. But I'd just like to know if he's dead or alive."

He drew a quick breath. "What was your mother's maiden name?"

"Glynis Dryden."

"I'll see what I can find out."

She jumped up and hugged his neck. "Thank you for being so nice." Kissing the side of his face, she whispered in his ear. "Do you think we'll ever have a chance to be alone?"

"Maybe it's best this way," he said instead of answering, not responding to her touch. Her heart sank.

"Maybe." She straightened. "I better go to bed. I don't want the kids to wake up and find me gone. Good night."

"'Night," he called.

She walked to her room with feet that felt like lead. She wasn't planning to stay here that long so getting involved with Wade would only hurt him. Hurt her.

So why was she hurting now?

WADE SAT IN A STUPOR. Dale Collins was her father. How could he tell her who Dale Collins was? God, this just kept getting worse.

He reached for his phone and called Virgil. Everything was under control and Odell had finally sent the Harvey boys home. He walked out onto the patio, sat down and propped his feet on a chair. Crickets chirped and a couple of june bugs buzzed around the screen door.

Yep. June Bug had a big crush on Callie. Wade did, too. And he wasn't going to do anything about it. He wanted to. He wanted her like hell. She was unlike any woman he'd ever met. She cared for others more than she cared for herself and she had a beauty that went straight through to her soul. A man couldn't ask for more, but pain was still fresh in his heart and he couldn't endure another parting.

So many obstacles stood between them.

There were two floodlights around the corral to keep coyotes away. In the light, he could see Lucky walking the fence. She'd seen a boy today and the horse thought Zach was back. Back and forth she marched the fence.

It was time.

He'd been taught all his life not to ride at night unless it was an emergency. This was an emergency. He stood and headed for the corral. He'd been waiting for someone else to ride Lucky, but that was his job, his responsibility. Zach was his son and he'd been avoiding riding the horse.

In the barn, he flipped on a light, grabbed a bridle and walked to the gate. Lucky stopped marching and he slipped the bridle on and led her into the barn.

He rubbed her face. "I miss him, too."

Lucky reared her head as if she understood.

Wade swung a saddle blanket then a saddle onto her back and cinched it tight. Tonight he was going to outride the pain on a horse called Lucky. And outride everything that awaited him in Homestead.

CALLIE COULDN'T SLEEP. She kept thinking that Wade had reacted strangely to what she'd told him. He'd seemed turned to stone. She had to talk to him again. She crawled out of bed, wondering if he was asleep. The kitchen light was still on, but Wade wasn't there. As she turned, she saw something out of the kitchen window and she looked closer. Wade rode out of the barn on Lucky and disappeared into the darkness.

What was he doing?

Trying to outrun the pain, she answered her own question.

She went back to bed, knowing it would be a long time before he returned.

IT WAS ALMOST MIDNIGHT when Wade came through the back door. Jock was waiting for him at the kitchen table.

"You rode him, didn't you?"

"Yes. It was time. It was long overdue."

"You keep saying that like we should have a timetable."

Wade leaned against the cabinet. "All I know is that I can't keep grieving. It's killing me. I have to find a way to live in the present."

"Have you talked to Kim lately?"

"Not since she called to say she's getting married in July."
Jock scratched his head. "And you're okay with that?"

"Yeah, Pop. I'm okay with that. What Kim and I had is
over. When we look at each other, all we see is sadness. Neither of us can live like that. She's found someone and I'm
happy for her."

"When you two were younger you couldn't keep your
hands off each other. You had a gleam in your eyes when
you'd see her."

"Yeah, but all that love and passion got derailed with the
reality of life."

"You have that same look in your eyes when you look at
her." Jock thumbed toward Callie's room.

"Her name is Callie."

"How long she staying here?"

"Until she can move back into her house."

"Are you sure you don't want her to stay longer?"

Wade pushed away from the cabinet. "I'm tired. I'm
going to bed."

In his room, he fell across the bed fully clothed. So many
emotions churned inside him and he was struggling to handle all of them.

Riding Lucky, he'd felt a release he couldn't explain. This
was a step into the present without all that past's pain dragging him down. Now he was better equipped to deal with the
problems in town.

But what could he do about Callie? How could he tell her that
her father lived in Homestead? And how could he keep her safe?

The questions ran around in his head like children at play,
taunting, cajoling, until he fell into an exhausted sleep.

CHAPTER ELEVEN

SOMEONE WAS SHAKING her.

"Callie. Callie."

It was Mary Beth. Callie quickly roused herself, thinking Mary Beth had probably wet the bed.

She pushed hair out of her eyes. "What is it, sweetie?"

"Where's my jeans?" Mary Beth stood by the bed in nothing but her underwear.

Jeans? Mary Beth always wore shorts or capris in the summer.

"Why do you want jeans?"

"I have to check on Babe and I don't want my knees to get brown again."

"Oh." She looked around the room. Brit looked all set to go and she assumed Adam was in the bathroom dressing. Crawling out of bed, she rummaged through the suitcase, pulling out a pair of Mary Beth's jeans.

"Yay." Mary Beth clapped and quickly slipped them on. "I need boots, Callie."

"Really?"

"To walk in the corral you have to have boots. Wade and Mr. Jock have boots."

"I see," she said. They were becoming cowgirls and a cowboy and it appeared that Nigel was becoming a distant memory. But he was always at the forefront of Callie's mind. She needed to call her lawyer, although that could wait until she was back at her house. She didn't want to disturb the quiet they'd found here with the reality that was waiting for them. It would come soon enough.

The house seemed very quiet and she wondered where Wade and Jock were. Callie quickly dressed in jeans and a T-shirt, brushed the girls' hair into ponytails, as well as her own. Then she headed for the kitchen.

Adam came out of the bathroom dressed in his jeans and sneakers.

"You think Mr. Jock will let me ride again today?" he asked, eagerness filling the voice that was usually tinged with worry.

His hair was parted on the side and combed neatly and he looked like the happy boy he'd been less than a year ago. She kissed his forehead. "We'll see."

"Can we have pancakes?" Brit asked.

Callie turned to Brit. "Yes. I think we have everything to make pancakes. I don't think Mr. Jock will mind."

In the kitchen, Jock sat at the table, drinking coffee. "Made the coffee," he said.

"Mind if I have some?"

"Help yourself."

She poured a much-needed cup as the kids slid into their chairs.

"Oh, my goodness," she exclaimed as she took a big sip.

"I like my coffee strong," Jock said to her shocked expression.

"Yes. You do." She was sure her lips were curled back. "This will remove paint and I'm sure the lining of my mouth. Not to mention my stomach."

His mouth twitched. "Put some hot water in it and it'll be fine."

"Wish you'd told me that before I took a swallow." All of a sudden she didn't want any more coffee. She'd had enough caffeine to last her all day—probably all week.

"We're having pancakes for breakfast, Mr. Jock," Brit said. "If it's okay with you," she added quickly.

"I want steak and eggs," Jock replied, his eyes on Callie. "And before you say the steak has to thaw, I already took it out. It's ready to cook. Throw it in a pan, sear it on both sides, drop in a couple of eggs and it's done."

"Sounds as if you could do that yourself."

Jock's eyes narrowed. He might have washed a dish or two in his time, but it was clear he'd never cooked anything.

"Okay," she said, pouring milk and juice for the kids. "I'll cook your steak and eggs."

"Might stir up some of those biscuits and gravy, too."

She stared straight at him. "If you say *please*."

His eyebrows knotted together and he muttered something that sounded more like a cuss word than *please*.

"Can I please have one of your bananas, Mr. Jock?"

"Kid, I'm having steak and eggs. You can have anything you want."

"Thank you."

"Where's Wade?" Brit asked.

Callie was wondering the same thing. Had he gone to work without telling her? She wanted to go home today.

"Yeah," Mary Beth chimed in. "We have to check on Babe and she might need us to feed her. We don't know how and Wade will have to help us."

"That calf is going to suck or she and her mama will go to the auction barn," Jock informed them.

"No." Mary Beth pouted, then frowned. "What's an auction barn?"

"It's where you sell animals."

"No. No. No." Mary Beth stood on her knees in the chair in agitation. "You can't do that."

"It's my calf and we don't have time to fool with her. Other work needs to be done."

"Callie!" Mary Beth wailed.

WADE WAS SHAVING in the utility room, not wanting to disturb Callie and the kids in the other bathroom. He could have used Jock's in the master bedroom, but he thought it was easier this way. Wiping his face, he slipped into his shirt, hurrying to get into the kitchen before Jock had all the kids crying.

"Wade," Brit shouted as he entered.

"Morning, everyone." He glanced at Callie and had the urge to kiss her, which he curbed. Her eyes sparkled and her skin glowed and he had a hard time looking away.

"We're having pancakes." Brit took a swallow of milk.

"I love pancakes." His eyes clung to Callie's. "Anything I can do to help?"

"No. Take a seat and play referee." A smile curved her mouth.

She had the biscuits in the oven and turned her attention to the pancakes. With two frying pans going, she did the pancakes and Jock's steak at the same time. She flipped the pancakes and turned Jock's steak, then broke the eggs into the pan. Working efficiently, she had everything on the table within minutes, including butter and maple syrup.

Brit said blessings and Mary Beth pushed her pancake around on her plate. "Mr. Jock says he's gonna sell Babe."

Wade looked at his father. "I don't think Mr. Jock meant that, did he?"

"Damn well did. That calf better suck this morning."

Callie stood and grabbed Jock's plate with the partially eaten steak and eggs.

"What do you think you're doing?" he growled.

"If you can't cook this, then you can't eat it."

Jock's face wrinkled into a leathery frown. "What the hell are you talking about?"

Callie put her hand on one hip, the plate was in the other. "This is the way it is, Mr. Jock. Babe stays and you get your food back. You insist on selling her and this goes in the garbage and you can cook some for yourself."

"You wouldn't dare."

Callie took a step toward the trash can.

"Okay. Okay. The damn calf can stay, but these kids are going to help feed her."

"Deal." Callie laid the plate in front of him. "And one more thing—I'd appreciate it if you wouldn't use cuss words in front of the kids."

"Listen, gal—"

"I'm sure Pop will watch his language," Wade interceded, resisting a smile. No one handled Jock like that.

"Like…" Jock stopped when Callie reached for his plate. "You're one tough lady."

"Remember that."

This time, Wade smiled right into her gorgeous eyes, as blue and inviting as the Texas bluebonnets that covered these hills in the spring. She'd said she planned to stay a year. In a year, he would be so in love with her that…

Love? Was he in love with Callie?

She smiled back and he knew he was.

But there was no happy ending for them.

AFTER BREAKFAST, THEY WALKED to the corral to check on Babe. The kids ran ahead.

"I'd like to go home today," Callie said.

"Why don't you give it another day?" Wade suggested. "By then Odell will have most of the repairs done."

If she stayed here one more day, she might never want to leave. "I have so much to do at the house."

"It'll be there tomorrow and you'll have a hard time getting the kids away from Babe."

He was right. The kids were happy and another day wouldn't hurt. Another day to be with Wade. A stolen day, but she'd take it.

They reached the corral and the kids climbed the fence to the top. "There they are," Adam shouted, pointing to Sadie and Babe in a corner.

Even from a city girl's eye, she knew Babe hadn't sucked. Sadie's udder was huge again and Babe was butting it with her head, unable to get the big teat in her mouth.

Tex and Jock came from the barn. "Don't look good, Sheriff. Time to get this one to the auction. Poncho and me'll load her up."

Before Wade could respond, Jock said, "Milk her again. I promised the lady."

Brit and Mary Beth clapped in excitement. Tex had a puzzled look on his face, as if he wasn't hearing right. But he and Poncho opened the gate and herded Sadie into the chute, shoving the pipe behind her.

The kids crawled through the fence to Babe, who was bellowing for her mother. She tried to suck their arms and fingers and butted them, searching for food. They giggled—a wonderful sound. Adam stroked Sadie in the chute and the cow remained still, not fighting wildly like she had yesterday.

After Tex milked Sadie, she was released to her calf. Babe latched onto a teat without a problem, shaking her tail in delight.

"She should be stronger in a few days and able to suck on her own," Wade told Callie.

"I've never seen the kids this happy." They were behind

Jock, chattering away as he walked into the barn. And the strange thing was Jock didn't seem to mind.

"We have to make sure they stay that way."

Her eyes held his. "What if we can't?"

That note in her voice twisted his gut and he wanted to promise her that nothing bad would ever happen to them. But he couldn't. All he could do was try. He touched her cheek. "I'm going to give it my best shot."

She caught his hand. "I saw you riding Lucky last night. That had to have been hard for you."

"Yes. But in a way it was cathartic."

"I'm glad."

They stared at each other for endless seconds, then Wade cleared his throat. "I better get to work. I'll try to get back early."

"Okay." She kissed his knuckles, and his arm felt weak from the touch. With extreme effort, he turned toward the house.

"Wade. Wade." Mary Beth came running. "Where you going?"

He swung her up in his arms. "To work, little bit." Her blond hair was escaping from her ponytail and her cheeks were red, her eyes bright. Callie had probably looked just like that at six years of age.

"I'll miss you," she said, hugging his neck.

He swallowed. "I'll miss you, too. Take care of Babe."

"I will." She slid to the ground. "Bye."

Before he could reach his car, Adam shouted, "Wade."

He turned to him. "Do they have boots in town—cowboy boots—like yours?"

"They have them at the feed store."

"If we gave you money, could you pick me up a pair?"

"Don't worry about the money. I'll pick up a pair. What size?"

"I don't know. Callie buys my shoes." He slipped off a tennis shoe and showed Wade.

It seemed as if Callie had always been a mother to them. She was there for them and they depended on her. Not many big sisters would go that far for her half siblings. But then Callie was different. He'd known that from the first moment he laid eyes on her.

"Got it." He handed back the shoe.

"Thank you," Adam said and ran to the group.

Wade didn't get in his car because there was one child left and in a second Brit came running from the barn and threw herself into his arms.

"Mary Beth said you're leaving."

"I'll be home later."

"Can I please ride Fancy then?"

"Yes. We'll go riding."

She kissed his cheek and headed back to the others.

His eyes caught Callie's a moment before he got into the car. A year? Hell, he was already in so deep that the thought of them leaving haunted him.

But he'd survive.

He didn't have much choice.

WADE CHECKED IN at the office first. Ray was leaving from the night shift and soon Virgil came through the door.

"Odell's working at the house and I picked up the Harvey boys and drove them over to finishing cleaning. Getting rid of that red paint's gonna take a while."

"Good work, Virg."

Virgil took a seat across from his desk. "What do you think this means? Is this gonna keep happening to the newcomers?"

"I hope not, but we'll watch the new residents closely."

The front door opened. "Wade."

"In my office, Miranda."

Virgil stood. "I'm going over to the Kolache Shop to get breakfast. Want anything?"

"No. I already had breakfast. Thanks."

Miranda came in with Dusty at her heels and took Virgil's seat. "How are Callie and the kids?"

Leaning back in his chair, he folded his arms behind his head, a glint in his eyes. "You mean Callie Lambert?"

She eyed him for a second. "If you're going to give me a lecture, you can save your breath. Everyone approved her application—single mom, three kids, just what we needed in Homestead. At the time I didn't know Callie Austin was Callie Lambert. When Callie called me, I didn't see any reason to change my decision. No one wanted that old house and it was falling apart. Callie gave me her word to fix it up and I trusted her. Before the Harvey boys did their little job, it was looking really nice. When Callie returns to New York, I'm sure we can get a good price for it."

"Aren't you worried what Clint, Rudy, Arlen and people like them are going to say when they find out we have a wanted criminal on the Home Free Program?"

"She's not a criminal," Miranda countered. "She got those kids out of an abusive situation and I applaud that. I'd do it again if I had to."

Wade leaned forward. "Miranda, you always amaze me with your uncanny ability to take risks but not see them as risks."

She frowned. "Is that a compliment?"

"Yeah, and your secret is safe with me. I don't want Callie and the kids hurt either. I just have to find a way to defuse the situation."

"Thanks." She paused. "What is your real feeling about the vandalism? Just sour grapes on Howard's part or something more?"

Wade took his time answering, not wanting to alarm her unnecessarily. "I'm not really sure what to think, but I just told Virg that we'll keep a close eye on the newcomers."

"Good. I hope that helps."

Wade picked up a paperweight. "Has Callie ever mentioned anything about her family?"

"Not really. She said she was born here, but her family moved away when she was about five I think."

So Callie hadn't told Miranda about her father, and Wade didn't see any need to, either. Not until he figured out how to handle telling her what he knew.

Miranda got to her feet. "Tell Callie if she needs anything to just call."

"I will. And Miranda…"

She turned around.

"Thanks for what you did for Callie."

One eyebrow lifted. "Oh, so that's the way it is."

"Go to work, Miranda."

"I'm gone."

WADE CHECKED HIS MESSAGES—none from Simon. He was hoping to have heard something by now, but it had only been a day. When Barbara Jean came in, Wade drove over to Callie's house.

As he got out of his car, he did a double take, staring at the house. He didn't even notice the fence or Delbert until he spoke up.

"What do you think, Sheriff?" Del asked.

He looked down at the fence. It was back up.

"I cemented all the corner posts—makes it a little harder for someone to destroy."

"Good job, Del."

"When's Callie coming back?" Little Del asked.

"Soon."

Wade walked up to the house where Odell and the Harvey boys were painting. He couldn't take his eyes off the color.

"Odell," he called.

Odell jumped down from the scaffold. The boys were painting the lower part of the house.

"Looks good, huh, Sheriff?"

"Did Callie pick out this color?" Wade kept staring at the very, very blue house.

"No, sir. She was thinking white, but the hardware store didn't have that much white. Mrs. Effinfelt ordered this to paint her house, but she passed away. Somehow the order got doubled and it was just sitting there. I got it real cheap." He glanced at the house. "You think Callie'll like it?"

"I'm not sure. You should have asked her first."

"Well." Odell fidgeted. "I wanted to have everything done when she came back and it would take time to order the white paint. If she doesn't like it, I'll paint over it. These boards haven't had any paint on them in forty years." He frowned. "You don't think she'll like it?" There was worry in his voice.

Wade had to be honest. "Mrs. Effinfelt's sight was bad and I'm not sure she could really see that color clearly. In my opinion it's a little bright. Could you tone it down with white maybe?"

Odell stared at the house. "It is a little bright, isn't it?"

That was an understatement. It was a shade short of neon.

"A pale blue would be better."

"No problem," Odell said. "I'll take the paint back and have Myron mix white with it until it's paler."

Wade thought they should ask Callie, but he knew Myron well enough to know he wasn't taking the paint back. Mrs. Effinfelt had died almost a year ago. The boards needed paint and he'd explain this to Callie before she saw it. It could be changed if she absolutely hated it. But really, this was the least of their worries.

"Good deal," Wade replied. "How are the Harvey boys working?"

"After they got over their little attitude problem, they're fine. Their mama keeps checking on them. She's afraid they might have to go to juvenile detention."

Wade didn't think Callie would press charges, but a little fear might keep them in line.

"Has their father been here?"

"No, and I'd just as soon not see him."

"If he shows up, call the office."

"Don't worry."

"How's the inside coming?"

They walked into the house. The new windows had been installed and the red paint had been removed from the house and the kitchen floor. The ruined sleeping bags were gone and Callie's furniture and belongings were back in place. The house looked in order. In the kitchen, the appliances were in and more cabinets were in the process of being built.

"Damn, Odell, you've been working."

"Yes, sir. Hired two more people to help," Odell ran his hand over the stainless-steel refrigerator. "They delivered the appliances yesterday and I stayed until I got 'em all in. They're supposed to deliver the mattresses today and Mama's comin' to make up the beds."

"What about sheets?"

"Callie ordered 'em and they're already here. Mama's gonna wash 'em in the new washer and dryer I just installed."

"When do you sleep, Odell?" Wade was amazed at the work he'd done in two days.

Odell straightened the bill of his baseball cap. "I got four hours last night, but I don't need much sleep. I want the house to be in good shape when Callie and the kids come home."

Wade watched him for a moment. "You really like Callie."

"Yes, sir. She's real nice to me—treats me like a person, not a misfit."

Wade patted his shoulder. "She'll appreciate everything you've done." Not many people had ever been kind to Odell and Wade regretted all the times he'd treated Odell like the rest of the town did. He wouldn't make that mistake again. "I'll check in later."

He went outside to talk to Howie and Cliff. "Morning, boys."

"Morning, Sheriff," they said in unison, both continuing to brush paint onto the house.

Howie paused to look at him. "Are you gonna take us to jail?"

"Your dad and mom will meet with me in my office first thing Monday morning. We'll talk about it then."

"Yes, sir."

"Keep up the good work. I'll be by later."

As he walked away, his cell phone buzzed. It was Simon. They talked for a few minutes and Wade sat in his car going over the information he'd just learned.

Now he had to tell Callie.

CHAPTER TWELVE

TEX PUT BABE IN ONE PEN and Sadie in the other, explaining that if the calf got full she wouldn't suck. The cow's udder would swell and they'd have the same problem. They'd let the calf suck at intervals and the kids were to help—that's was Jock's plan. Adam carried a bucket of feed to Sadie, and Brit and Mary Beth watched over Babe, unable to leave her alone.

Tex and Poncho left to check the herd, but Jock stayed behind and Callie wasn't sure why. Maybe he was afraid to leave them alone with the cow and the calf. That had to mean he was beginning to like them here. Or, she might be reading too much into it.

The kids came into the barn and Jock showed them how to take care of a saddle. "It's a piece of equipment a cowboy uses every day and he has to keep it in good condition. Don't want it getting dry and cracked. Have to clean it at least once a month or so with some good saddle soap, then rub it with neat's-foot oil until it shines." He grabbed a spray bottle off a shelf. "This is glycerin saddle soap. In my day I used a bar, but now you can just squirt it on. Just a little. Don't want it running all over the saddle." He handed the kids pieces of cloth. "I'll spray and you rub the saddle real good." The kids rubbed without a word of protest and Callie joined in. Jock kept giving instructions.

Then Callie noticed something out of the corner of her eye

and looked up to see a cat slinking along the rafters in the hay-loft. Callie pointed and the kids followed her finger.

"A cat," Mary Beth cried, darting to the ladder for the loft. Brit and Adam were a step behind her.

"Is it safe?" she asked Jock.

"Yep." He sank onto a bale of hay. "But they'll never catch that cat. She's none too friendly."

"Be careful," she called to the kids.

"I'll watch them," Adam called back.

Callie sat beside Jock. "What's the cat's name?"

"Just call her cat."

"Don't you name anything on this ranch?"

"Nu-uh. Didn't even name my own son."

Callie was surprised. He figured a strong, stubborn man like Jock would definitely have a say in naming his son. "You didn't?"

"My wife, Lila, named him. She was one of five girls and Wade was the first boy born and she wanted to use her maiden name in memory of her father—so his name would live on and all that stuff."

"Her maiden name was Wade?"

He shook his head. "Wadeinhiemer."

"She shorten it?"

He shook his head again. "He's Wadeinhiemer Montgom-ery. That's what's on his birth certificate. I refused to call him that so I called him Wade and it stuck. Very few people know his real name."

Callie was totally engrossed. "What was he like as a kid?"

"He made friends easily and was popular in school. He and Jud Ritter had the young girls hopping in this county, then he met Kim and that was it for Wade. Jud, I'm not sure where he is, but I'm sure he's still chasing women."

Wade was a heartthrob. She could picture that easily

with his dark good looks. His marriage must have been happy for a while.

"He and Kim became parents early, too early I think sometimes, but my wife and me supported them and helped all we could. We doted on Zach. We'd lost a son in sixty-four and a girl in sixty-eight—both stillborn. Wade was our whole world and that grandson just plumb made it perfect. I guess it was too perfect." He swallowed noticeably. "When my son called and he couldn't talk, I knew it was bad. As I listened to his words, my world just stopped turning and I still don't understand. Why Zach? Why my perfect grandson?"

His voice cracked on the last word and Callie wanted to hug him, but she didn't. She was just glad he was talking to her.

"I know that kind of pain," she found herself saying. She knew it well, losing John and her mother in a short period of time and still not understanding. "I don't think it's for us to understand. It's how we handle it that counts."

He nodded. "You could be right."

"Callie." Mary Beth came running, holding the big cat in her arms. And she was big, gray and white—and purring.

"We found her."

"Well I'll be a sonofa…" At Callie's glance, Jock stopped. "That cat won't let anybody get near her. She just gets fat off the rats in the barn."

"Rats?" Callie looked around and had the urge to draw up her feet. She was not particularly fond of those little creatures.

"She likes us. What's her name?" Brit asked, stroking the cat.

"Cat."

Brit frowned. "That's not a name. You have to start naming your animals, Mr. Jock."

"You name her," he said.

"We're calling her Kitty." Mary Beth ran her hand gently along the animal's back.

"Isn't that the same as Cat?"

"No," Mary Beth snapped. "It's special."

"Whatever."

"Mr. Jock, do you think it's time to feed Babe?" Adam asked.

"Yep, sure do." Jock got to his feet and Adam handed him his cane. Callie wasn't sure how this was going to work without Tex and Poncho so she went along. Mary Beth was enthralled with the cat, but Brit hurried to help.

Brit opened the gate and Adam pushed Babe through it. Sadie immediately trotted over, making grunting sounds, and Callie held her breath, worried the cow might charge the kids. But Jock stood there with his cane and the cow didn't come any closer. Sadie had probably felt the sting of that cane before and sensed when to back off. She knew Jock had the situation under control and the kids weren't in any danger. Babe latched onto a teat without a problem. She was getting stronger.

As Adam closed the gate, Lucky galloped to the fence. Adam climbed onto the fence and patted her. Callie expected Jock to shout at him, but he didn't. He just stared with a sad expression on his face.

Yolanda drove up to the barn in an old truck, smoke puffing out of the tailpipe. Chester and Peanut jumped out of the front seat. The girls ran to meet them.

"Isn't that the damnedest sight you've ever seen?" Jock asked, his eyes now on Yo and her animals. "Hauling a pig inside the truck. That woman doesn't have a lot of good sense."

Callie just shook her head and went to greet Yo, who was carrying two buckets. In one were the best-looking peaches Callie'd ever seen. In the other was a chicken, plucked and cleaned, a very big chicken—had to be a hen.

"What's this?" Callie took a bucket from her.

"We got several peach trees—thought y'all might like some. And—" she tilted her head toward Jock, who was standing with the kids "—he asked me to kill a hen. Always wanting me to fix chicken and dumplings, but I done told him more times than I can count that Mexicans don't make chicken and dumplings. At least not in my family. So, *niña,* I hope ya can make 'em cause I ain't taking this chicken back home."

Callie glanced at Jock and he had the good grace to look embarrassed. "Yes, I can make them."

Yo handed her the other bucket. "Well, have at it. I don't work on Saturdays or Sundays."

"Lazy bit—"

"Thank you," Callie called, frowning at Jock.

"Chester, Peanut," Yo shouted. "Casa." Chester darted away from Brit. Peanut jumped from Mary Beth's arms and followed Yolanda. Kitty had disappeared at the first sign of more people.

Before Callie could say anything to Jock, Wade walked into the barn. Her heart did a rhythmic flip-flop.

He glanced at the buckets in her hands. "Had a busy morning, huh?" His eyes twinkled and a smile curved his sensuous lips. She couldn't look away and the urge to kiss him was strong. In a short amount of time, she'd come to depend on this man. And it wasn't that she needed anyone to depend on—it just felt good. He made her feel good. About herself. About the future.

Would there be a place for Wade in her future?

She didn't get to ponder the question as Brit and Mary Beth threw themselves at him, chatting about their morning. For the first time, she realized Adam wasn't in the barn.

Hurrying to the double doors, she saw him on the fence still stroking Lucky. Wade came to stand beside her, his eyes on Adam and the horse. Jock joined them. No one said a word and the silence became so still she was sure she could hear the ticking of her watch.

Wade looked at his father and they stared at each other for endless seconds. Then Jock nodded. Wade swung toward the tack room for a bridle and walked steadily toward Adam and Lucky.

Slipping a bridle on Lucky, Wade led her into the barn. Callie needed to carry the chicken to the house, but a few more minutes wouldn't hurt. In no time, Wade had a saddle on Lucky and cinched it tight.

"Keep talking to her, Adam," Wade said. "I'll be right back."

Puzzled, Callie watched him jog to his car and come back with a bag. He set the bag on a bale of hay and pulled out a box. "You might want to put on these before you saddle up."

Adam tore into the box like a hurricane. "Boots. Real cowboy boots. Wow!" He sat down and pulled off his sneakers and slipped them on. Carefully, he stood with a big-eyed look. "These are cool."

Wade pulled out two smaller boxes. "Come see if yours fit," he said to the girls.

Ohs and *ahs,* echoed around the barn as Brit and Mary Beth pranced around in their new boots. Brit's old boots were quickly forgotten.

"You ready, Adam?"

"Yes, sir."

"You remember everything I taught you yesterday?"

"Yes, sir."

Wade laid the reins over the saddle horn. "Put your left foot in the stirrup and swing up. Today we'll ride in the corral until you and Lucky become accustomed to each other."

"Okay."

Wade guided the horse into the corral, then let go of the

reins. Adam took Lucky around the corral, turning and stopping her. Callie couldn't tear her eyes away from the look on Adam's face. He was excited and happy.

She realized she still had the chicken in her hand and had to get it to the house. Glancing at Jock, she saw all that sadness on his face—sadness he was trying to hide. Unable to stop herself, she patted his arm.

"Are you okay?"

He focused on her with surprise on his face, surprised that she might actually care. No one, but Wade, had cared about him for a long time.

"Wade said it was time. He was right." The words were low, but Callie caught them.

"If you don't want Adam riding Lucky, you just tell me."

"It's okay, gal."

She could see that it was. "Come on, girls. I have to carry this chicken to the house." She grabbed the peach bucket Yo had set down.

"Ah, Callie." Brit stomped her foot. "We want to watch."

"Brit…"

"I'll look after them," Jock offered

"Thanks," Callie said, and hurried to the house. In the kitchen, she saw that it was one o'clock. She hadn't even realized the time and no one had eaten lunch. But then they'd had a big breakfast. If they were going to have dumplings tonight, she had to put the chicken on to boil. She was busy in the kitchen when Wade walked in.

She swung from the stove. "Is something wrong?"

"No. We're just taking a break. I'm fixing to saddle Fancy for Brit, but I wanted to talk to you for a minute."

She wiped her hands on a dish towel. "What is it?"

He leaned against the cabinet. "I talked with Simon, the investigator, this morning."

"Oh." She waited with her breath hitched in her throat.

"Seems Mr. Tremont has been married a couple of times to older women—older wealthy women."

"So he's been divorced?"

"Not exactly. Wife number one is dead. Number two is in a health-care facility in Philadelphia."

Callie sank into a chair. "He never mentioned being married before and my mother never said anything. She said he was from Seattle and didn't have any family." She frowned as something registered. "Is he divorced from wife number two?"

"That's what Simon is trying to find out. He can't find anything on record, but I want him to dig a little further on how his first wife died, too."

"Do you think…" She couldn't even put into words what she was thinking.

"I'd say a lot of this isn't adding up."

"Oh, Wade." She launched to her feet. "This could be the break I need. Thank you." She threw her arms around him and squeezed.

He held her for a second. She smelled of hay, lavender and sunshine, and he had to force himself to let her go. "There's a lot of questions that have to be answered. But if Tremont is still married to wife number two then that's going to give you a lot of leverage."

"When will your investigator know?"

"Not sure. Research and digging out records take time. He's trying to expedite things as fast as he can. In the meantime, let's hope the FBI doesn't come calling."

She kissed his cheek. "Thank you," she said again.

He swallowed hard. "We better go before the kids start screaming for us."

"But they haven't had lunch."

"I don't think you'll get them in here for lunch."

"You're probably right."

They slowly walked to the barn.

"Do you have to go back to work?"

"It's Saturday and I've taken the afternoon off. But Saturday is a big night at the beer joints and I might get called out."

At least she had him for a little while.

THE KIDS SPENT THE AFTERNOON riding in the corral, taking time to bring Babe in to her mother. Wade had an easy way of doing that. He just picked Babe up and carried her to the other pen.

Wade saddled up his horse, Maverick, and Brit and Adam followed him into the pasture enclosure on their horses. They were both riding very well.

Mary Beth pulled on Callie's hand. "Callie."

"What, sweetie?"

"I wanna ride. I got boots."

"Oh." She hadn't even thought that Mary Beth might want to ride.

Hearing Mary Beth, Jock shouted, "Wade."

Wade spoke to Brit and Adam then trotted over. Callie never thought she'd be attracted to cowboys, but looking at Wade in the saddle, tall and lean, energized her senses.

"Little bit wants to ride," Jock said.

"Hand her to me." Wade motioned to Callie.

Callie lifted Mary Beth into the air and Wade settled her in front of him, then they joined Brit and Adam. Callie watched for a while longer then headed to the house to prepare supper. She knew her siblings would be well taken care of.

SUPPER WAS A CHATTY AFFAIR; even Jock joined in, telling the kids how well they were riding. Sitting around the table, they seemed like a normal family and, for a brief moment, Callie let herself believe that dreams did come true. But then the moment was gone and the world outside loomed, reminding her that dreams were for fools. She didn't mind being a fool, though, if Wade could share her life in any way. And that was so unrealistic. His life was here. Hers wasn't. So why couldn't she stop what was happening between them? Was she being selfish? Naive?

"This is the best chicken and dumplings I've ever eaten, gal," Jock said. "You've outdone yourself."

"Thank you," she said, getting to her feet and pushing unpleasant thoughts away. She brought the peach cobbler to the table.

"Wow. Look." Mary Beth kneeled on the chair to see the cobbler.

"I found vanilla ice cream in the freezer. Who wants some?"

Everyone held up their hands.

Wade stood and gently pressed her into a chair. "Sit. I'll serve this."

Callie smiled. "I like a strong, take-charge kind of man."

"Me, too," Mary Beth said. "I like Wade." Then she giggled and Brit joined in. Callie was still smiling as she got the kids ready for bed. They were exhausted from the day and Callie knew they'd be asleep within minutes.

But as always, she was wrong.

"Tell us a story." Mary Beth stalled.

"Yeah, the one about the girl and the horse and the sheriff." Brit snuggled into her.

"Once upon a time, there was a sheriff who owned a horse who needed to be ridden."

"Lucky," Adam said from his cot. Callie smiled in the darkness. Adam usually thought storytelling was childish, but tonight he was participating.

"And Fancy," Brit put in her two cents.

"Then some children arrived from far away who desperately wanted to ride a horse."

"That's us." Mary Beth wiggled beside her.

"And the sheriff decided it was time for the horses to be ridden."

"You know why, Callie?" Mary Beth touched her face.

"No, why, sweetie?"

"Because the sheriff loves us."

"Yeah. Wade loves us and we love him." Brit's voice grew drowsy.

"Yeah," came a murmur from Adam's direction.

Callie's heart stopped. Out of the mouths of babes. Why couldn't it be? she asked herself. Why couldn't there be happily ever after in Homestead, Texas—with Wade?

Callie knew the answer, but chose to ignore it—for now. For tonight.

WADE STOPPED OUTSIDE the bathroom door, listening to Callie and the kids. Mary Beth hit the nail on the head, but he'd never tell Callie that he loved her. It would only complicate things and make parting that much more difficult. That might be the coward in him, but that's the way it had to be.

Pop had gone to bed and he walked into the den to turn off the TV. He thought he'd never feel these emotions again, was sure they'd all died with Zach. As the memory of his son ran through him, he realized, for the first time, that he didn't brace himself against the pain. It was there, but it didn't paralyze him with crippling emotions. Zach was always going to occupy a part of his heart, but now he was letting other people in. He was living again—all because of Callie and the kids.

Sitting down to take off his boots, he saw Callie standing in the doorway. She had on some sort of pajamas and a T-shirt.

Her blond hair hung loosely around her shoulders. Silhouetted in the doorway, she looked like an angel.

He cleared his throat. "Thought you'd gone to bed."

She walked in and perched on the footstool at his feet. "Need some help, Wadeinhiemer?"

A grin split his handsome face. "Very few people know my real name." Wade found it interesting that Pop had told her his name, because these days Pop talked to no one. He stayed locked within himself, but Callie and the kids were working their way into his heart, too.

"It's your mother's maiden name."

"Yeah. My mom's family were some of the first settlers in Homestead, as were the Gallaghers, the Ritters, the Kelleys, the Wrights, the Cantrells and several more. Pop worked cattle for my grandfather, that's how he met my mom. Sheriff Whitaker was impressed with his rough, take-no-prisoners type of attitude and hired him as a deputy. When Whitaker passed away, Pop ran for the office and won. He made a lot of friends and a lot of enemies during that time."

"There's a lot of history in Homestead."

"Yeah. Some good. Some bad." Tonight he didn't want to think about the bad. There was just too much of it. He rested his head against the chair.

"Jock seemed okay with Adam riding Lucky."

"Mmm." That was one of the good things.

"Would you like me to remove your boots?"

He raised his head, the grin in place. "You know what they say about a woman removing a man's boots."

"No." She tucked her hair behind her ears. "I don't believe I'm familiar with the saying."

"If a woman removes a man's boots, she has to warm his bed." His eyes never wavered from hers.

She stood, placing a hand on both sides of his chair. "I can do that," she whispered, leaning in close.

"You can?" He breathed in her scent and reached up to cup her face. He wasn't thinking, only feeling.

"Mmm."

He took her lips slowly, pulling her onto his lap, savoring, tasting and just enjoying her. Her mouth opened readily with an eagerness that surprised and elated him. The kiss went on and nothing was heard but gentle sighs and groans. He slipped his hand beneath her shirt, caressed and stroked until they both were consumed with a need that was escalating out of control. A need too long denied in both of them.

From out of nowhere an annoying sound persisted. A sound he knew well—his cell phone. Damn! He rested his forehead against hers with a long sigh.

"I have to get that."

"Mmm." She kissed his neck.

The thought of not answering did cross his mind, but he was the sheriff. A little fact that irritated him at the moment.

"Yes," he bellowed into the phone. "Okay, Herb. I'll be right there."

"Business?" Callie pulled down her T-shirt.

"Yeah. Some ranch hands are getting rowdy at the Lone Wolf Bar. Herb thinks it's getting out of control. I better get over there."

Callie climbed off his lap. "Do you go by yourself?"

"Yep."

"Isn't that dangerous?"

"Sometimes. But I can handle it." He touched her cheek. "Don't worry."

"Just be careful."

"I will." He reached for his hat. "I'll see you in the morning."

"I really need to go home tomorrow."

"Okay." He placed his hat on his head, hesitating. "About tonight…"

"Please don't say you're sorry."

"I wasn't, but…"

"We're adults, Wade, and can handle a personal relationship."

"I need to tell you some things first."

Her lips parted in surprise. "What?"

"I can't get into it now, but we'll talk tomorrow." He quickly kissed her nose and headed for his car.

He had to tell her about her father and that wasn't going to be easy. But she had to know he was still alive.

CHAPTER THIRTEEN

THAT NEXT MORNING after breakfast, they all went to check on Babe. They'd let her in with her mother during the night and when they reached the corral, there was no doubt that Babe had sucked. Sadie's udder wasn't swollen with milk. The kids cheered, but their faces became long when Callie told them they were going home.

"Can we vote on it?" Adam wanted to know.

"No. This isn't something we vote on. We have to go home. We've imposed on the Montgomerys long enough."

Jock's face was long, too, and he didn't say much. As they drove away, Callie saw him ride out of the barn and gallop into the woods.

The car was quiet on the ride into town. Three kids were pouting in the backseat. Callie felt like pouting, too. She stole a glance at Wade. His face was set, staring at the road. He hadn't tried to persuade her to stay and she was a bit disappointed about that.

Last night she couldn't sleep after he'd left to go check out the bar. She couldn't stop herself from worrying and it crossed her mind that's what it would be like married to a lawman. It was one of those sneaky thoughts that slipped by unaware, surprising her, yet it felt natural—like so many things had while she'd been here with him. When she'd heard him come in, she'd turned over and fallen instantly asleep. He was safe.

As they neared town, they could hear the bells of St. Mark's ringing. "I told Noah I'd bring the kids to church, but so far I haven't had a chance."

"Why not this morning?" Wade asked.

"But we're not dressed."

"Dress is casual here in Homestead. Y'all are fine."

Callie wore white capris and a yellow-and-white tank top. The girls also wore capris—Mary Beth in pink and Brit in purple. Adam was in shorts and flip-flops. Their cowboy garb was in the suitcase.

"Are you sure?"

"Trust me." He glanced at her, smiling.

That made everything better. "Okay."

As soon as Callie entered the small church with the dark wood, marble floors and stained-glass windows, she saw that Wade was right. Everyone was dressed casually. They took their seats in a pew, the kids sandwiched between them.

Noah's sermon was moving and Callie enjoyed it. There were a lot of people there she recognized. Kristin and Ryan sat two rows ahead with Cody, who turned around to wave at the kids. Delbert and his family were there, along with Walter, Buddy, Ethel Mae, Millie and her husband, Miranda and her mother. The familiar faces made it feel like home.

Later, outside the church, people offered comforting words. Miranda hugged Callie and said she'd talk to her later. Ethel said she'd see her at the house, as did Walter and Delbert. Kristin and Ryan walked up with Cody.

"Mom, can I go play with Adam and Brit?" Cody asked.

"Not today. It's Sunday and Mrs. Austin is just getting back into town."

"'Kay. How's Fred?" Cody asked Mary Beth

Mary Beth's mouth fell open and Callie suppressed a groan.

"What?" Kristin looked as if Cody'd done something wrong.

"We forgot Fred at the ranch." Lately Fred had taken a back seat to all the other animals and, in the rush this morning, they had just forgotten him.

"Callie!" Mary Beth cried.

Callie gathered her close and explained to Kristin what had happened.

"We'll go back and get him," Callie told her. "I'm sure Mr. Jock will watch out for him in the meantime."

"'Kay."

Kristin and Ryan said goodbye and Callie shook hands with a lot of people. Everyone said they were glad she was back and it seemed as if she'd been gone longer than three days.

Mary Beth darted through the crowd to Buddy. "Where's Rascal?"

"At home," Buddy replied. "I'll bring him over to play this afternoon. How's that?"

Buddy shook Callie's hand. "Glad you're back, Callie."

"Thank you, Buddy."

Noah was busy greeting his congregation and made his way to them. "So you gave the church a try."

"I told you I would."

"It's good to have you. Now we have to get the kids enrolled for Sunday school classes."

"Fine."

"Next Sunday." Noah moved off to talk to other parishioners. A couple came out of the church with three children. The man was tall and lanky. The woman was also tall with auburn hair. One of the girls had red hair and looked like the woman, so she had to be a daughter.

Wade spoke to the man and motioned Callie over. "This is Ethan Ritter and his wife, Kayla, and Kayla's daughter, Megan. And this is Heather and Brad, the new additions to the family."

"Nice to meet you." She shook hands again.

"We heard what happened at your place," Kayla said. "I had a similar thing happen to me when I first moved here."

"You did?"

For the next few minutes, they talked about the mischief they'd experienced. The kids sized each other up and soon were chattering away—all about horses.

"Have you heard from Jud lately?" Wade asked.

Ethan's friendly expression hardened. "No, nor am I likely to. My brother'd call you before he'd ever call me." He turned to his wife. "We better go. Luella probably has lunch ready."

"It was so nice to meet you," Kayla said. "We have to get the kids together for a play day. They seem to be getting along fine." The kids were talking like they'd known each other forever.

"Are your kids in Sunday school?" Callie asked.

"Oh, yes."

"I'm planning to enroll mine."

"They'll love it and it will give them a chance to get to know each other better."

"Let's go, Kayla," Ethan said again.

"See you later," Kayla called, linking her arm through her husband's as they walked off.

IN THE CAR, CALLIE ASKED, "Does Ethan have a problem with his brother? He seemed to tense up when you asked about him."

"Yes. There's a lot of sadness in the Ritter family. Ethan's sister died from toxic levels of lead poisoning in her system."

"How did she get something like that?"

"From eating tamarind candy from Mexico. It was contaminated with lead. Ethan got the candy from a kid in school and Angela loved it so he kept giving it to her. Angela kept it hidden in her closet because her parents wouldn't let her eat that much candy. The housekeeper found it one day and since she's from Mexico, she knew about the lead contamination.

Luella immediately told Zeb and Valerie. They had Angela tested, but the damage to her system was irreversible and they had to watch her slowly die. It tore the family apart, especially Ethan because he was the one who'd given her the candy over a long period of time. Ethan ate the candy, too, but not near as much as Angela. He was given a clean bill of health."

"How sad."

"Yes. Ethan's mother died a year later from a broken heart and Zeb committed suicide two years ago. He shot himself and Ethan was the one to find him."

"Oh my God! How awful. Now I understand that sadness in his eyes." Callie's heart went out to Ethan, who'd endured so much but still managed to survive.

"Yeah. Ethan found happiness with Kayla and I'm happy for him. The therapeutic riding school I mentioned is for kids with special needs and Ethan and Kayla are very good with them."

"It takes special people to do something like that. But when you mentioned his brother, he changed completely."

"Yeah. Family issues that they can't seem to get past. Jud and I grew up friends and we both went into law enforcement. We've stayed in touch over the years, but I haven't heard from him lately. I'm getting a little worried."

"Your dad mentioned that you had a friend named Jud and that you both had a way with the ladies."

"Pop seems to have told you a lot. Believe me, he exaggerates."

The corners of her mouth twitched. "I don't think so. I believe everything he said about you and your friend, Jud." She reached across the seat and touched his arm. "Up to a point. Since you were married at seventeen, you couldn't have done too much chasing."

"That's one thing about small towns, there's very few secrets. Everyone knows my past."

"And they seem to have a connection to each other."

"I told you it was close knit."

"Yes, and I'm really beginning to feel a part of it."

But you're not staying, a little voice whispered.

Her eyes caught Wade's and she saw her thoughts echoed there.

She looked away, hating what stood between them. It would be there until Nigel was out of the kids' lives and out of hers. There was a chance that would never happen, if the court ruled against her. The thought of hiding in Homestead forever was beginning to sound good.

But she couldn't do that—she had to keep her word to John.

WHEN WADE TURNED onto Bluebonnet Street and stopped at her house, she could only stare. Slowly, she got out and the kids tumbled out beside her.

"Our house is blue," Brit said.

"Yes. Our house is blue," Callie echoed. "Why is that, Wade?"

"I was going to explain," Wade said in an hesitant tone, "but it slipped my mind. You see, Odell wanted to do the job as fast as possible and this was the only color he could find at the hardware store in a large quantity. It looks a lot better than yesterday."

"What did it look like yesterday?"

"Brighter. Bolder. It's kind of a soft baby-blue now."

"Mmm." Callie studied the house, trying to make up her mind. She'd planned on white and the blue took some getting used to. Odell's heart was in the right place and she didn't want to hurt his feelings.

"I like it," Adam said

"Me, too," Brit added. "But it would have been really cool if it was purple."

Callie cringed at the thought. Wade laughed at her expression.

"Callie." Mary Beth pulled on her arm. "I gotta go potty."

They ran up the walk to the front door and Callie noticed her white picket fence was in place, the grass mowed and the awful red paint was gone. Her home was back to its former state, except it was now blue.

Ms. Millie came out of the house with a camera around her neck. Callie didn't know how she'd gotten here so fast. They'd just seen her at church.

"Smile everyone." She snapped their picture and Callie didn't even think of turning away, and she should have. What if someone saw her photo? This was Homestead and the paper didn't go far. Or at least she hoped it didn't.

"Be in the next edition," Millie said. "Everyone wants to see that you're home and safe." She waved as she strolled down the steps.

"Bye, Ms. Millie."

Callie stopped as she entered the house. Mary Beth sprinted to the bathroom. The house was clean, too, and everything in its place. Odell and Ethel came from the kitchen.

"About time you got yourself back here," Ethel said with her wry humor. "Odell's about to work himself to death."

"Thank you, Odell," Callie said. "You've been very busy."

"Come look at the kitchen." She followed him into the kitchen and forgot about the blue exterior. The kitchen was perfect. All the appliances were in and he'd taken out the wall they'd talked about to make the kitchen bigger. Even the utility room and the extra cabinets he'd had to build were finished. She walked around touching things, hardly able to believe her kitchen was finished.

"How did you do this in such a short amount of time?"

"He didn't sleep," Ethel informed her.

"What!"

"Mama!"

"You didn't have to do that, Odell," she said, but she was touched by his loyalty.

"Well, your furniture and dishes started arriving and I figured it was time to get it done. I hired two extra men to help."

"That's fine." She'd ordered things from an antique house in Austin to match the decor of the house and had probably paid too much, but the breakfast-room set looked like something that had originally been in the house.

"Your mattresses and bedding came yesterday and Mama made up the beds."

"We have mattresses?" She clapped her hands, staring at the kids, who looked back at her with wide eyes. "Aren't you excited? Let's go look."

"We moved the beds upstairs like you wanted."

"Thank you," Callie called as they scurried for the stairs.

"Callie."

She turned to Wade.

"I'm going over to the office to check messages and relieve Virg."

"You will come back?"

"Yeah, later. You okay with the blue?"

"Of course, it's hard to be upset with someone who works as hard as Odell."

Wade nodded and left.

Suddenly her excitement was gone. She was becoming too involved with Wade and the people in this town. How was she ever going to leave?

THE DAY PASSED QUICKLY. Callie put away their clothes and it was nice to have a dresser and an armoire.

Miranda came by and they chatted for a while. She told her nothing had changed and Callie should continue on with her plans. But Callie hated putting her friend in this awkward position.

Buddy brought Rascal, and the kids played in the yard with him. Buddy stayed until Wade arrived. He brought Fred home and then had to leave on a call to a nearby town. Two neighbors were fighting over a fence line.

Callie and the kids went to sleep in their new beds. The girls slept with her, since they only had two beds. She planned to buy another bed as soon as she could afford it. Her finances were dwindling and she had to open the café soon.

She worried about Adam sleeping alone and went into his room to check on him.

"Are you okay in here?"

"Sure."

Adam had been subdued since their return from the ranch. He wasn't a talker like Brit, but he hadn't said much all evening.

"It's okay to say you're not."

"I'm fine."

"I'll leave the door open."

"Okay."

"If you feel afraid, you can sleep in our room."

Callie turned out the light.

"Callie?"

"What?"

"You think Mr. Jock's okay?"

So that was it. He was worried about Jock. "Yes. Mr. Jock is tough. He's a cowboy."

"Yeah." Adam turned onto his side. "Good night."

"Night."

THE NEXT MORNING as Callie was fixing breakfast for the kids in her new kitchen, she heard a car honking, but she didn't pay it any attention. Then a loud knock came at the door.

She set the blueberry muffins on the table and went to answer it. Jock stood there with two buckets, one in each hand, and his cane hooked over one arm.

"Didn't you hear me honking, gal?"

"I didn't know you were honking at me."

"Well, I was. Yo sent these vegetables and I brought a steak and eggs."

"Oh." Callie was speechless.

"Figured turnaround was fair play."

"Yes. Yes. Come in." Callie tried hard not to smile. He missed them. Or did he miss her cooking? She'd rather believe the former.

The kids came running. "Mr. Jock. Mr. Jock."

"Here, boy. Take these to the kitchen."

"Okay." Adam took one bucket and Callie the other, and they walked into the kitchen. Jock took a seat at the breakfast table and the kids bombarded him with questions.

"How's Babe and Sadie?" Brit asked.

"Turned them out into the pasture this morning."

"And you didn't have to sell her." Mary Beth bit into a muffin.

"Nu-uh. What's that, kid?"

"It's a blueberry muffin," Callie answered. "Would you like one?"

"Sure. You got my steak going?"

"Say *please*."

"Please with sugar dripping all over it."

The girls giggled and Callie went to prepare his steak and eggs. She could still hear the conversation.

"How's Lucky, Mr. Jock?" Adam asked.

"Walking the fence line. She needs to be ridden so get your boots and we'll go right after we eat."

"Wait a minute." Callie's stern voice stopped Adam in his

tracks. "That's a little high-handed, Mr. Jock. I have a lot of work to do today and I can't leave just yet."

"Nobody asked you. The boy can go with me."

"Me, too," Brit and Mary Beth said together.

"Please, Callie. Please," Adam begged.

Callie glared at Jock for putting her in this position, but she knew he was just lonely. Without her, she couldn't let the girls go and they weren't going to understand.

"Okay, Adam, you can go, but girls, you have to stay here with me. Buddy's bringing Rascal over again, remember?"

"Ah, Callie. I have to ride Fancy." Brit slumped in her chair.

"I'll take you this afternoon."

"Promise."

Callie placed a kiss in her palm, then made a fist and held it against her heart. "Promise."

"What's that?" Jock was curious.

"See." Brit kissed her palm and held a fist to her heart. "A promise is a message kept in the heart and never forgotten. Right, Callie?"

"Right."

They finished breakfast and Adam hurriedly dressed in his jeans and boots and left with Jock. As they drove away, Callie knew that Adam had formed a special connection to Jock—something they both needed. But it wasn't easy to let him go. Her protective instincts were strong. There was no safer place than the ranch, though.

Buddy brought Rascal, then left to open up his gas station. The girls tumbled in the front yard with the dog, giggling.

Ethel jogged up the walk from her morning run, waving to the girls. When she reached Callie, she asked, "What are we doing today?"

"Washing all the new dishes."

Ethel groaned. "Oh, crap. I shouldn't have gotten out of bed this morning."

Callie laughed. "Would you mind watching the girls for a few minutes? I have to run over to the sheriff's office."

Ethel sank into a rocker. "Don't mind a bit."

"I'll be right back," she called to the girls, who barely raised their heads in acknowledgment. They weren't afraid anymore and didn't care if she was out of their sight. That was very good.

CALLIE WAS RUNNING LATE. She'd told Wade she'd be in his office to meet with the Harveys at nine and it was past that now. Cooking breakfast for Jock hadn't been in her plan this morning, but she didn't mind. She hoped Wade wouldn't either.

The courthouse was less than three minutes from her house and the sheriff's office and jail were around the back. She parked in the designated spot and hurried in. It was late June and the hot sunshine warmed her face and arms. By July the heat would be unbearable.

Inside, a woman sat at one desk and Virgil sat at another. Everything in the room was very simple and rustic. Wanted posters hung on the wall and the sight gave her a chill. If Wade hadn't intercepted hers, it would probably be there. Not for the first time, she realized the enormous risk he was taking.

"Mrs. Austin." Virgil got to his feet. "Good mornin'."

"Morning," she replied. "And please call me Callie."

"This is Barbara Jean, our secretary," Virgil introduced the woman at the desk. She was somewhere in her late thirties with brown hair and a kind smile.

"Nice to meet you," Callie said, shaking her hand.

"Same here. The sheriff's waiting for you. Go right in." She pointed to the left.

Callie opened the door and stepped in. A man, a woman and two boys sat in front of Wade's desk. "I'm sorry I'm late."

Wade rose. He didn't have his hat on, and the rugged lines of his face kicked her heartbeat up a notch. The thought of running her fingers through his dark hair crossed her mind.

"Mrs. Austin," he said. "This is Howard and Melba Sue Harvey and their boys, Howie and Cliff."

The woman was very thin and gaunt and Callie's heart went out to her. "I'm so sorry for what my boys did to your house, but I made sure they were there, like the sheriff said, for them to help clean up the mess they made. June Bug worked them hard."

"His name is Odell."

"What?" Melba Sue looked confused.

"Please call him Odell. That's his name."

The man snickered and Callie glanced at Howard Harvey. With his sullen expression, small eyes and unkempt appearance, he reminded her of a cornered ferret. A cruel, foraging ferret with claws.

"Oh. Okay. I wasn't aware he wanted to be called by his name."

"He does, Mama," Howie said. "He told us he don't like to be called June Bug 'cause he don't eat bugs no more."

"We laughed and he got mad," Cliff continued. "He's got a real temper and he's a little scary, but we don't call him June Bug no more. He knows a lot of stuff about carpentry and he said when we got older, he might hire us."

"Well now, ain't that somethin'," Howard snapped in an angry voice. "My boys ain't working for June Bug Stromiski."

"We're getting off track," Wade broke in. "Mrs. Austin, do you want to press charges against these boys?"

Callie looked at the boys. "Why would you destroy my place like that?"

They looked at their feet. Howie shifted restlessly. "Because Dad…"

"Shut up!" Howard shouted. "You're not blaming this on me. Now I have to pay for the goddamn damages."

With a father like that, Callie suspected the boys had more than their fair share of trouble. But Melba Sue's expression was the deal breaker. It was obvious she loved her sons and the thought of them in jail was breaking her heart.

"Please do not destroy another person's property out of spite."

"Yes, ma'am." Howie hung his head.

"We cleaned it up real good," Cliff added.

"Yes, and I'm happy about that, and—" she glanced at Wade "—I can't press charges."

"Oh, thank you, Mrs. Austin," Melba Sue gushed. "Thank you. They're good boys, just a little misguided at times."

"Shut up, Melba Sue. Nobody wants to listen to your sniveling." Howard pulled out his wallet. "What's the damages?"

"Mostly Odell's labor. He traveled to San Antonio for the glass and replaced it himself." Wade pushed a piece of paper across the desk.

Howard pulled out four one-hundred-dollar bills. "That should cover the damages."

That took Wade by surprise—how did Howard have that kind of money in his back pocket? Wade stood, his eyes on Howard. "Where'd you get the money?"

"Took a draw on my wages. That's what you want, Sheriff, isn't it? Me to pay my bills?"

"Yeah. I'd like for you to pay your bills, adjust your attitude and stop blaming everyone else for your problems."

"Let's go," Howard said to his family.

"Boys, I'll be keeping a close eye on you. So behave yourselves," Wade said to Howie and Cliff.

"Yes, sir." The family walked out of the office.

"Thank you," Wade said as the door closed. "They didn't need to go to juvenile detention."

"I didn't think so either. Their father is a fine piece of work and I feel so sorry for Melba Sue."

"She's had several chances to get out of that relationship, but she always chooses to stay. Typical pattern. It's hard to break." He came around the desk and handed her the money. "This should help with the expense of the cleanup."

With the money in her hand, she said, "I feel bad taking it. They need it more than I do."

"Don't go soft on me. Those boys broke the law and I'm hoping they've learned something."

"Me, too."

"And Odell worked nonstop, so he deserves overtime."

Her fingers closed around the bills. "You can bet he'll get it." Odell had gone above and beyond what was expected of him and it was only right he received compensation. He probably wouldn't want it, but she'd make sure he took it.

Wade leaned against the desk, watching her. "Where are the kids?"

She tucked a stray strand of hair behind her ear. "Jock stopped by this morning. That's why I was late."

An eyebrow rose. "My dad stopped by your house?"

"Yes. With steak and eggs in hand. Wanted me to cook his breakfast."

"You're joking."

"No."

"I saw the steak out when I left. Thought he was going to cook it himself."

"There's more. Jock told Adam that Lucky needed to be

ridden and wanted him to come to the ranch. It put me in an awkward position because the girls wanted to go, too. So I promised to take them later this afternoon and I have so much work to do with getting the café ready to open."

"So Adam's with Pop?"

"Yes. That's okay, isn't it?"

"It's wonderful. My dad hasn't taken an interest in anything in years. And don't worry about the girls. I'll come by later and take them out to the ranch so they can ride and I'll bring them back. That way you can get all the work done you need." His eyes flickered with amusement. "Or you could just come with us."

"Don't tempt me." She glanced at her watch. "I have to go. Ethel's watching the girls."

She stopped at the door and turned. "I saw those wanted posters out there and it made me realize the enormous risk you're taking with your future."

"It's my choice."

She saw that it was. She was so incredibly lucky to have found this man—this very good man. He would protect them—keep them safe.

But what did he gain in return?

CHAPTER FOURTEEN

THE DAYS SETTLED into a routine. Every morning Jock showed up for breakfast, and now Wade came, too. They ate the meal like a normal family, but Callie had to keep reminding herself that they weren't.

Adam continued to go to the ranch with Jock and was learning to work cattle. Brit wanted to go, too, but Callie didn't think the ranch was the place for a small girl. Brit could go when either she or Wade could go.

Wade hadn't received any more information on Nigel and, as the days passed, Callie was hoping that he wouldn't. She knew that was the child in her wanting to have it all. Sooner or later they'd have to face Nigel—in court or in person.

The Fourth of July arrived and they spent it at the ranch. To the kids' way of thinking, there was no other place to go. And she had to admit she was in total agreement. Tex and his family were having a big barbecue, but Callie and Wade decided that a picnic would be nice.

They were going to an old deer cabin on Spring Creek and they had to ride there on horseback. Callie hadn't been on a horse in years, but she adjusted quickly. She'd packed a picnic basket of fried chicken, rolls, fruit, cheese and her double fudge walnut brownies for dessert.

Mary Beth rode with Wade and they trotted through green coastal pastures into the hills of brushy mesquite, cedars and scrub oaks. Whitetail deer and wild turkeys could occasionally be seen eating beneath oak and pecan trees. Squirrels and rabbits were plentiful, too. At times, the horses picked their way slowly over rocky crevices and cacti, then they rode down into a valley of tall grasses with a glistening creek meandering through it.

A small cabin was nestled on the bank under a sprawling live oak. They dismounted and Callie sucked in the fresh air, feeling the sunshine on her skin and experiencing a high of pure pleasure.

It was a magical afternoon. They fished in the creek and the kids squealed with delight when they actually caught a perch or catfish. They ate on a blanket under the live oak, except Jock, who sat on a chair Adam brought from the cabin. A tire was attached to a rope and hung from the tree. The children took turns pushing each other, laughing and being kids again.

As the sun began to sink, they saddled up and headed back. When they reached the barn, they took care of the horses, then made their way to Tex's for the fireworks display. The Mexicans were having a big party and relatives spilled out onto the yard and pasture. The girls sat in a group of other children. Jock took a seat on the porch steps, Adam beside him like a shadow. Callie and Wade sat on a tailgate.

Wade held her hand and neither spoke as fireworks lit up the sky. All too soon, it was time to return to town—and reality.

CALLIE WAS BUSY getting the café ready to open. The two bedrooms downstairs were big and she figured she could get four or five tables in each one. But she'd start out with four in each because she didn't think business would be that brisk at first. She found a few tables at a local antique store and Wade knew the people who owned the old furniture store that had closed—a lot of furniture was still inside. She was able to buy the rest there. Then she ordered linens, All-Clad pots and pans and good knives from the Internet. Next she worked on a menu and tested recipes on Wade and her friends. She soon discovered that her gourmet ideas weren't going to fly in Homestead. Her hollandaise and béarnaise sauces didn't go over very well. Wade didn't say anything, but Odell and Ethel said plenty.

"What's that?" Ethel wanted to know.

"It's a sauce."

"Is it like gravy?" Odell asked.

"In a way," she answered with a long sigh.

"Why not just make gravy?"

They didn't think too much of her tarts and crepes either and she knew, for the café to be a success, she'd have to prepare meals the Southern way—like Mrs. Heinbacker had taught her. So she adjusted her menu to some down-home good food. Later, she would introduce some of her favorite recipes. *Later*—that one word pulled her up short. She was thinking like she was going to be here forever. But she wasn't. She had to make the most of the time that she was here.

Her thoughts turned to her father. She still hadn't asked anyone else about him and Wade hadn't mentioned him either. She intended to bring up the subject again, but they never seemed to have any time alone. Once she opened the café, they'd have even less time. There had to be a way….

While Callie was in the kitchen washing some votive candleholders she'd found at Tanner's, Ethel walked in with a box of napkins. "Here's the napkins folded that fancy way."

"Thanks, Ethel."

"Why you're using cloth napkins is beyond me. Nobody in this town knows how to use one. And who's going to wash all these things?"

"I intend to hire a few more people."

"That's good. I do a lot of things, but washing and ironing are not my favorite chores."

Callie set a candleholder on a towel to dry. She took a long breath. "Ethel, have you ever heard of a Dale Collins?"

"Sure. He died years ago. Drank himself to death. Why are you asking about…?"

Callie pulled the sink stopper and the soapy suds swirled down the drain with a swishing sound, blocking out Ethel's voice.

Her father was dead—just like Glynis had said. For a second, she couldn't breathe and she felt a pain in her chest. She hadn't even known her father, so she didn't understand why it hurt so bad. Maybe because she'd hoped for so long that one day she'd get the chance to meet him, to see his face. Maybe that's why she'd waited to ask. It was better thinking he was alive. That way she could still hope. Now she knew for sure that she would never see him.

Dragging in a breath, she turned to ask Ethel where he was buried and saw a young girl standing in the doorway. In her twenties, she had bright red hair, freckles and thick glasses. She was about fifty pounds overweight and her hair pulled back into a tight ponytail made her face appear rounder.

"Wanda, what are you doing here?" Ethel asked sharply.

"I came to…to speak to Mrs. Austin."

Callie wiped her hands on a dish towel. "I'm Mrs. Austin."

"I…ah…Father Noah said you…you're opening a café and…he…I mean…I thought you might need…some help."

"Wanda, stop clucking like a nervous chicken about to be dinner. Mrs. Austin can't understand a word you're saying."

Wanda was very shy and Ethel wasn't helping. Callie took her arm and led her into the café area to sit at a table.

"Tell me about yourself," Callie invited.

"I...I..."

The girl was visibly trembling and Callie reached out to touch her. "You don't have to be nervous of me. Take a deep breath and tell me about yourself."

"My name is Wanda Krauss and I've lived in Homestead all my life. My dad had a stroke and my mama had to take care of him, then she got cancer and became really ill. I had to drop out of school when I was sixteen to care for them. My sister and brother live in another state and there was only me. My mama passed away three months ago and my daddy's been gone six weeks. People say I'm not too smart, but I can clean and cook and I need a job."

Callie's heart went out to this young girl who'd never had a life of her own. "I'll need someone to bus tables, wash dishes and help with the laundry."

"I can do that. I'll do anything you ask."

"Then you have a job." Callie didn't need any references. She could almost see into this girl's heart and all she saw was good.

"Oh, thank you, Mrs. Austin. Thank you. I'll work real hard and I'll always be on time and I'll stay until you want me to leave."

"Fine. And please call me Callie."

Wanda left with a big smile and Callie felt she should be thanking her because she felt Wanda was going to be a great asset.

She sat at the table, not moving, just absorbing the knowledge that her father was dead. She wished Wade and the kids would come back from riding. It was too lonely without them and she needed to hold someone.

THE KIDS CAME BACK talking ninety miles an hour and it was some time before Callie could get them in bed.

"Pop says I'm getting better and better," Adam said, hopping into bed.

She lifted an eyebrow. "Pop?"

"Well, I called him that and he didn't tell me not to."

She tucked him in. "I'll have to talk to Jock about it." She kissed his forehead, knowing what she had to say wouldn't be easy. "You can't be a replacement for Zach."

"I know. Just like he can't be a replacement for Daddy. We like each other—that's all. And he's teaching me a lot. I almost roped a calf today." It was so uncanny to see her brother who was always glued to his computer or listening to music becoming almost a different person.

"And he almost fell off his horse, too," Brit shouted from the other room.

"Girls don't understand roping," Adam whispered. Callie had a feeling that was one of Jock's sayings.

She kissed him again. "Good night."

In the other bedroom, she said, "I have to speak to Wade, so you girls go to sleep."

"I want a story," Mary Beth said.

Callie noticed that Miss Winnie wasn't clutched in Mary Beth's arms and hadn't been lately. Nor did she talk much to Fred. She was changing, too.

"Brit can tell you a story."

"Yeah. I'll tell you one about the bestest cowgirl in Homestead."

Mary Beth made a face. "I don't want a cowgirl story. I want a princess one."

"Okay." Brit snuggled down. "Once upon a time there was a sheriff…"

Smiling, Callie took the stairs two at a time, thinking that suddenly there was a sheriff in all their stories.

And in their hearts.

WADE WASN'T IN THE KITCHEN so she went out to the front porch and found him lounging in one of the rockers. Slipping onto his lap, she wrapped her arms around him and rested her head on his shoulder.

"Hey, something wrong?" He stroked her hair.

"He's dead."

"Who's dead?"

"My father. I finally asked Ethel about him and she said he died long ago. Drank himself to death just like my mother had told me. But I was still hoping…."

"Callie…"

"It's okay. I can accept it now." She raised her head. "He gave up all his rights to me and I don't remember him, so that must mean he didn't have much to do with me when I was small. Maybe he just didn't want a child."

"Callie…"

"No. I don't want to talk about it anymore." She rested her head in the crook of his neck. "It's nice out here just you and me. This is the first time we've been alone in days."

"Mmm." Wade was at a loss for words. He hadn't had time to do anything about her father and now Ethel had beat him to it. It twisted his gut to see her hurting like this, but it wasn't his secret to tell.

"Look at all those stars," she said. "We could be anywhere in the world."

He rubbed his head against hers. "I'd rather be right here."

"Me, too." Her hand slipped beneath the buttons on his shirt. "We need some time alone."

"Are you sure?" He wanted her to be sure about the next

step in their relationship, even though he wasn't sure about it himself. Could he love Callie then watch her go back to New York? But how could he not love her and spend the rest of his life with what-ifs?

"Yes," she breathed as her lips met his.

He kissed her briefly then said, "Let's not get carried away. I'm on duty tonight. Let's make a date. We have plenty of babysitters and you and I will go out for an evening before the café opens."

"Are you asking me out, Wadeinhiemer?"

He grinned. "Yes. Now I have to get back to the office."

She crawled out of his lap and he slowly got to his feet.

"When you line up a babysitter, maybe we'll go to San Antonio and catch a movie…or whatever."

"Or whatever." She stood on tiptoes to kiss him. He tasted her lips for a moment and he had to force himself to leave.

But he had to do something he'd been putting off. That meant divulging Callie's secret about her real identity. Was that safe?

It wasn't much of a decision. Callie had to know.

CALLIE PUT AWAY THE LAST of the dishes in the kitchen then went upstairs to bathe and get ready for bed. In her pajama bottoms and T-shirt, she went to check on the kids. Adam was sound asleep and she could almost see a smile on his face.

The girls were all over the bed, also asleep, and Callie was trying to figure out a way to get in without disturbing them. She had to buy another bed. They couldn't continue to sleep like this. The girls needed their own room. And she definitely needed some privacy.

As she was climbing between the sheets, she heard a knock downstairs. It was late. Who could it be? *Wade*. That's the only person it could be. She flew down the stairs, her feet barely touching the floor, and swung the door open.

"Buddy," she said in disappointment.

"I know it's late, but could I talk to you for a minute?"

"Sure." She stepped aside. "Come into the kitchen and I'll fix us something to drink."

"Thanks. But I don't need a thing."

Rascal wasn't with him, so that meant something must have happened to him. "Did something happen to Rascal?" she had to ask.

"No. He's at home."

Callie couldn't imagine what Buddy wanted to talk about. They took seats at the breakfast table and Callie thought she should go put on a robe, but she didn't feel uncomfortable and the clothes covered her. And she didn't think Buddy noticed what she had on.

"The house is looking real nice." He glanced around. "Odell did a good job."

"A lot of people helped, including you."

"It was fun. Gave me something to do after work." He removed his baseball cap and set it on the table. His hair was a deep blond with streaks of gray. His hand shook.

"Buddy, are you okay?"

He took a deep breath. "I…ah…just had a long talk with Wade."

"You did?"

He looked at her, and for the first time, she noticed his eyes were hazel-green.

"You don't know a lot about me."

She smiled. "I know you're a good person."

His eyes clouded over. "My real name is Dale Collins."

What! The smile vanished and Callie gaped at him, not quite able to take in what he was saying. Dale Collins? That was her father's name. Could…?

"What did you say?" Her words came out low and hoarse.

"My name is Dale Collins."

"Ethel said you were dead."

"That's my father. I'm a junior and no one has ever called me Dale, but Glynis."

Glynis. Oh God!

"But I asked you…and you said…"

"I know. I couldn't tell you the truth, so I lied."

She swallowed hard. "You're my father."

"Yes. I married Glynis Dryden in high school because I had to. She was pregnant. I resented her and I resented the baby. I was young and I didn't want to be tied down. I wanted to have fun."

Callie had trouble breathing.

"But when you were born, my attitude changed. I couldn't take my eyes off your beautiful face. You had blond hair with curls and the most gorgeous blue eyes. Mary Beth looks a lot like you." He ran a nervous hand through his hair. "I wanted to be a father. I tried, but nothin' I ever did was good enough for Glynis. We lived with her mother because we couldn't afford anything else and I worked as a mechanic. Didn't make a lot of money and Glynis complained all the time. The more she complained, the more I drank. It wasn't all Glynis's fault, don't get me wrong. I wasn't mature enough to be a father or a husband."

Gentle, kind Buddy was her father. That thought was quickly followed by another that surprised her—Buddy was uncaring, irresponsible, a deadbeat dad who hadn't wanted her, who'd given her up.

"You gave up all rights to me. How could you do that?"

He closed his eyes briefly as he seemed to struggle for control. "That didn't mean I didn't love you. There wasn't much love in my family and I didn't know how to love anyone. That doesn't excuse what happened though." He fidgeted uncomfortably. "Glynis and I had a big fight because I'd lost my job. I was too drunk to go to work most days. She packed her things and left, saying she was going to find someone to take care of her and you. I never saw her after that. About three months later I got divorce papers and Glynis asked for full custody of you. I was so drunk and angry that I just signed the papers. Then I headed out to West Texas to work in the oil fields. Made good money, but spent it all on liquor and a good time."

Callie didn't know what to say, so she just listened.

"Fell off the top of one of those oil rigs and didn't break a bone 'cause I was stone drunk. My boss got me into rehab and I was sober for the first time in years. After that I had one thing on my mind, so I hired an attorney. I wanted to see my kid. The lawyer said my rights to you had been terminated with the divorce. Guess I didn't read those divorce papers close enough. Probably would've gone on a drinking binge, but I got a call my mom was real sick and I came home to take care of her. Been here ever since."

"You hired an attorney to see me?"

"Yeah. My lawyer said I had a snowball's chance in hell of doing that." He reached into his back pocket and pulled out his wallet. Flipping it open, he removed a small picture and laid it on the table.

Callie stared at herself when she was about four and her throat closed up. The photo was worn and tattered, as if someone had handled it a lot. *He did care about her.*

"When you were that age, I'd take you down to the drugstore to get an ice-cream cone. Then we'd sit on the bench at the courthouse and you'd ask all kinds of questions about the clock in the tower. You had a fascination with it."

Through the fuzziness of her mind, she could almost hear that little girl's voice. "Daddy, how did the clock get up there?…Daddy, what time is it now?" That's why the clock tower had jogged her memory when she'd first come to town. She'd remembered it from the times she'd watched it with her father.

Buddy. Dale Collins.

"I knew who you were the first moment I saw you. You favor Glynis. She was very beautiful."

"You knew who I was?" She gulped.

"Yep. Been waitin' a lot of years to see that face, but I was a coward. I couldn't tell you who I was. Didn't think you really wanted to know, but I kept coming here just to get a glimpse of you."

Her hand trembled against her mouth, tears stung the back of her eyes. "You're the reason I came here with the kids. Glynis said you were probably dead, but I had to know."

Silence filled the room. So many emotions swirled between them, but neither knew exactly how to handle them.

"How's Glynis?" Buddy finally asked.

Callie stared at him. "Wade didn't tell you?"

He shook his head. "He said you had a lot to tell me and that I was to keep everything quiet."

Obviously Wade wanted her to be the one to tell him the truth about herself. He was leaving it up to her and she knew why. Telling another person could jeopardize their safety. Callie looked into Buddy's eyes. She could trust him, of that she was certain. He was her father. So she told him their story.

His face changed to dismay then horror. "So they're not your youngins?"

"No."

"They're Glynis's?"

She nodded."

"Damn. Never would have guessed that." His face suddenly hardened. "How could Glynis marry a bastard like Nigel Tremont?"

"I've asked myself that so many times in the past few months and I just don't have an answer."

"But you had a good life up until then?" The question seemed important to him.

"Yes. Things were rough at first, but after Mom met John our lives got better. He adopted me and took good care of me."

"Always thought you were too young to have three young-ins and I knew your age."

"Wish you'd said something earlier."

Silence dragged again, then Buddy cleared his throat. "Didn't figure I had that right."

"When I needed a hiding place, I thought of the land give-away deal in Homestead, mainly, I see now, because I needed to come back. I had to find out if you were still alive, and you were the first person I met when I drove into Homestead. Fate works in funny ways sometimes."

"Yep." He picked up the photo and put it back in his wallet. "I made some real bad decisions and choices, but what I'll always regret the most is not being a part of your life."

"Me, too," she admitted. "I couldn't understand why you'd give up all rights to me. It made me feel unwanted."

He moved with slow, tired motions. "It's hard to explain the actions of a drunk and that's what I was. Every day's a struggle, but I haven't touched a drop in twelve years. In all those years, even when I was drunk, a day didn't go by that I didn't think of you and wonder where you were. If you were happy, if…" He stopped. "The photo kept me sane in rehab. I kept telling myself that once I was sober for good that I could see my kid, my baby girl."

She swallowed the lump in her throat. "But I'm not a kid anymore."

He raised his head. "No. You've turned into a beautiful young woman and I'll do anything to help you, to keep those youngins safe."

She knew that he would. It was clear in his voice and in his eyes.

"I hope in time you'll be able to forgive me."

Suddenly, all the years she'd hated this man who hadn't wanted her seemed nonexistent. He cared, kept her photo and hadn't forgotten about her. That's all she really needed to know—for now.

Her eyes filled with tears. "I don't need time. I just need to know my father."

His eyes also rimmed with tears. "Oh, Callie, that's more than I deserve." He blinked away a tear. "Do you know your grandmother, Hettie Dryden, used to work for the Hellmuths as a maid? Glynis had a job at the Dairy Queen and sometimes Hettie would bring you to work with her. You were a quiet little thing and no trouble at all."

Her eyes grew wide. "My grandmother worked here?"

"Yep."

"The rockers and the house seemed so familiar and I couldn't figure out why."

"You loved those rockers. You'd sit out there and rock away."

"Oh, my." Now she knew why she loved the house just by looking at the photo. It was her past—a tiny, unforgettable part of her past.

Buddy's hand reached across the table and she placed hers in it. He squeezed tightly, and in that instant Callie knew she'd made the right decision in coming to Homestead.

She'd found her father.

And so much more.

CHAPTER FIFTEEN

WADE KEPT GLANCING at the clock, wondering if Buddy had told her yet. How was she taking it? He thrust his hands through his hair. Buddy was Callie's father. That was still a little hard to digest. But if anyone deserved some happiness, it was Buddy. He didn't want Callie hurt, though. She was dealing with enough.

His cell buzzed and he clicked it on, to get the latest from Simon. This investigation was taking longer than he'd expected. Nigel Tremont was good at covering his tracks.

The bell on the front door jingled and he went to see who was having a problem tonight. Callie stood there, her eyes bright and she was smiling. He let out a long breath. Evidently things had gone well.

He grinned. "What are you doing here this late? Where are the kids?"

She walked closer. "I had to come and thank you, so Buddy is staying at my house in case the kids wake up."

"From the look on your face, I'd say you and Buddy had a good talk."

"The best."

"I'm glad. When you said Dale Collins was your father, I couldn't believe you didn't know that was Buddy."

"Mmm." She moved closer and ran her hands up his chest to his neck. "I decided I couldn't wait to see you."

"Callie," he groaned as she pressed her body closer. "I'm on duty."

"Does a lot happen at night?" She kissed his neck.

"No, but I have to be ready if it does."

"How ready?" She wrapped her arms around his neck, gazing at him with love in her eyes—a look he couldn't resist.

He took her lips with a fierce need and the kiss went on until they were both breathless with wanting. Her skin smelled of lavender and she tasted of sugar—the sweetest sugar he'd ever had.

Sliding his hands beneath her T-shirt, he cupped her breasts. Tiny moans left her throat and he knew they were getting close to the point of no return. He didn't have to think about it. He knew loving Callie was better than never loving her.

He broke the kiss and moved toward the front door, locking it. A smile split her face and she threw herself back into his arms.

Kissing the warm hollow of her neck, her cheek, her nose, he whispered, "Ever make love in a jail cell?"

She shook her head and released a bubble of laughter. Swinging her up in his arms, he carried her down a small hallway and kicked open the door to the cell with his foot. The door clanged against the bars as they sank onto the cot and they dissolved into laughter like two teenagers.

Wade hadn't felt this great in years and for tonight, for this time out of time with Callie, he wasn't the sheriff. He was a man.

Their hands eagerly found each other, and he pulled the T-shirt over her head then tasted every inch of her smooth, soft skin, lingering over her sensitive nipples. She moaned and he captured her mouth in a heated kiss.

Her fingers undid the buttons on his shirt and trailed across his chest and shoulders with tantalizing strokes. Emotion, strong and sure, swept through him and he yanked off his gun, then his boots in a split second. Their clothes followed and soon they were skin on skin, hearts beating wildly as they lay on the cot entwined.

They didn't speak—they didn't need to. They both knew what they wanted.

All their problems faded away with each kiss, each caress, and there was just the two of them finding comfort in an age-old way—with each other.

When Callie knew she couldn't take any more, she shifted onto her back and spread her legs, accepting Wade with a white-hot urgency that both shocked and excited her. She held him tight as each movement, each thrust bound them tighter and closer until spasms of pleasure welded them together forever. She loved him. But the words never left her throat and she felt deprived of the greatest gift of all—knowing her love was returned. She couldn't be that selfish though. She'd already taken what she needed and they understood that. They were adults.

Wade pulled her to his side, breathing in her scent for a moment longer. Sex in his teens had been awesome, but making love with Callie was unlike anything he'd ever experienced and he suddenly knew that nothing would match this moment. He'd made a decision to love her and he wouldn't regret it. Not for a second. He wouldn't let himself think about the day she'd walk away from him to her other life in New York.

For now, she was his.

They sat up, leaning against the wall, just holding on to each other. "Are you going to tell the kids about Buddy?"

"No, not yet. Too many secrets for them to handle. I'll tell them later."

"That's probably best." He caressed her arm. "You okay?"

"Mmm. I just want to go to sleep in your arms."

"Me, too." He kissed the top of her head. "But can you imagine the headline in the *Homestead Herald* if we were discovered like this?"

"Mmm. Newcomer a Floozy. Seduces Sheriff." She laughed out loud and he caught the sound with his lips and again they were lost in the magic of love.

WADE STOOD AT THE DOOR, fully dressed, with his arms around Callie as she lingered over goodbye.

"I heard from Simon earlier," he said, kissing her forehead. "He's gone to Philadelphia to see if he can speak with the woman in the health-care facility who was married to Nigel and try to get more details. Her daughter won't talk to him over the phone."

"This is taking so long."

"I know, but we should have something soon to help your case."

"Then I can take the kids back to New York to face a judge."

"Yes."

She held him tight, wondering if she was going to be able to do that now. After a long leisurely kiss, she darted out the door to her car hoping Millie wasn't lurking outside with her camera. But Millie had gone to bed a long time ago. Everyone in Homestead had.

On the way to her house, she knew she wouldn't be able to sleep tonight. Too much had happened. Too many wonderful things that would forever bind her to this small town.

FRIDAY WAS TO BE THE GRAND opening of the café and Callie was in a tizzy getting everything ready. Wanda was truly a find and Callie didn't know what she'd have done without her. She'd hired a waitress, Janet, and Ethel's daughter Essie to seat people and to work the cash register.

Essie had returned to Homestead after separating from her

husband and Ethel had figured she needed something to do. As Ethel had put it, Essie couldn't sit in her house watching soap operas all day.

Odell was putting the finishing touches on the heating and air-conditioning system. It was July and the rooms had to be cool for people to eat in comfort.

The rest of the dishes she'd ordered had arrived, and she and Wanda were busy washing and stacking them on open shelves Odell had built for that purpose.

When Odell went outside to his truck to get something, Callie noticed Wanda watching him.

"People say he's not too bright, but they're wrong. He can do all kinds of things."

"Yes." Callie laid a dish on the stack. "A lot of people underestimate Odell."

"Why do you call him that?"

Callie looked at her. "Because that's his name."

"I know, but I never heard anyone call him that until I came to work here."

"Please call him Odell. It's an insult to call by that other name."

"I will. I'd never hurt his feelings." Wanda paused, then asked, "Callie, how do you lose weight?"

Was Wanda interested in Odell? Callie's matchmaking instinct went into high gear, but she quickly shifted it back to neutral. She had to let things happen naturally.

Callie put away a dish. "For starters, you can stop having soft drinks and candy bars for breakfast." When Wanda arrived in the mornings that's usually what she had in her hands.

"But I always eat that."

"Too many calories. Try a whole-grain cereal and low-fat milk and a piece of fruit, then have salads, vegetables and lean meats for lunch and supper."

At Wanda's frown, Callie added, "Dieting is all about will-power. If you want something bad enough, you'll do it."

"I guess." Wanda put the last of the dishes on the stack. "What about my hair? I don't know what to do with it."

Again Callie's heart went out to this young girl who had no one to guide her. Callie studied the long stringy hair that hung down Wanda's back. "How about getting it cut into a shorter style? I believe Kristin's aunt has a beauty shop in town."

"Ms. Raejean, but I've never been in there."

"I'll make an appointment and I'll go with you. Would that help?"

"Oh, yes, ma'am. Thank you. You're so pretty and I knew you'd know all about these things."

Buddy came in the back door, stopping the conversation. "Are you ready for a trial run?" He was helping Odell and Bubba Joe so the air could be in by the opening.

"Yes." She smiled. "And thank you for helping."

"No problem. When are the youngins coming back?"

"Not until dark I'm afraid, but Mary Beth will be glad to see Rascal."

"He's laying on the front porch, watching the gate."

Rascal was very attached to Mary Beth, as was Buddy. They were all forming bonds here in Homestead. Callie was glad to get to know her father. They talked a lot about the past, the mistakes and the heartaches. They both treasured this time together.

Odell and Bubba Joe came in and Odell screwed the last vent into place, then Buddy switched on the control. Odell held his hand toward the vent because he couldn't actually reach it without a ladder. Throwing his baseball cap into the air, he shouted, "It's working."

"Thank you, Odell," Callie said. "Thank you, Buddy, Bubba Joe."

"This calls for a celebration," Bubba Joe said. "Odell and me are headed to the Lone Wolf for a beer. Anyone else want to come?"

Buddy shook his head. "Not exactly my kind of thing anymore."

"Sorry, Buddy, I…"

"Don't worry about it," Buddy said. "You boys have a good time."

Wanda picked up Odell's cap and handed it to him.

Ask her to go. Callie was mentally urging him. But he and Bubba Joe disappeared out the door without a glance at Wanda.

CALLIE HAD A ROAST on for supper and she finished the vegetables while talking to Buddy. The house was so much better with the air-conditioning on. The heat from the stove wasn't so oppressive and cooking was going to be an even greater joy.

Soon the kids came charging in, all talking at once. After hugging Buddy and Callie, Mary Beth and Rascal hurried upstairs. Callie assumed she had to go to the bathroom, but she usually announced it.

Wade slipped an arm around her waist at the sink. "Mmm. Air. Nice. You smell good."

"That's beef, I believe," she replied with a twinkle in her eyes.

"With gravy?"

She nodded.

"My kind of woman."

She so desperately wanted to kiss him and the desire was echoed in his eyes. Leaning closer, she whispered, "Anyone in that jail cell tonight?"

"I'll check—later," he said with a grin, and walked into the breakfast area where Buddy was listening to Adam and Brit.

"We had a roundup today, didn't we, Wade?" Brit asked

for Wade's confirmation, just in case Buddy didn't believe her.

"Sure did, cowgirl." Wade sank into a chair and Brit slid onto his lap.

"It was very exciting," Brit added. "Cows and babies were everywhere bellowing 'cause they weren't real happy we were taking care of them."

"Yeah." Adam joined in. "We branded some calves and sprayed cattle for flies and ticks and things. Pop let me help."

Callie froze. Was that something Adam should be doing? She glanced at Wade and knew that neither he nor Jock would let the kids do anything they shouldn't. And Adam lived for the times he could be on the ranch. He hadn't even mentioned Nigel lately.

Mary Beth walked slowly into the room carrying Fred in the goldfish bowl, Rascal behind her. Callie ran to help her, not understanding why she'd bring Fred down.

The bowl safely on the table, Mary Beth announced, "We have to brand Fred."

Silence engulfed the room, broken only by a few snickers.

Wade pulled Mary Beth onto his lap beside Brit. "Little bit, we don't brand fish."

Mary Beth looked at him with serious eyes. "Pop says you have to brand your animals 'cause when people steal them, everyone will know who they belong to. So we have to brand Fred in case anyone breaks into our house again and takes him."

"Don't be a doofus, Mary Beth. You can't brand a fish," Brit said.

"I'm not a doofus," Mary Beth snapped back. "And why not?"

Before Brit could formulate a response, Adam took over. "Because Fred's too little. Those branding irons are really big and are not for fish. They're for cattle."

"Then we have to get a fish branding iron."

"There's no such thing." Adam's voice rose as he was losing his patience.

"We know where Fred is at all times." Wade took over. "He's in his bowl swimming around. That's just the way it is with fish. With cattle, they have wide-open spaces and rustlers sometimes take advantage of that. But Fred, he's pretty safe and if anyone takes him, I'll bring him back."

"Promise?" Mary Beth wanted proof and Callie knew what was coming.

"I promise."

Mary Beth made a face. "A real promise."

Wade glanced at Callie for help.

"You have to kiss your palm and hold it to your heart," she told him.

Wade did as instructed.

Mary Beth nodded. "My daddy always said that a promise is a message kept in the heart and never to be forgotten."

"You got it, little bit."

Callie watched Wade with Mary Beth. He was good with kids and she knew he was a good father. And he deserved to be a father again with a family and a home —something she couldn't give him. Suddenly all the hope and joy she was feeling dissipated. But she would never let it show.

After supper, the kids went to take their baths and Wade and Buddy helped with the dishes. That done, Buddy reached for his cap.

"I'll mosey on to my place, that is unless you need me to babysit."

Wade's cell buzzed and he answered it. "Okay. I'll be right there." He replaced the cell on his waist. "Virgil arrested Norris at the Saddle Up beer joint for drunk and disorderly. I have to get over to the jail. I'll call you later." He gave her a quick kiss and was gone.

She watched him go with a sad expression.

"You care for him a lot," Buddy remarked.

"Yeah. It happened so quickly and I let my emotions get involved when I shouldn't have. I'll be leaving as soon as the custody hearing is settled and that's going to hurt him. Hurt me and the kids. That's the last thing I wanted. I just…"

Buddy put his arm around her and patted her shoulder. Callie leaned on her father for the first time in her life and she felt an incredible joy from that.

"Sometimes you have to let your heart lead you," Buddy said. "Wade's a good man. I remember him as a kid following Jock around, watching his every move. There was little doubt that he'd go into law enforcement. Then his son died and he came home. Never saw a sadder man, the light had completely gone out of his eyes. But when he looks at you and those kids, it's back. Wade Montgomery can handle anything, but I think if you had your way you'd stay here in Homestead."

She drew back. "I can't, Buddy. I have to take the kids back to their life in New York. A life John had planned for them. It was his wish and I have to honor it."

"And what about your happiness?"

"Oh." She blinked away a tear. "I'll put that on hold for a while."

He touched her cheek. "You're an unbelievable young woman. Now, I better get going. Rascal," he called. They could hear thumping upstairs but Rascal didn't come down.

They exchanged an amusing glance. "Mary Beth is probably trying to hide him under the bed again. Mary Beth," Callie shouted. "Bring Rascal down this instant."

"He can stay. I'll pick him up tomorrow."

"No. Rascal is your dog." Callie knew Rascal was the only company he had and she wasn't taking that away from him.

"Mary Beth," she shouted again.

Silence, then the patter of bare feet sounded on the stairs. Soon Mary Beth and Rascal appeared. Mary Beth had on her Barbie pajamas and her blond hair was hanging loose down her back, a pitiful expression on her face.

"Does Rascal have to go home now?"

"Yes," Callie answered.

"Maybe—"

"Yes," Callie repeated, stopping Buddy before he could even make the offer.

"Bye." Mary Beth gave Rascal a hug, then Buddy.

Buddy kissed Callie's cheek. "At least she didn't want to brand him."

"Give her time. I'm sure she'll think of it."

"Yep." Buddy smiled, and Callie realized he didn't smile much. He looked so much younger when he did, probably similar to the boy Glynis had known.

Buddy stopped at the door. "Don't worry too much. Things have a way of working out."

As she locked the doors, she hoped those words were true. She took Mary Beth's hand and they went upstairs. With the kids tucked in, she took a long, hot bath, letting her muscles relax. But her thoughts kept straying to Wade and she wished she was relaxing in another way—with his body against hers.

Her cell phone buzzed and she quickly got out of the tub to answer it. It was her lawyer, Gail.

"How you doing?"

"Fine. What's happened?" Gail would only call if there was some progress in the case.

"I called in some favors and a judge has finally agreed to a hearing in three weeks. I just wanted to let you know."

"Thanks. This is good, right?"

"Yes. This is sooner than I expected. I just wish I had something concrete against Nigel. That would help tremendously."

Callie told her about Wade and the investigator.

"Let me get this straight. You have the local sheriff helping you?"

"Yes," Callie admitted, smiling. "He's a very nice man and he'll help us all he can. But I do not want his name used in anyway. He could lose his job."

"Well, honey, give me this nice man's name and phone number. All I want from him is info and maybe soon you can bring the children home to New York."

She gave Gail the number and hung up, sinking onto the edge of the bathtub. Three weeks. That wasn't much time. What was she doing opening a café? She wouldn't even have time to get it off the ground.

Three weeks. Suddenly that was too soon. She wanted that year. She needed that year. Or maybe she needed to face reality.

She put on her pajamas and trudged down the hall to her room and heard the girls giggling.

"Callie, make them go to sleep," Adam called from his room.

She turned on the light and climbed into the bed, sitting against the headboard. "Time for a meeting."

Adam jumped onto the bed and sat cross-legged. The girls pushed up beside Callie.

"I want to tell you something."

"I vote yes." Brit quickly raised her hand.

Callie frowned. "Yes, what?"

"I vote yes that you marry Wade."

"Me, too." Adam's hand shot into the air.

"You're marrying Wade? Oh, boy. Oh, boy." Mary Beth threw her arms around Callie. "I want to be a flower girl."

Callie closed her mouth that had fallen open at Brit's announcement. "Wait a minute. Where did you get an idea like that?"

"I saw you kissing Wade," Brit informed her.

"When?"

"When we came back from the ranch the other day. He kissed you and you kissed him back."

"A lot of people kiss, Brit, but it doesn't mean they're getting married."

Her face fell. "Then you're not marrying Wade?"

"No." But she wanted to, and she had to hide her inner desires. That wasn't in the cards for them. "Have you guys forgotten why we're here?"

"Nu-uh." Adam plucked at the sheet.

She let out a patient breath at the word. *We're not Texans. We're New Yorkers*, she wanted to shout. But deep down she so desperately wanted to be Texan. She had to focus on what was important. "My lawyer called and a hearing has been set. We may be able to go home sooner than we thought."

There was no yelling or shouting for joy. Just total, absolute silence. Adam jumped up and ran into his room.

"Go to sleep, girls." Callie got out of bed. "I have to talk to Adam."

Brit and Mary Beth snuggled down in the bed.

"I still vote for marrying Wade," Brit muttered.

"Me, too."

Callie heard Mary Beth's response as she entered Adam's room. He had his back to her. She sat on the edge of the bed.

He flipped over. "I can't go back. Pop needs me. I need him." His voice trembled with unshed tears and it made what she had to do so much harder.

"Our life is in New York. The life Daddy planned is in New York. You and he talked about it lots of times. You'd go to his private school that excels in academics then on to Harvard like he did."

"I...I..."

She gathered him in her arms and held him tight. "I know you like it here, but look at this like a vacation and we can come back."

"We can?" he mumbled.

"Sure."

He pushed away and looked into her eyes. "Promise?"

She made the special promise. That was all he needed—reassurance that he could return.

Tucking him in, she knew she was lying. For the first time, she'd lied to them. Once they left, they'd never return. She'd promised John and she'd keep her word—even though it was breaking her heart.

CHAPTER SIXTEEN

IT WAS AFTER TWELVE when Wade finished at the courthouse. Norris was in the holding cell and the two men he'd been fighting with were in the jail in the basement. Keeping them apart for the night was the best course of action. After they sobered up, Gil Schafer, the district attorney, would decide what to do with them. Norris wasn't getting off easy this time. He was going to learn a lesson the hard way. When Wade called Cora Lou, she said to keep him locked up or she might kill him. Seems the good ol' boys were fighting over a waitress.

Exhausted, he thought of going over to Callie's, but knew she was already in bed. That knowledge didn't keep him from watching the door earlier, hoping she'd stop by. But Norris was in the holding cell, so it would have been a waste of time. He could become territorial over that jail cell. He had other uses for it these days.

He grinned as he got into his car. Straitlaced Wade Montgomery was breaking the rules, and in the days to come he might have to break a few more. Suddenly, keeping Callie and the kids safe was more important than anything—his job, his future. He didn't even pause to question his actions. He just headed home.

Driving to the back of the house, he noticed a light was on. Pop was in bed long ago and he always turned off the lights. Wade went through the kitchen to the den. Pop was hunched over in his chair, staring at a piece of paper on his lap. Something was wrong.

Walking farther into the room, he saw what the problem was. The FBI bulletin on Callie was in Pop's hand.

Jock looked up at Wade, but he didn't say anything. His brow was wrinkled and his eyes worried.

"Where did you get that?" Wade asked.

"I was going to show Adam my .45 Colt revolver I used when I was sheriff—the one I shot that bank robber with. When I opened the safe, this was laying on top." He held up the paper. "Her husband was abusing those kids, wasn't he? That's why she kidnapped them, right? You can't let the FBI take her. They'll put her in jail. Someone like Callie doesn't need to be in a place like that."

Wade dropped to the sofa, facing his dad, not at all surprised that Jock was taking up for Callie. She'd broken through his hardened defenses when no one else could—not even Wade.

Removing his hat, he said, "It's not her husband, but her stepfather she's running from."

Jock shook his head. "I don't understand."

"The kids are not hers. They're her half siblings."

"What the hell's going on, Wade?"

Wade told him Callie's story, confident that Jock would do nothing to harm them.

"Why would her mother do such a thing? Anyone can see how much Callie loves those kids."

"I believe she was coerced by Nigel Tremont, that's the stepfather. You remember Simon Marchant—I used to work with him in Houston.

Jock nodded.

"I have him checking out Mr. Tremont and it seems the man has a pattern of marrying older women with money."

"Good. That will help Callie in court."

"That's what I'm working on, trying to gather enough evidence to prove Tremont is an unfit stepfather."

"You can do it, son, then they can live here in peace."

Wade's gut tightened. His next words weren't going to be accepted graciously. "As soon as Callie is granted a hearing, they'll be leaving for New York. That's their home. They're only hiding in Homestead until the hearing."

Jock's brow knotted into a fierce line. "And you're going to let that happen?"

"Yes."

Jock kicked down the footrest with his good leg. Grabbing his cane, he stumbled to his room.

Wade ran both hands over his face with a tired sigh, then he followed Jock, who was sitting on the side of his bed in the darkness. Moonlight streamed through the window, silhouetting his slumped figure.

Wade's gut tightened more. "The kids attend a private school in New York, the one their father attended. Their roots are in New York. Callie was a chef in a New York restaurant, something she's worked very hard to achieve. But she left it all behind to get them away from Tremont, who was using them like a punching bag."

Jock made a distressful sound, but didn't say anything.

"Actually Callie was born in Homestead—that's why she came back. Her mother was Glynis Dryden."

"Hettie Dryden's daughter?"

"Yeah."

"After Hettie's husband was killed, she worked for the Hellmuths to make a living for herself and her daughter. But the girl was wild. I remember that. Hettie had lots of problems with her. Now Callie has the Hellmuth house. Ain't that somethin'? Wait a minute."

Wade could almost hear the wheels clicking in his dad's head.

"Glynis married Buddy in high school. Does Callie know Buddy's her father?"

"She does now."

"Then Callie has roots here. She could decide to stay."

Wade could hear the hope in his voice.

"She won't, Pop. She going to do what's best for those kids. That's been her goal from the start." Wade knew that better than anyone.

"But you could persuade her to stay, son. I can see how you feel about her."

Wade swallowed the knot in his throat. "I'm not going to do that to her. It would only make the situation more difficult."

"Sometimes a man has to fight for what he wants."

"And sometimes a man has to be strong enough to let go."

He heard a snort. "Your rational reasoning always aggravates the hell out of me. Got that from your mother."

"Sorry, Pop. I want her and the kids to stay, but it has to be her decision. Right now Callie needs our help and that's what you and I are going to give her."

"While they're here, she'll still let them come to the ranch, won't she?" Worry coated every word.

"I don't think you can keep the kids away."

"Adam's gettin' awful good on a horse. He was born to ride. And little cowgirl, she's gettin' as good as her brother. She has a lot of grit, nothin' is ever going to get her down. Now, little bit, she just loves the animals. Doesn't care that much about ridin'. She'll probably be the vet in the family." His voice dropped. "But we'll never know, will we?"

Wade sucked in a breath, feeling the truth of that statement spear him. "Guess not."

Silence, then Jock said, "You just make sure they don't put Callie in jail."

"I'm doing my best. Night, Pop." Wade turned toward his room, wondering if his best was going to be good enough.

CALLIE WAS SO BUSY she didn't have time to do anything but concentrate on the café. In a way, that was good. The day before the opening, she made an early appointment for Wanda at Raejean's Snip and Curl Beauty Shop.

Raejean was a colorful lady in her late sixties, with flaming red hair and nails and a personality to match. With the pink-flamingo wallpaper and fluffy pink curtains, the salon was like a floating cloud and it took a moment for Callie's eyes to adjust.

Raejean took Wanda in hand and Wanda seemed comfortable with her, so Callie went back to the café to work.

Jock picked the kids up early and Brit and Mary Beth went, too. Yolanda was going to watch them and Callie had a feeling Wade had something to do with that. She missed him—how much was something she didn't want to dwell on.

Callie and Ethel were busy going over the menu and recipes. Callie had spent a lot of time going over ideas of what people would like in Homestead. Chicken-fried steak was a favorite so Callie decided to open with that. Green beans, garlic mashed potatoes and sautéed vegetables would go with it. And peach cobbler was the dessert.

She had hamburgers, grilled cheese and salads, too, but the house special would be the deal for the day. Ethel tried to add her spin to things and Callie had a hard time convincing her that they had to do it Callie's way. Ethel was always a good sport, though.

When Wanda came back from the beauty shop, Callie and Ethel stared. Wanda's hair was cut short and fluffed up in the back in one of the new styles. Bangs softened her face and she looked like a different person. She actually looked pretty. Raejean had done a wonderful job. Callie had been afraid Wanda might come back with the helmet look.

At their stares, Wanda asked, "What? Is it too short?"

"No. No." Callie immediately went to her. "It's very nice. I like it."

Wanda held up a bag. "I bought a lot of products to keep it this way. Think I spent half my paycheck."

"Very nice," Ethel added her praise.

Odell came through the back door and stopped, also staring at Wanda. "What you cut your hair for?" he asked, frowning. The words came out as a criticism and Callie wanted to shake him because she knew he didn't mean it that way.

Wanda's face crumbled.

Ethel saved the moment. "I wouldn't be talking about hair if I were you, Odell. You're starting to lose yours."

"Mama." Odell was embarrassed.

"Well, it's true. Show Callie your head."

"Mama!"

"I don't want to see anyone's head," Callie said. "I want us all to go back to work."

The day passed quickly. The refrigerator was stocked with food and they'd gone over the routine for tomorrow a dozen times. Ethel balked at a few things.

"Why do you have to do green beans that way? Just put 'em on the plate."

"Ethel." Callie drew a quick breath. "I have fresh green beans and Wanda has already cut the ends off. I'll sauté onions and bacon first, then add the green beans and seasoning. When the beans have been fully coated, I'll add water, white wine, put a lid on and let simmer until they're almost done. Then I'll gather about eight beans in a bundle and wrap a slice of bacon around them. For an added touch, I'll tie the ends of the bacon into a bow and place in a baking dish. Melted butter with brown sugar goes over the top with a little garlic salt. When the bacon is crisp, they're done."

"You're joking?"

"No, Ethel. I'm not joking. Presentation means a lot to me."

"This is Homestead," Ethel reminded her.

"I'll do it, Callie," Wanda offered. "It sounds real nice."

"Oh, you're always sucking up," Ethel grumbled.

"Am not."

"Okay," Callie intervened. "Are we together on this or not?"

"Yeah," Ethel mumbled. "Guess it's never too late to teach an old dog a few new tricks."

Callie hugged her. "Thank you, Ethel."

Essie and Janet came in later and Callie went over their duties. Essie looked a lot like Ethel except she was thin and had shoulder-length brown hair. Like her mother, she was a talker, a good attribute in a hostess. And Essie knew everyone in Homestead.

Callie showed her the mints and Texas pecan kisses she'd made from Miranda's mom's recipe to give to customers as they left.

"Oh, how cute," Essie said. "Blue-and-white mints in a basket with a blue gingham bow. Mama said you did things fancy."

"Just be sure when people pay that you offer them a mint or a pecan kiss."

"Don't worry. I can do that, and I can wait tables, too, if you need someone."

"Thank you. I'm not sure how busy we're going to be. I'm just opening for lunch tomorrow. But Saturday, I'm opening for lunch and dinner so I might have to take you up on that."

Essie leaned in close. "As long as Mama's not bossing me around. Nothing makes me madder."

"Ethel will be busy in the kitchen."

"Yeah, right. Sometimes I think she has eyes in the back of her head."

Callie suppressed a laugh. Staying out of the Stromiski family disagreements seemed wise.

CALLIE COULDN'T WAIT for the kids to come home. She was so used to having them around, she missed them terribly. Buddy had a car to work on so he hadn't been around much today either.

Everything was set for tomorrow, so everyone went home. Callie couldn't help but notice the way Wanda and Odell were looking at each other. A romance was blossoming for sure. But again, Odell and Bubba Joe went to the Lone Wolf without asking Wanda. Callie had heard from Ms. Millie that the Lone Wolf wasn't the place for a lady. It was probably better if Odell took Wanda some other place.

She had to stop matchmaking.

She sat in a rocker, waiting for the kids. It was already dark and Wade had called and said that they were on the way. When she saw the headlights stop at the curb, her heart accelerated. They were home safe. And Wade was with them.

Her world was perfect and uncomplicated—for the moment.

THE KIDS CAME RUNNING up the walk, all three plopping into her lap at the same time, even Adam.

"I missed you," Mary Beth murmured against her.

"I missed you guys, too." She kissed warm cheeks that smelled faintly of something Callie couldn't identify.

She wrinkled her nose. "What's that smell?"

"It's coastal hay. Right, Wade?" Brit looked up at Wade, who was leaning against a pillar, watching the scene.

"Yep. It's coastal." His eyes clung to Callie's and she knew she loved him more than she would ever love again. Why did love have to be so difficult?

"We baled hay today," Adam enlightened her, sinking to the porch floor.

"And it was neat." Brit joined her brother on the floor, her eyes bouncing with excitement. "Tex cut the hay a few days ago 'cause it has to dry first. Right, Wade?"

"Right."

"Then today, Tex raked the hay into long rows with a tractor and a funny-looking thing. And Pop, he drove a bigger tractor with a big old machine behind it and the machine gobbled up the rows like this." Brit made a sucking in motion with her mouth. "And a big round bale of hay popped out. Then the machine would eat more and another bale would pop out. It was so neat. We had a whole field of round bales of hay."

"I got to help," Adam said. "I rode on the tractor with Pop and he showed me how to do everything. Tomorrow we have to get the bales off the field so the coastal can grow again. It takes a lot of hay to feed cows all winter."

Another one of Jock's sayings, Callie was sure.

"Mary Beth and I rode in the truck with Yo, but Pop let me ride the tractor, too."

"Me, too," Mary Beth said, "except I rode with Wade." She walked over to him and he picked her up and held her.

Callie thought again how good he was with them. It was all so natural to him.

"Time for baths then we'll decide what to have for supper." Adam got to his feet. "Is everything ready for tomorrow?"

"Yes." Callie stood. "I just hope someone shows up."

"They will," Wade said as he followed them into the house. "Even if I have to arrest a few people and bring them over here."

They all laughed and Callie wished she could let go of the

ALL ROADS LEAD TO TEXAS

fear in her. This feeling was different than before—now she was afraid of hurting Wade. That was the last thing she wanted.

LATER, AFTER THE KIDS WERE in bed, she sat in Wade's lap on the porch. Her head lay on his shoulder and he idly caressed her arm.

"I talked to your lawyer today."

She tensed, feeling guilty. She hadn't told him about the hearing and she didn't understand why. Then she knew—she wanted more time with him. "I told her to call you."

"I put her in touch with Simon. Between the two of them, I think they can build a strong case in your favor." His hand stilled on her arm. "She said she has a hearing in three weeks to present your case to a judge. Why didn't you tell me?"

She sat up, knowing it was time for the truth. "Because I was selfish. I wanted to keep on pretending that I have all the time in the world here. But we'll probably be leaving soon, that is, if Gail can persuade the judge to listen to my side and see that Nigel is a threat to the children's well-being. If not…" She shrugged. "I'm not sure what's going to happen." She drew a deep breath, needing the strength to say what she had to, not what she wanted to. "I think it's best if we don't get any more emotionally involved. It's going to be hard enough when the times comes." She slid from his lap, suddenly feeling alone again.

"I'm a big boy and I can take care of myself." He stood beside her. "I don't regret what happened between us, but you're probably right. We need to cool things."

"Yes," she mumbled.

He touched her lips with his forefinger. "Smile. Tomorrow's a big day for you."

His touch ignited that flame of desire inside her, which she quickly disguised. "I don't know what I'm doing opening a café when I may not be here long."

"Because you need to keep busy and it's good for Homestead."

"Yes. I owe this town a lot, especially the people who have been so good to me."

"Then make this café a success, and in the meantime I hope Simon can uncover something that will help your lawyer." He kissed her forehead. "Pop'll pick the kids up early and we'll keep them the rest of the day."

"No, that's not necessary."

"Night." He strolled down the steps.

"Wade."

"It's a done deal," he called over his shoulder.

Callie wrapped her arms around her waist, bracing herself for a new relationship with Wade—one of a friend, an acquaintance.

That's the way it had to stay.

THE NEXT MORNING, Callie had rolls rising and peach cobblers made before the kids woke up. She heard a truck honk then the clatter of feet running down the stairs. All three kids charged into the kitchen, dressed and ready to go.

"We gotta go, Callie," Adam said. "Pop's waiting."

"Why isn't he coming in?" Callie asked. "You haven't had breakfast."

"Yo's fixing breakfast so you can open the café," Adam told her. "Bye." He gave her a hug and a kiss and the girls followed.

"Don't you want to stay home with me, Mary Beth?" She didn't want her to go unless she really wanted to.

Mary Beth shook her head. "Nu-uh. I gotta go. I'm naming all the cows and babies and I have to feed Kitty."

Nu-uh.

Callie groaned. Now they were all talking Texan.

The kids were happy, though, and that's what she wanted.

The tearful, frightened kids of a few weeks ago were gone and Mary Beth hadn't wet the bed since they'd been here. She didn't go to bed worrying about it anymore either. They were blossoming in the warm sunshine of Homestead.

Then why did Callie feel so cold?

Wanda came in munching on an apple and they began the other preparations for the meal. She left Wanda making green salads and hurried upstairs to make up the beds. Inside the rooms, she received a shock. The beds were made and the children's clothes were picked up. Everything was in its place. Her eyes grew misty. They were helping in their own way.

She hurried down the stairs and stopped as she saw Ethel outside, enjoying a last drag on a cigarette before coming into the house.

"Mornin', Callie," Ethel said as she walked inside.

"Morning," Callie responded.

"Are you just gettin' up?"

"No. Been up since five."

"I guess show-off is here already?"

"If you mean Wanda, then yes, she's here. She's a very good worker, just like you."

"Guess I better get to it then."

Callie put an arm around Ethel. "Tell you what. I'll make a deal with you."

Ethel frowned at her. "What kind of deal?"

"If you stop smoking…"

"Saw me, huh?"

"Yes."

"But I'm not smoking in the house."

"I know and I appreciate that, but getting back to the deal. This is it. If you stop smoking, I'll find Odell a girlfriend."

Ethel stopped in her tracks and stared at her. "What? I'm

Odell's mama and I love him dearly, but there ain't no girl in Homestead going out with him." Her eyes narrowed. "Unless you plan on going out with him yourself and I've seen the way you and the sheriff look at each other and I don't think that's happenin'."

Callie sighed. There were no secrets in this town. "No. I'm not talking about me and I'm not talking about one date either."

"I don't know what the hell you're talking about. I think you've had your head in the oven too often and the fumes are gettin' to you."

"Oh, Ethel. I love your sense of humor." She lifted an eyebrow. "Deal?"

Ethel hesitated.

"I know you can stop." Callie pressed her point. "You don't smoke all the time."

"No. Just when I get stressed out. Essie's driving me crazy. Kids shouldn't move back home with their mamas. It just doesn't work. She's in the bathroom for hours. I couldn't even get in there this mornin'. And all that perfume and hair spray—enough to choke a horse."

"Deal or not?" Callie asked, trying not to smile.

"You find Odell a girlfriend and I'll never touch another cigarette again."

Callie held out her hand and they shook on it.

"When can I expect results?"

Callie hid a secret smile. "Oh, it won't take much time."

"I still think you've had your head in the oven too long."

They walked into the kitchen and Odell was taking a large tray of salads from Wanda to carry to the refrigerator. Ethel couldn't see what was going on under her nose. By the glances Wanda and Odell were sharing, Callie knew it wouldn't be long at all. And Ethel would stop smoking in the process. That might have been sneaky, but when sneaky worked, you took it.

How she wished her problems could be solved so easily.

CHAPTER SEVENTEEN

THE CAFÉ OPENED without a problem. Callie had intended to call it La Maison Bleue, the Blue House, but Odell, Ethel and Wanda had gone together and bought a mat for the entry door as a gift. On it was Callie's Café and that's what it was officially christened. It was perfect. That's what everyone called it anyway.

Ms. Millie had run an article about the café opening and the day's menu, so Callie was hoping a few people would show up.

Kristin, Ryan and Cody were the first to arrive. Callie came out of the kitchen to greet them.

"Thank you for coming."

"Oh, please," Kristin laughed, taking a seat. "This is going to be so great having a nice place to eat lunch, and I get to spend more time with my husband." She touched Ryan's cheek.

Ryan smiled. "I want you to know, Callie, that I drove all the way in to have lunch with my wife."

"Are Brit and Adam here?" Cody asked, looking around.

"No, I'm sorry. They're at the Montgomery—" Her voice stopped as she saw who was coming up the walk. Jock, Wade and the kids strolled in and Callie looked at them, puzzled. What were they doing back?

"Excuse me," she said to Kristin and Ryan, and met the group in the foyer. "What are you doing here?"

Wade carried a large bouquet of mixed flowers. "Happy grand opening," he said, placing the flowers on an entry table.

"Oh, my."

"We brought you flowers," Mary Beth exclaimed.

"And we're here for lunch," Jock said. "My treat."

"Yeah. We're customers." Brit held on to Jock's hand.

"You didn't have to do this." She was so touched she wanted to cry.

"Gal, are you going to stand here quibbling all day or are you going to get us some food? I'm hungry as a coyote on the prowl."

"Me, too," Adam said.

"Cody." Brit ran to her friend.

Callie gathered herself. "Okay. Essie will show you to a table. I need to return to the kitchen."

"Callie, can Cody and me go outside and play?"

Callie kissed the top of Brit's head on the way to the kitchen. "Not today, sweetie. It's time for lunch."

"We can't stay long," Kristin said. "I'm busy at the clinic. Maybe another day."

"Okay. Bye, Cody." Brit ran to join her siblings at a table.

Wade followed Callie into the kitchen. "Whoa." He grinned at all the activity going on. "It's busy in here."

"Yes." She paused from arranging a plate. "Thank you for bringing them. The flowers are beautiful."

"Thought we'd lend our support and when Pop saw in the paper that chicken-fried steak was on the menu, well, that cinched it."

Ethel had gone around Wade twice to get a spoon, then a bowl. Suddenly, she stopped. "Now, Sheriff, you're a big man and you're starting to get in my way. Either do something or move that gorgeous body elsewhere."

"Yes, ma'am." He winked at Callie. "Talk to you later."

A steady stream of people kept coming and Callie was so busy she didn't even realize when the kids had left. She vaguely remembered them saying bye. She, Ethel and Wanda worked well together. Ethel fried the steaks that Callie had prepared, added gravy and handed it to Callie, who put a scoop of garlic mashed potatoes, green-bean bundles and sautéed vegetables on the plate. She garnished it with a sprig of green onion and a radish cut into a flower. Wanda took care of the salads, tea and desserts.

They'd scooped the peach cobbler into bowls earlier, and Wanda heated them slightly before topping them with ice cream and handing them to Janet. Out of the corner of her eyes, Callie saw Odell helping scoop the ice cream. No one spoke. They were all too busy.

When Callie went out to chat with some of the people, Wanda took over her spot. Ms. Millie and her husband, Hiram, came, as did Noah, Miranda and her mom, Virgil, Barbara Jean, Walter, Del and Little Del, Frances Haase, Arlen Enfield, Ed Tanner and his wife, Myron Guthrie, Gil Schafer the D.A., and several people from the courthouse she didn't know. She shook hands and smiled and received a lot of compliments.

Afterward she was exhausted, but it was a good exhaustion. She, Ethel, Wanda, Janet, Essie and Buddy sat at the kitchen table going over ways to improve their work. Buddy had helped with the dishes to keep the kitchen from getting so cluttered. He didn't have to. Callie had large containers for the dirty dishes, but she appreciated his help.

"We need another waitress," Janet said. "I ran my butt off today."

"I can help with the waitressing," Essie volunteered. "But then there's no one to take money."

"I can do that," Buddy said. At Callie's frown, he added, "I'll put on my good jeans and my white shirt. I'll even take off my baseball cap. Heck, I'll even wear a tie if you want me to."

"But what about your station?" Callie asked, not wanting him to do it if it was going to hurt his business. She could see that he wanted to, though.

"I close it up all the time when I have to go somewhere. I make my money fixing cars and the big Exxon up the street gets all the gas business. That's fine with me. I can come and go as I please."

"Okay, then. Buddy will take the money, but a tie won't be necessary."

"Thank God."

Odell came through the back door. "We got a problem."

"What?" Callie turned to Odell.

"The cars were parked all over the street and Mrs. Miller couldn't get her car out. We have to do something about the parking."

"Let's look out back and see what we can come up with." Buddy and Odell headed outside and the women went to work on the dishes.

The kitchen clean once again, the women went home, but Wanda lingered. "I'll be here early tomorrow to help you."

"Thank you, Wanda. You did a great job today."

"I didn't get nervous or anything."

"No…" Callie stopped as Buddy and Odell returned.

"This house sits on about an acre and a half so there's plenty of room to make a parking lot. Don't have to do much of anything, but put up some signs and Odell will direct traffic a few times and everyone will figure out where to park. Now I'm going home to make sure my white shirt is ironed and finish a car I need to get out." He kissed Callie's cheek. "See you tomorrow."

"Bye, Buddy."

"Callie."

She turned to Odell.

"There's the old servant's quarters out back and it's in real bad shape. Could I fix it up in my spare time? Then I could rent it from you. I'd have my own place away from Mama."

Callie paused as so many emotions ran through her. She was a phony, a fake. She'd lied to all these wonderful people who'd welcomed her to their town and into their hearts. She wasn't really who they thought she was and she would be leaving. She shouldn't allow Odell to do anything to the place. But how could she tell him no? It would be good for the town to have Odell restore the quarters. It was falling apart like the house, so it couldn't be wrong to give Odell some freedom. Ethel would have a different viewpoint, but...

"Sure, Odell. Go ahead."

"Thank you." He glanced at Wanda. "Wanna see it?"

"Yes." Wanda's eyes lit up.

As they went outside, Callie wondered where Bubba Joe was. He and Odell were usually inseparable, but Odell now had another interest. And it was wonderful to watch.

Callie sighed, then grabbed her purse and headed over to Tanner's to pick up the prime ribs she'd ordered for tomorrow. She wanted to season them and put them on before she went to bed that night. Putting the beef in the refrigerator, she felt a stab of loneliness and knew where she had to go. It didn't take her long to reach Spring Creek Ranch.

As she parked by Wade's squad car, she saw Yolanda's truck pull up to the barn. She walked toward it. Yo climbed out and Chester and Peanut followed.

"Hi, Yo," she called.

"Hey, *niña*. How did the opening go?"

"Great. Where are the kids?"

"Oh. They comin'." She waved toward the pasture. "Little bit usually rides with me, but when Mr. Wade's around she's stuck to him like glue. Sure is good to see." Yo leaned against the truck. "Even the old *bastardo*'s different. After Zach died, things were pretty bad around here. Never thought it'd change. Mr. Jock's done stop drinking and Mr. Wade he's smiling again. *Niños* sure been good medicine. Life come back to Spring Creek."

A stab of guilt almost paralyzed Callie. When her true identity was revealed, so many people were going to be hurt. She had to put a stop to it now before she hurt anyone else. But how did she do that? How could she break that old man's heart?

And Wade's?

She heard the thunder of hooves, and looked up to see Adam on Lucky and Brit on Fancy racing for the barn. Adam stood in the stirrups, leaning forward with his hat pulled low. Brit's hat bobbed on her back, as she and Fancy sprinted after him. Dust spiraled behind them like a cloud and Callie was amazed at how well they could ride.

Adam pulled up a moment before he reached Yo's truck and jumped off, patting Lucky. "Good girl, we beat Brit again."

Brit was a second behind him, but undeterred by her defeat. "I'll beat you someday."

"Hi, Callie," Adam shouted, leading Lucky into the barn. "I have to take care of my horse."

"Callie," Brit called as she rode in behind Adam and dismounted.

She saw two more riders coming at a slower pace, Jock and Wade. Mary Beth rested in front of Wade, and Callie just watched for a moment, soaking up this peace, this joy that she was about to shatter.

Chester snorted.

"Gotta get Chester home and feed him," Yo said, climbing back into the truck with Chester and Peanut on the front seat.

Callie waved bye and walked into the barn. Adam and Brit already had the saddles off and Callie wasn't sure how they'd done that so quickly. They were brushing the horses down and talking soothingly to them, then they led them into the corral.

"C'mon," Adam said Brit. "We have to get the feed."

They ran to the storage shed and, between the two of them, they carried a sack of feed and dumped it into a trough. The horses neighed and moved around them and Callie's heart leaped into her throat, but Adam and Brit were unafraid, stroking the horses as they ate.

Wade and Jock rode in.

"Callie, Callie, look at me," Mary Beth called.

"I see." Callie held up her arms and lifted Mary Beth from the saddle.

"We been checking cattle and we saw Sadie and Babe," Mary Beth said. "Now I have to help Wade take care of the horse. If you ride, you have to take care of your animal 'cause he's got feelings, too."

Mary Beth slipped from her arms and Callie stood back as the horses were unsaddled, rubbed down and fed.

Wade came back into the barn. "Things looked like they went well today."

"Yes. Thanks for bringing the kids and the flowers."

"My pleasure." Her eyes clung to his and all she could see and feel was warmth—a cozy, candlelit, just the two of them, skin-on-skin kind of warmth. She wished she could freeze this moment in time and not think about the future, just enjoy the present. But she couldn't. She had responsibilities.

She looked away. "I came to pick up the kids."

"You didn't have to do that. I was fixing to bring them home."

Jock and the kids strolled in.

"Get your things. Let's go," she said more sharply than she'd intended.

"But it's early," Jock complained. "They can stay a while longer."

"No, they can't. I've imposed on you long enough."

"It's not an imposition, gal."

Jock wasn't making this easy. "Thank you, Jock, but it's time I started taking care of my kids again. They won't be able to come out here so much because I want them at home."

"What!" erupted from the kids simultaneously.

Wade and Jock exchanged a glance and Callie quickly herded the kids toward her car. They kept grumbling, but Callie was steadfast. She had to do this for everyone's own good.

WADE AND JOCK WATCHED her drive away.

"What's going on, son?"

"I don't know."

"Did somethin' happen today?"

"Not that I'm aware of."

"Callie's acting strange."

"Yeah." Wade nodded. "And I'm going to find out why."

THE KIDS WOULDN'T EAT supper. They just pushed their food around until Callie told them to go take baths. With the girls tucked in, she went to talk to Adam.

With a mutinous expression, he sat cross-legged on his bed. She took a breath. "Please try to understand that we're getting too involved with the Montgomerys. We'll be leaving as soon as I hear from my lawyer and—"

"Please don't hurt him, Callie. He doesn't deserve it."

Callie knew he was talking about Jock and she should have stopped all this before it ever had started. Now she was the bad guy, hurting everyone. She kissed his forehead because she couldn't promise anything.

Feeling spent, she went downstairs to the front porch. Wade marched up the walk and she slowly sank into the rocker, bracing herself.

He leaned against a pillar. "What's going on, Callie?"

"Nothing. I've just decided that I can't involve you and your father any further in our lives."

"Don't you think it's a little late for that?"

"Maybe, but it's my decision."

His eyes darkened. "So all of a sudden you're going to keep them away from Pop and me."

She stuck out her chin, determined to be strong. "They need to be with me. I have to do what's best for them."

"Callie…"

"No." She fought against the softness in his voice. "You're not the one who abducted them and took them across the country. You're not the one who the FBI is looking for. And you're not the one who has to face the consequences."

"That's where you're wrong. I'm the one who aided and abetted you. I could have turned you in to the FBI and ended it then."

"I know and I appreciate —"

"Do you?"

"Please, I'm trying to keep all of us from getting hurt."

"You're too late." He turned and hurried to his car.

Callie drew up her knees and rested her forehead on them. The tears came and she didn't try to stop them. She cried for everything she was losing and the tears echoed an ache in her heart that was never going to go away.

I'm sorry, Wade.

THE NEXT MORNING, THE KIDS were still sulking. She gave them chores to do, which at least kept them busy. The girls helped Wanda with the laundry and Adam was with Buddy and Odell figuring out the parking. He came back in for paper and Magic Markers to make signs. This was difficult, but it would be better in the long run.

At least that's what she kept telling herself.

By the time Ethel arrived, the rolls were rising and two large banana puddings were in the refrigerator. The prime rib had been cooking all night on a very low temperature. They went to work on the rest of the menu: roasted red potatoes with rosemary, corn casserole and a sautéed vegetable medley of squash, eggplant, green peppers, tomatoes, onion and garlic.

She gave the kids jobs while the rush hour was on so they wouldn't be pouting. The girls handed out the mints and pecan kisses while Adam helped Buddy at the cash register.

The lunch crowd was larger than Callie had expected, but she was pleased. She met more of the Gallagher clan—Trevor and his wife, Donna, and their two kids, Hayden and Sara, were with Kristin and Ryan and Cody. Ethan and Kayla and their kids came, along with Kayla's father, Boyd.

The kids were busy chatting and getting acquainted, so Callie asked Odell to carry two small tables that were in the utility room to the front veranda. She made hamburgers, fries and fruit wedges for all the kids and they ate outside, talking about horses.

She saw a lot of new faces and some familiar ones. Noah arrived with his mother, Ruth. Callie had met Ruth, as she was on the Home Free Committee. A dour, prim-and-proper type lady, she didn't smile much.

Callie greeted them at their table.

"This is so nice, Callie," Ruth said, arranging her napkin in her lap. "And good for Homestead. We've needed a place like this for a long time."

"Thank you, Mrs. Kelley."

"And thank you for hiring Wanda," Noah said. "I've been trying to get her out of that house since her father's death, but she was scared to even apply for a job. I told her you were a real nice lady and for her to come over here and ask. I was surprised when she actually did it."

"Don't thank me. I should be thanking you. Wanda is a jewel."

Janet came to take their order and Callie made to move on.

"Oh, Callie." Noah stopped her. "Wanda never finished high school and I'm trying to talk her into the GED program. If you could help me influence her…"

"I'll be glad to." Callie saw Ethel waving to her from the kitchen. "I'll talk to you later."

Callie hurried into the kitchen.

"We've run out of fried onion rings and carrots to garnish the plates and I know how you like to garnish everything," Ethel said.

"I have some sliced in the refrigerator. Won't take but a minute to flour and fry them."

She didn't have time to take a breath until about two when the crowd thinned out. Going into the dining room, she saw Ethan and Kayla sitting close together at a table, watching the kids outside on the veranda.

Adam, Brit, Brad, Megan and Heather were chatting and laughing away. Callie took a seat. "They seem to be having fun."

"Yeah," Ethan said. "That's why we're still here."

"Dad left a while ago, but when Ethan mentions leaving to the kids, we get that look. You know that how-can-you-be-so-cruel look, and of course, Ethan's been served a second helping of banana pudding so we may never leave."

They shared a laugh and Ethan got to his feet. "This time we have to go."

"It was lovely." Kayla reached for her purse. "We'll be back often."

"Thank you." Callie waved as they walked away.

Mary Beth met them, offering the goodies, then came and crawled into Callie's lap. The other kids were older and she was feeling left out again.

"Can Rascal come into the house now?"

"Yes." She kissed her forehead. "Go get Rascal."

In a flurry, she was gone. Callie toyed with the napkin on the table. Wade hadn't come and she wasn't surprised. It didn't keep her from being disappointed, though. To keep those thoughts at bay, she headed for the kitchen.

The evening meal was as busy as lunch and Callie was exhausted by the time the kitchen was clean and she closed the door on the last person. The kids were back in their pouting mode and she was feeling the pressure of hurting everyone.

The next morning, they went to church and the kids were excited they were going to see the other kids again. Wanda was in church and Callie sat by her. She looked for Wade but she didn't see him. Was she always going to be looking for him?

After church, they visited with all the new friends they'd made, then went home to a very quiet house. The pouting mode had shifted into high gear. So Callie decided to do something they really enjoyed; making individual small pizzas and letting them choose their own toppings. Chocolate s'mores were next. Usually this was a fun time with lots of giggling, but today there was stony silence. She fought tears and every adult emotion in her. By the afternoon, she couldn't fight it any longer.

"Okay," she said to three very sad faces. "I'll call Jock and see if you can come riding."

Three faces beamed back at her. So easy. Then why was it so hard?

She poked out Jock's number and he answered on the third ring.

"Yeah," he bellowed.

"Jock, this is Callie."

"Yeah, so what?"

The grouchy, irrepressible man she'd first met was back. "The kids would like to come riding and I'm calling to see if it's okay."

There was a slight pause. "You don't have to call to ask that. They're always welcome here."

"Thank you. I'll bring them shortly."

She turned to tell the kids, but they'd disappeared. Upstairs, she heard thumps and noises and soon all three were back in jeans and boots. And they were smiling.

Grabbing her purse, she thought that in the cool light of day, hard decisions made in haste and guilt could come back to haunt her. Or was it their cool faces?

Or was it Wade?

Once in college, a professor had told her that happiness was an elusive thing. But if one was lucky enough to find it, to hold on tight and enjoy the rare sensation that few people experienced. With everything going on in her mind, she'd somehow forgotten that.

Maybe it was time to hold on tight and enjoy the ride.

CHAPTER EIGHTEEN

IN THE DAYS THAT FOLLOWED, Callie didn't regret her decision. The kids were happier, Jock was happier, and she and Wade had reached a new understanding.

That Sunday afternoon, they sat on a bale of hay watching Mary Beth play with Kitty. Jock had taken Brit and Adam riding to check on some heifers.

"I'm sorry," she whispered.

"I know." He reached out and took her hand. "You had reasons for doing what you did and we agreed to just be friends. I never said it would be easy though."

She looked into his warm eyes. "But can we *just* be friends?"

He rubbed his thumb over her palm. "Probably not." His eyes hovered on her trembling lips. "I want to kiss you like hell."

She licked her lips. "Please don't. I don't have the strength to resist."

"And we have to be adult, responsible."

"Yes."

His expression grew somber. "I'm really beginning to hate that phrase. I liked it better when we threw caution to the wind and went with our basic instincts—in a jail cell."

"Hmm. It's nice to be in—" The word froze on her tongue as she realized what she was about to say. Her eyes flew to his and she could see he was thinking the same thing, but neither of them would say it. They couldn't. Parting would be that much harder.

Callie's professor had never said how to hold on to a love that wasn't meant to be. Maybe it wasn't possible. Maybe…

"Please let the kids continue to see Pop while they're here."

"I was trying to protect everyone."

He squeezed her hand. "I know."

And she knew he did. He probably understood her better than anyone ever had. That's why loving him was so easy.

"I talked with Simon this morning," he said. "And the daughter, Candace Avery, finally agreed to speak to him. She hesitated because she wanted to be sure he wasn't working for Nigel."

"Did he find out anything?"

"Yes. Tremont divorced her mom."

Callie sagged with disappointment.

"Seems Tremont got her mother to sign a power of attorney a week before the accident. With her mother in a coma, Tremont told Candace he was now in control of the estate and showed her the power of attorney. Candace was shocked, but immediately went to the banks where she was a cosigner with her mother and withdrew all the money, leaving a small checking account. The bank people knew her and didn't question anything. Tremont was furious when he found out and tried to have her arrested. The police did a lot of investigating, but Candace was never arrested."

"It's basically like my situation," Callie murmured.

"Yes. But Tremont learned his lesson and made sure everything was in his name before you found out."

"Yeah." She sucked in a breath. "I still can't believe my mother was taken in like that."

Wade shifted uneasily and she knew there was more. "What?"

"Candace told Simon that her mother came out of the coma and was coherent for awhile. By this time, Tremont had filed for divorce. Mrs. Wagonner told Candace that Tremont threatened Candace and her children's lives if Mrs. Wagonner didn't do as he wanted. That's the only reason she signed the power of attorney. Evidently he'd hit her a couple of times and she was afraid of him."

"Oh my God!" Callie turned to Wade. "Nigel probably threatened to harm the kids if Mom didn't agree to a new will giving him control. She was crying when she called me, saying she'd made a terrible mistake and had to explain. That has to be it. That would explain so much. My mother had an impulsive nature but her kids always came first. I just couldn't understand, but now…" She gripped her hands together. "What kind of accident did Mrs. Wagonner have?"

"Car wreck. She was forty-seven."

"At night?"

"Yes."

"This is all too similar."

"That's why I have Simon doing more checking. But he got a piece of information from Candace he wants to check out first."

"What?"

"There's another wife in Seattle. Candace found a letter in her mother's house from April Gantor to Nigel Gantor asking for money, so Candace called her to see what it was about. The lady wasn't too friendly and wouldn't talk to her, but she did say she'd been married to Nigel Gantor and didn't know who Nigel Tremont was."

Callie frowned. "Another wife? Another name?"

"That's what Simon is going to find out and to see why she needs money. Candace saved the letter and gave a copy to Simon."

"So we wait."

"You stay busy running your café. I'll tie up all these loose ends and get them to your lawyer, and please let the kids continue to enjoy themselves while they're here."

She touched his cheek. "You're a special man and I've been so rude to you."

"I know those protective instincts. I was once a parent."

A shadow crossed his face and he turned his cheek into the comfort of her hand.

They sat that way for a moment until Mary Beth demanded their attention.

CALLIE ADJUSTED HER SCHEDULE a bit, but Jock didn't seem to mind. He came to the café for lunch and the kids would go back with him to the ranch. He'd bring them home for supper and he and Wade ate with them after the café closed at eight. This way the kids were with her in the mornings and helped out around the house. No one complained.

Callie threw herself into the café, changing menus to suit her customers. Monday was her mesquite-smoked-ham day. Tanner's had exceptional hams and Callie had to try them. With black-eyed peas, corn bread and sweet-potato casserole, the special was a favorite. Bread pudding was also becoming very popular along with her cobblers.

Tuesdays there was always a line for chicken and dumplings. On Wednesdays she prepared stuffed chicken breast, and Thursdays featured pork tenderloin. There were so many fresh vegetables in Homestead that she had a variety of choices. People were beginning to expect certain dishes on each day of the week so she stopped changing the menu and concentrated on making the food as good and as attractive as she could.

The days slipped into August and Wade still had no con-

crete evidence on Nigel. April Gantor refused to talk to
Simon, but he still worked diligently on the case. Gail was
growing restless as the hearing loomed closer and closer and
they still had nothing but a string of marriages to older
women, except April. She was the same age as Nigel. Simon
and Gail were still trying to piece together the details of that
relationship.

In spite of how busy she was with the café, Callie
couldn't keep her mind off Nigel. Mostly, she thought about
her mother and the torment she'd been going through before
her death. How Callie wished she'd dropped everything and
gone to her that night, but Glynis had insisted on meeting
somewhere other than the brownstone. The restaurant had
seemed logical. What-ifs pounded inside her head.

AUGUST WAS HOT. That Saturday, Odell and Wanda made
homemade peach ice cream and served it to anyone who
wanted some. Wade, Jock and the kids were enjoying theirs
on the veranda as Callie finished up in the kitchen with Ethel,
Wanda and Essie.

Yo now came in to work in the kitchen since she said she
had nothing to do on the ranch. Callie was glad for her help
and amazed how she kept the dishes washed with terrific
speed. Yo had left long ago to take supper to Tex and Poncho.

Coming out of the utility room where she'd put table linens in to wash, Callie saw Odell and Wanda whispering by
the back door. Callie smiled. Odell was spending a lot of
time restoring the servant's quarters, and he spent an equal
amount of time showing them to Wanda.

"Go ahead, you two," she said. "We're through here."

Wanda turned to her with a big smile. "Odell's going to
church with me in the morning."

The pot Ethel was drying clattered to the floor. Essie's jaw dropped to her chin. Were they blind, or what? Surely they'd seen this coming.

Callie hugged Wanda. "That's very nice. I'm sure Father Noah will be happy to see Odell."

"You're going to church with Wanda?" Ethel's voice was high and squeaky.

Odell held his head high. "Yes, I am, Mama."

Ethel picked up the pot and slammed it onto the counter. "How many times have I asked you to go to church?"

"I'm not going to church with my mama."

"And you'd rather go with her?" Ethel flung a hand toward Wanda.

Wanda trembled and Odell's face turned red in anger, so Callie stepped in before Ethel completely alienated her son.

"Wanda, would you get the bowls from the kids on the porch, please?" The kids could bring in their own bowls, but she needed to get Wanda out of the way.

"I think I'll help," Essie said and quickly followed Wanda. Odell stormed out the door.

Callie put her hands on her hips. "Ethel, what are you doing?"

Ethel blinked, as if she were in a daze. "What?"

"When I first came here, you told me your greatest wish was for Odell to find a girlfriend. Now he has. Why aren't you happy?"

"It's Wanda." Ethel said under her breath.

Callie was taken aback. "So?"

"It's Wanda," Ethel said again.

"I'm getting the impression that you don't think Wanda is good enough for Odell."

"You said you'd find him a girlfriend," Ethel reminded her.

"Who did you think I was talking about? A movie star? A model? Or the next Miss America? Because if you did, I think you need to look around. There aren't any of those women in Homestead. I could see what was happening between Wanda and Odell. Why couldn't you?"

Ethel's lips disappeared into a thin line.

"Oh, wait a minute." Callie walked to Ethel. "You don't really want him to have a girlfriend, do you? You want Odell to come home to his mama."

"He's my baby," Ethel muttered.

Callie put an arm around her. "Ethel. Ethel. Let Odell be happy. He deserves it and Wanda does, too."

"She has red hair."

Callie laughed. "She's kind, sweet and a very caring person. She's all alone and needs a family."

"I suppose."

"And Odell's happy. Doesn't that make you happy?"

"I'd be happier if he was back home with his mama."

"Ethel! You told me yourself that kids shouldn't move back with their parents."

"I wasn't talking about Odell. He's my baby."

"Ethel…"

"I'm a clinging mama and I know it. I just thought Odell would be with me forever."

"And he will be. He lives in Homestead and you'll see him every day. Make the most of this opportunity. Accept Wanda. If you don't, you'll push Odell away."

"You go through excruciating pain to have kids, then they step on your toes and mangle your heart. After that, they're ready to throw you in the grave."

"Well, Ethel." Callie patted her shoulder, trying hard not to laugh. "If I were you, I'd make sure they were crying when that happens. If you keep this attitude, they'll be smiling."

"Kids," Ethel snorted in disgust, marching to the back door and yanking it open. "Odell," she shouted. She glanced at Callie. "Tell Wanda to meet us in the backyard."

"Now Ethel…"

"I'm letting go, Callie, and I'm going to do it nicely." She frowned. "Can you imagine a passel of redheaded grand-babies?"

Callie sighed. "They're going to church. That's all. But I, for one, think they're perfect for each other."

"You would, and if I think about this long enough I'm sure it's all your fault."

Callie grinned. "Be careful what you wish for, Ethel, because sometimes it comes true."

"Yeah, yeah, yeah."

Callie went to the veranda to give Wanda the message and debated whether she should go with her. But she'd let Odell handle his mama. She had a feeling he wasn't letting Ethel browbeat Wanda.

Jock had gone home and Callie sent the kids to take baths. Wade pushed to his feet. "I better get to the beer joints and make a round just to let all the cowboys in town for a good time know that I'm on duty and watching them."

"Have you heard anything else from Simon?"

"He's still trying to get April to talk to him, but she's re-sisting. Simon feels she knows something and is too afraid to tell him what it is."

"I'm running out of time."

Wade looked up to the big moon hanging in the sky. "I spoke with Candace and she's agreed to testify on your be-half if you need her."

"Oh, Wade." Unable to resist, she hugged him. "Thank you."

Wade breathed in the scent of her hair, her skin, and his mouth trailed from the side of her face to her lips. Gently, achingly, he tasted her sweetness. With a tiny moan, she opened her mouth and he was lost in the wonderful sensa-tion that was Callie.

The kiss deepened, then lingered. He slowly stepped back. "Night," rasped out low and husky. He wasn't going to apologize for something he wanted so badly. He strolled away before primitive needs overtook his good sense. But for the life of him he couldn't equate good sense with not loving Callie.

He drove over to the Saddle Up beer joint thinking that life sometimes was just too cruel.

CALLIE WENT TO BED with Wade's kiss fresh on her lips. As the mindlessness of sleep claimed her, she wondered why she was depriving herself of something she needed. The answer eluded her.

The next morning, Wade wasn't in church. She'd talked to him earlier and he'd said there'd been a stabbing at the Saddle Up and he was going to be busy most of the day. But he made it out to the ranch by late afternoon. He looked tired, and all Callie wanted to do was hold him. *Once you find happiness, you better hold on tight.* Tonight she was going to do just that—hold on to the best man she'd ever known.

She was almost delirious with excitement at her decision and couldn't wait to get the kids home and in bed. But it was still daylight and she stopped at Buddy's for gas. She hadn't seen him today and she missed him.

Polishing an old red Corvette convertible, Buddy waved and the kids bailed out to see what he was doing. Rascal barked in a frenzy when he saw Mary Beth.

Brit and Adam climbed into the Corvette while Buddy filled up her car. "Missed you in church this morning," Callie said, leaning against her car.

"Had a bit of a situation and couldn't get away."

"Are you okay?" Callie was immediately worried.

"Sure."

Out of the corner of her eye, she noticed a movement and saw two Mexican boys hiding behind Buddy's house. "Buddy..."

"It's all right. They're just illegals waiting for a ride."

Callie waited for him to explain. "Rolando Diaz over in Buttermilk Flat sends for a lot of his family—the illegal way—and he tells the coyotes to drop them at my station. Rolando got tied up this morning and these boys are scared half out of their minds. He should be here any minute." He twisted the cap in place. "Just don't mention them to Wade. If he knows, he has to do his job."

"Okay." She spared the boys a glance. "Is this safe?"

Before Buddy could answer, a battered truck drove up close to Buddy's house and the boys jumped into the bed. The driver nodded to Buddy and they disappeared down the highway.

"Rolando and a few of his compatriots build fences at a reasonable rate. They're good people looking for a better way of life."

"Buddy," Brit called, interrupting the maudlin thoughts running through Callie's head. "Can we please go riding in the Corvette?"

Buddy glanced at Callie.

"Okay. I'll meet y'all at the house."

Buddy climbed into the driver's seat with Mary Beth and Rascal beside him. Adam and Brit were in the back seat.

Callie smiled at the picture. "What model is it?"

"Nineteen fifty-eight. Ain't she a beaut?"

"Definitely."

He started the motor and it hummed like a new car. "We'll take a leisurely spin through town."

Callie waved and watched them drive out of the station. She was going to miss her father, but she couldn't think about that now. She tried to keep her thoughts focused on tonight.

Tonight and Wade.

She hurried home and waved to Odell and Wanda as they drove out of her driveway. They'd been in church this morning with Ethel sitting right beside them. Poor Odell. He was going to have a hard time getting rid of his mama. But Odell and Wanda had spent the afternoon working on his apartment and Ethel was nowhere in sight.

Smiling, Callie walked through the back door. The big house was quiet, very quiet, and Callie sensed that something was different. Her cell buzzed and she dug it out of her purse. It was Wade. Her smile widened. She'd take the call in the parlor with her feet propped up.

Hurrying into the parlor, she stopped in her tracks. Her heart jackknifed into her throat and her cell slipped from her hand to the floor with a thud.

Nigel stood just inside her doorway with a leering smile on his evil face.

CHAPTER NINETEEN

"HI, THERE, CALLIE. I've been waiting for you."

The sound of his voice scraped across her skin like sharp fingernails. How did he find her? Where was the FBI? She took a step backward, gauging her distance to the door. She had to get to Buddy and the kids before Nigel did. That was her only thought.

"Where are the spoiled brats? Did you think you could hide them forever?"

He moved closer and she knew her means of escape were dwindling. His blond good looks and well-built body were striking, but something about him always made her skin crawl.

"Cat got your tongue, sweet Callie?"

"How did you find us?" she managed to ask.

"You should be careful who takes your picture." His lips twisted into a cynical smile. "The FBI were dragging their heels so I hired a P.I.—a good P.I. He discovered that good ol' Glynis was from Homestead, Texas. A little more checking and there was your picture right on the front page of the local newspaper."

The picture Millie had taken the day Callie had come home after the vandalism. She'd gotten careless and now it was costing her—and the children.

"You can have the money. Just leave us alone."

"Ah, sweet Callie. I'd love to do that, but your cautious father put in his will that whoever was guardian of the children had control of the money. Of course the guardian was Glynis and the stupid bitch said she couldn't get that changed."

"Don't call her that," Callie said between clenched teeth.

"Tut-tut. Watch your temper." He wagged a finger at her and she wanted to bite it off.

"You forced her to write that crazy will. I know you did."

"*Force* is such a harsh word, and if Glynis knew how to take orders, we wouldn't be in this mess."

"What are you talking about?"

"Do you think I want to be saddled with those kids? I wanted control of the money, not the kids. But she insisted the lawyer wouldn't budge. John had cemented his wishes in stone. I even threatened the poor bitch and she became hysterical that her precious babies would be harmed."

Suddenly it made sense. Her mother had been coerced, just like she and Wade had suspected. There was nothing she could have done about the money. John had already made all the arrangements. All she could have done was change the children's guardian—that's why Glynis had been so upset. She'd been worried about the children and she'd had a right to be. Evidently Glynis had realized how evil Nigel really was.

Nigel touched her cheek and everything in her shriveled up in revulsion. "Why do you have to be so difficult, sweet Callie? You and I could have a grand old good time."

Her stomach churned with nausea and she slapped his hand away.

He hit her across the face with his fist, knocking her sideways into the wall, her head slamming against a table. She heard someone screaming and realized it was her.

"Shut up, you bitch."

Her head felt as if it were dislocated from her shoulders

and she reached up to stop the floating sensation. Something wet oozed through her fingers. Blood. She was sinking, going somewhere she didn't want to go. *No.* She had to remain conscious. She had to get to the kids and warn them.

"Get up, bitch." Nigel kicked her with his shoe. "The FBI are on the way. They're talking to the sheriff."

Sheriff. Wade. The room swayed and she held on. Wade was coming. He'd keep the kids safe.

"What's going on here?" That was Wade's voice.

"Damn bitch attacked me," Nigel said.

Wade ran to Callie and knelt on the floor, a suffocating sensation tightening his throat. Her forehead was bleeding and her face was turning blue. He gently brushed blond hair caked with blood away from her forehead. "Callie, can you hear me?"

"The…ki…"

"Ssh. Don't try to talk." That's why she hadn't answered her cell. That bastard was here. Wade had wanted to warn her to take the kids and get out of the house as quickly as she could. Now it was too late. *Where are the kids?*

He reached for his phone. Kristin was at the jail checking an inmate who'd gotten hurt in the fight at the Saddle Up last night. He was hoping he could catch her before she left to go home.

He gave a sigh of relief when she answered. "Kristin, get over to Callie's as fast as you can. She's hurt." Next he called Virgil. "I need you at Callie's," was all he said.

"Wade," Callie whispered.

"Don't try to talk. Kristin is on the way." With a bloody hand, she reached for his shirt to pull him closer. Her hand shook and he leaned down.

"What is it?" It was clear she was trying to tell him something.

"The…kids are with…Buddy. Keep…them….away."

"I'll take care of it." Her first thought, as always, was of the kids. He stroked her arm, his heart laden with fear. "Relax. Kristin is—"

Kristin hurried through the door, bag in hand, and Virgil was a step behind her. Kristen dropped down by Callie and Wade stood. Two FBI agents stood at the door with Nigel and Wade stepped into the breakfast area, quickly poking out Buddy's number.

When Buddy answered, Wade came straight to the point. "The FBI is here. Take the kids to Jock and wait to hear from me. Just get them quickly out of Homestead."

"Got it," Buddy said. "Nobody's taking these kids."

"Tell them to be brave and I'll be there soon." That was a big relief. The kids were safe for now.

He hurried back to Callie, kneeling by Kristin. "How is she?" Kristin had stopped the bleeding and Callie had a bandage on her forehead.

"She hit this table with her head and probably has a slight concussion. Callie, I'm going to help you sit up." Wade helped, too, and soon Callie was sitting upright against the wall.

"Thanks, Kristin," Callie said, and Wade could see that she was better. But the left side of her face was blue and swollen all the way to her jaw. Anger replaced the fear.

"Did hitting the table cause the damage to her face?" he asked.

Kristin pointed to the bandage. "In my opinion, that was caused by hitting the table. Her face appears as if she's been hit very hard with something else."

Wade stood, banking down the anger. "Nigel Tremont, you're under arrest. Read him his rights, Virg."

"What the…" Nigel spluttered.

"C'mon, Sheriff, what are you trying to pull?" Agent Rod Turner asked.

"He assaulted her and that's a crime in my town."

"You don't know that," Agent David DeLeon said.

"Take a look at her face and tell me he didn't hit her."

"That's just your opinion."

"The PA confirmed it and that's all I need for an arrest. Read Mr. Tremont his rights, Virg."

"You have the right to—"

"You can't arrest me," Nigel declared in anger. "She's wanted for kidnapping. Do something."

Rod put a hand on his shoulder. "When you do something stupid like this, it makes our job difficult. You shouldn't have come over here by yourself in the first place. Go with the deputy and we'll get this straightened out."

"Put your hands behind your back," Virgil instructed. Nigel complied and Virgil snapped on the cuffs. Going out the door, Virgil was reading him his rights. David followed.

Wade didn't miss that Rod stayed behind and he knew why. He was waiting to arrest Callie and Wade had to figure out a way to stop it.

"How is Miss Lambert?" Rod asked Kristin.

Kristin frowned. "Who?"

Rod thumbed toward Callie. "Callie Austin is really Callie Lambert and she's wanted for kidnapping her brother and two sisters."

Kristin looked at Wade and he nodded, hoping she got the message. "I don't know anything about that, but I need to get Callie to my clinic to check her over and I might have to send her to San Antonio for further evaluation. Your guy did a number on her."

Bless Kristin. She got the message loud and clear.

"No," Callie said to Wade's surprise.

"C'mon." Wade swung her into his arms. "Let's get you to the clinic."

Within minutes, they had her in one of Kristin's rooms. Agent Turner waited outside.

Kristin spoke to Wade. "She has a slight concussion and her face is blue and swollen and will hurt for a while, but otherwise she's fine. I can send her to San Antonio if you want me to."

"No," Callie said again, sitting up on the bed. "I can't go to San Antonio. I have to stay here with the kids." Her hand touched her forehead. "I'm fine—just a little dazed."

Wade knew the kids were the reason she was resisting. "But it will have you out of the way so I—"

"You once said I had to face this situation. Well, that time has come and I have to deal with it. We can't keep hiding for the rest of our lives."

"So you're going to turn the kids over to Nigel?"

A tear slipped from her eye. "No. I can't do that either."

"Okay." He put his arm around her. "I'll take care of this. Agent Turner is waiting outside to arrest you. I'll take you over to the jail and put you in the holding cell."

A smile ruffled her mouth and she winced as pain registered next. "I like the holding cell."

"We're not giving the kids over until Simon and Gail get here—and hopefully not then. Nigel might be spending a long time in my jail."

"You called Simon and Gail?"

"Yeah. While Kristin was checking you over. They'll be here sometime tomorrow."

"Thank you." She closed her eyes briefly. "Where are the kids?"

"With Jock and Buddy. Would you like to talk to them?"

"Yes, please."

Wade glanced at Kristin. "Would you check and see where the agent is?"

Kristin opened the door a crack. "He's sitting in a chair, flipping through a magazine."

"Good." Wade poked out a number. "Let me know if he comes near the door."

"Okay."

"Pop, how are the kids?" Wade asked as soon as Jock answered.

"They're scared and want Callie. How are things going?"

"Not real good, but I don't have time to get into it. Please keep the kids away from the house in case the FBI come looking."

"We're on horseback headed for the deer cabin on Spring Creek. They'll be well hidden."

"Thanks, Pop. Callie wants to talk to them."

"Just a minute. We have to stop. Little bit's riding with me and I'll put her on first."

Wade handed Callie the phone.

"Callie, come get me," Mary Beth cried. "I'm scared."

Callie swallowed. "It's all right, sweetie. Jock will take good care of you until I can get there. Be good for me. I love you."

"Love you, too."

"Callie, are you okay?" Adam's worried voice came on. "Are you in jail?"

"I'm fine and I'm not in jail." At least she didn't have to lie to him.

"Is *he* there?"

"Yes."

"Then I'm coming back."

"No," Callie shouted, and winced. "Your sisters need you. Help take care of them."

"I will."

"I wanna talk." She could hear Brit and in a second she was on the line. "Callie, I'm scared."

Tears stung her eyes. It wasn't like Brit to admit she was frightened. "I need you to be brave for me and help with Mary Beth. Soon we'll be together again."

"Okay. Buddy and Rascal are with us and Mary Beth likes that. Adam and me do, too."

"Good." Buddy was there and somehow that made her feel better. He hadn't been there for her when she was small and now he would protect Glynis's children as if they were his own. "Mind Buddy and Jock. I love you and I'll be in touch."

"Love you," she heard chorused in the background as she hung up.

She looked at Wade. "I'm ready."

Wade nodded to Kristin and she opened the door. Agent Turner was immediately on his feet, walking into the small room.

"How is she?" he asked Kristin.

"Slight concussion and a swollen and bruised face, but she'll be fine in a few days."

"Then there's no need for a trip to San Antonio?"

Kristin glanced at Wade and replied, "No."

"Okay, then. Callandra Lambert, you're under arrest for the kidnapping of Adam Lambert, Brittany Lambert and Mary Beth Lambert. You have the right to remain silent. You—" He reached for his handcuffs and Wade stepped in front of him.

"I don't think so. She's not in any condition to escape."

The two men eyed each other and the agent shrugged and backed off. "Where are the kids, Miss Lambert?"

"I'm not saying anything until my lawyer gets here."

"Suit yourself, but it will go a lot easier on you if you cooperate."

"We'll continue this questioning at the jail," Wade interrupted, helping Callie off the table.

At the door, Callie hugged Kristin. "Thank you.

"If you need anything, and I mean anything, just call me."

"I will."

Wade held Callie's elbow as they walked out to his car. She sat in the front seat and the agent crawled into the back. No one said a word as Wade drove to the jail. Virgil met them at the door.

"I put Tremont in the basement. Is that what you wanted?" Virgil asked Wade.

"Yes. That's fine." He went to the holding cell and held the door open. Callie walked in and Wade closed it.

Virgil frowned. "Why you locking up Callie? Did Tremont do that to her face?"

"In my office, Virg."

Wade closed his door and he told Virgil the whole story.

"So that's why she was so touchy when she first came here."

"Yes."

Virg's face contorted as he did some thinking. "You're not gonna let them have her, are you, Sheriff?"

"Not without a very good fight, and even then, I'm still not sure. Call Ray and tell him I need him for extra duty."

"You got it. That Tremont's causing a ruckus and the agent's trying to calm him down."

"Let him complain all he wants. He's staying put."

Virg nodded and went to call Ray. Wade dialed Miranda, figuring she had a right to know. Miranda was very understanding and said she'd be in as soon as she could. In a matter of hours, the whole city council was going to be barreling down on him like an eighteen-wheeler out of control. He was ready. There was no way they were going to force him to give up those kids.

The agents came in and took seats across from Wade's desk. "What are you trying to pull, Sheriff?" Rod asked the same question he'd asked at Callie's house.

Wade shrugged. "Nothing. I'm just doing my job—protecting the citizens of Loveless County."

"But it seems you have a personal stake in this," David commented.

"I always have a personal stake when I see an injustice being done," he answered without missing a beat.

Rod leaned forward. "Listen, we're not a fan of Tremont's. We're only doing our jobs, too. We have a warrant for Miss Lambert, and we'd appreciate it if you'd tell us where the kids are so we can take them back to New York and get the hell out of your town."

"Where would you take them?"

Rod blinked. "Excuse me?"

"Tremont is staying in my jail at least until Wednesday when the judge comes through. Bail will probably be set at that time. So I want to know exactly where will you be taking the children?" He held up a hand. "You don't have to answer because I know—Child Protective Services. I wouldn't wish them on any kid. The caseworkers are overworked and underpaid and the kids pay the price."

"It's the system, Montgomery," David replied. "You are familiar with the system, aren't you?"

"Yeah, but there's a woman out there who loves those kids more than life itself and that's who they should be with. Until that happens, one way or the other, I'm going to stall you boys until the cows come home."

"You're hindering our investigation," David pointed out.

"How?" Wade lifted an eyebrow. "Miss Lambert's in jail and she's not saying a word until her lawyer gets here. I haven't crossed any lines of misconduct."

"Yeah, Sheriff," David snickered. "It's a very thin line and you're skating close to the edge."

Rod stood. "Looks like we're stuck here until the lawyer arrives. Is there any place to stay in this one-horse town?"

"There's a motel out on the highway."

"Is it decent?"

"Depends on how you define decent. It has a bed and a bath."

David got to his feet. "And probably cockroaches the size of armadillos."

"Nah." Wade's mouth twitched in amusement. "Not quite that big."

Rod hesitated in the doorway. "Callie Lambert better be in that cell in the morning. If she's not, you can kiss that badge goodbye."

Wade nodded, understanding their viewpoint. He didn't like it, but he didn't see the situation quite the way they did.

Before he could think about it any further, Miranda came hurrying into his office. "I was just talking to Callie. She looks awful. She said her stepfather hit her."

"He bounced her off a wall and she hit a table."

"Was that the FBI who just left?"

"Yes."

"You're not going to let them have her and the kids, are you?"

"Nope. Not in my plans."

Miranda's brow wrinkled. "I guess I need to notify everyone on the council and the Home Free Committee."

"Why don't you wait until morning?"

"No. I have to do it now. I don't want this to be more difficult than it has to be."

"Fine. But I *don't* want them over here telling me how to do my job."

"That's your problem." She headed for the door. "I'll be in my office if you need me."

Wade kept waiting for the phone to ring from council members wanting answers. But only the usual calls came through.

Virgil and Ray finished up for the night and went home. Wade took the night duty, but wanted them back early in the morning. He went along to the holding cell and unlocked it. Callie was sitting on the cot, her back against a wall, and his heart twisted at the lonely sight.

"You okay?" he asked, sitting by her.

She went into his arms and he held her. "I don't know. My head hurts, but all I can think about are the kids. I don't want them to be afraid, but I can't do anything to stop this or their fears."

He reached for his phone. "Let's see how they're doing."

Callie talked for a minute then handed Wade the phone. "Buddy said that they played checkers for a long time and Mary Beth fell asleep in his arms. He said he'd hold her the rest of the night because he didn't want to wake her. Adam and Brit are asleep on a cot with their arms around each other. Jock is snoozing in a chair by them." She wiped away a tear. "I was so lucky to find such good people to care for them."

He pulled her closer. "Kristin said not to sleep for a couple of hours because of the possible concussion, but it's way past that now, so try to relax and go to sleep. Tomorrow will be a busy day. Your lawyer will be here and decisions will be made for the kids' future—and yours."

"Are you staying in here with me?"

"Wild horses couldn't drag me out."

"This will be our last night together." Her hand caressed the back of his neck and everything he felt for her ballooned inside him into a wad of intense pain.

"Go to sleep," he whispered, not wanting to think about a life without her. He had one night and he'd hold her until the darkness faded into the light of a new day.

As the jail became quiet and all he could hear was her steady breathing, he prayed for a miracle. A miracle that would keep Callie and the kids in Homestead.

Miracles were in short supply and the truth was that Callie would be leaving tomorrow to face her life in New York.

Without him.

And he had to let her go.

CHAPTER TWENTY

THE NEXT MORNING, the sheriff's office was a hive of activity, with concerned citizens making their opinions known. Most of them were supporting Callie, but there were also many eager to find fault with the Home Free Program.

Clint Gallagher was one of them. "Let the FBI have her," he thundered. "We don't need this kind of publicity for Homestead."

"I agree," Arlen piped up.

Kristin, who was there attending to Callie's wound, came into the office and linked her arm through Clint's. "I think it's time to take you home."

"Not until this is settled."

"It's settled. Wade will handle it," Kristin said in a voice Wade had never heard her use before. Evidently Clint hadn't either because he went with her without uttering another word.

"The whole city council is coming up the walk," Virgil alerted him.

"Barbara Jean…"

"I know. Hold your calls."

"Yes, and show them in."

"I'm going," Arlen said. "I'm sure the city council feels the same way I do—stop this before the publicity gets out of hand."

Wade had time for a couple of deep breaths before the council descended on him.

"What the hell's going on, Wade?" Rudy Satterwhite demanded. "Is it true she kidnapped those kids?"

"The stepfather was abusing them and she did the only thing she could."

"Oh, how awful." Frances Haase held a hand to her chest.

"Still, she's a wanted criminal," Rudy insisted. "We don't need that kind of element here. I vote that Wade let the FBI have her and get the focus off our town."

"I have to agree," Max Beltrane said. "I like Callie, but this isn't good for Homestead."

"I disagree," Miranda spoke up. "We support our citizens especially when they're in trouble. What's it going to look like if we turn our backs on her at the first sign of a problem?"

"I agree with Miranda," Hiram said.

"Me, too." Frances nodded. "We need to support her."

Everyone looked at Ruth, who once again had the deciding vote. It would either be a deadlock or they'd support Callie. Wade hated to tell them that this really wasn't up for a vote. He was the sheriff and this was his decision. That might be high-handed, but it was the way he felt. And they weren't going to change his mind.

Ruth took a moment. "I abhor abuse, especially of defenseless children. Callie's done a lot of good for this town in a short amount of time, so I vote to support her."

"Wake up, woman," Rudy shouted. "She's a wanted criminal."

Ruth bristled. "I do not appreciate being spoken to in that manner."

Miranda put an arm around Ruth. "I'm sure Rudy didn't mean it the way it sounded."

"Like hell. I made my position clear." Saying that, he stormed out.

"He was rather rude," Frances commented as they followed.

"I'll handle it," Miranda said, and left.

Wade looked up to see Ethan standing in the doorway. "Kayla's in with Callie," he said. "If you need a place to hide those kids, just let me know."

"Thanks, Ethan. I'm sure Callie appreciates the offer." There wasn't anything Ethan wouldn't do for a child. "For now they're in a safe place."

"Good."

As Ethan and Kayla left, Noah arrived and spent a lot of time with Callie and Wade knew that helped her.

Soon the agents were back in his office. "Ready to get this over with, Sheriff?" David asked.

"Just as soon as her lawyer gets here. Her plane landed and she's on the way from San Antonio."

"Good," Rod said. "Where can we get some breakfast in this town?"

"Bertha's Kolache Shop. It's on the square and easy to find."

They left and Wade thumped his fingers on the desk. Where was Simon? He hadn't called and he didn't answer his cell. Wade needed some evidence fast.

Ethel, Odell and Wanda came to visit Callie. She told them to open the café and they hurried to do what she wanted. When the office was empty, he let her call the kids. They were fishing in the creek and seemed calmer this morning. But Callie was worried and the wait was getting to both her and Wade.

Wade waited and paced, watching the clock. The agents were also waiting in the outer office. They all seemed to be in a holding pattern. But he knew the agents weren't going to wait much longer before they forced his hand.

Suddenly, a vaguely familiar woman's voice filled the room and Wade hurried to meet Gail Baxter. She was a petite woman with black hair threaded with strands of gray. They shook hands.

"I'd like to see my client, Sheriff," she said.

"Sure. Virgil," he called. "Show Ms. Baxter to Callie's cell."

"Yes, sir."

David walked over. "That's the attorney?"

"Yes."

"Now maybe we can get this show on the road."

In minutes, Ms. Baxter was back in his office with fire in her eyes, the agents trailing behind her. "I want every possible charge filed against Nigel Tremont. I thought she was safe here, but she's been battered and bruised by that maniac. How did that happen?"

"Mr. Tremont managed to slip away from the FBI agents," Wade said.

Gail turned to confront them, but David stopped her. "Listen, Ms. Baxter. We're not responsible for Tremont and we regret what happened to Miss Lambert. We have a warrant for her arrest and we're here to enforce it."

Gail placed her hands on her hips. "When hell freezes over."

"Don't make this difficult."

"I'm not. I'm going to make this quite easy." She glanced at her watch. "My detective will be here shortly."

David's eyes narrowed. "What detective?"

"The one investigating Nigel Tremont."

"We're not waiting on any detective because this isn't about Mr. Tremont. It's about a warrant we have for Miss Lambert. She's going back to New York to face charges with or without the kids."

"This is Texas and I believe Sheriff Montgomery has jurisdiction."

"Lady, we're the FBI."

"And I'm going to stop you any way I can."

"Let me speak to Ms. Baxter," Wade intervened.

"Make it quick. We're getting a little tired of this runaround."

As soon as the agents closed the door, Gail turned to Wade. "Have you heard from Marchant?"

"No. I was hoping you had."

"Not a word all night. Last I heard, he said he'd found something significant, but didn't say what."

"Damn." Wade slammed his hat on the desk. "This isn't like him."

The door suddenly flew open and Simon stood there, a big, raw-boned man, out of breath, disheveled and looking harassed, a briefcase dangling from his hand.

"Simon," Wade said in surprise and pumped his arm in gratitude. "Have a seat." Wade grabbed bottled water out of the small refrigerator and handed it to him. "What happened to you?"

Simon sat in Wade's chair with a groan. "An hour layover took three. My cell went out and the rental car broke down. I had to walk to Homestead and a sheep farmer gave me a ride the last mile or so." He took a big swallow of water. "Damn it's hot. I hate Texas in August. My clothes are soaking wet and I smell like sheep. To say I'm pissed at this point is putting it mildly."

"Did you find anything?"

"You bet, so get the big boys in here 'cause I only have enough breath to say this once."

Relief gushed from Wade's lungs. "Okay, and this is Gail Baxter."

"Howdy, Gail. Nice to meet you in person."

"I hope you have something good."

As the agents walked into the room, Simon took another gulp of water. Wade made the introductions and let Simon run the show.

Simon plopped his briefcase on the desk. Gail and Wade looked over his shoulder.

"Everyone in this room is interested in justice, right?" He laid several folders on the desk.

"What are you up to, Marchant?"

Simon looked up. "Damn, Rob. Didn't recognize you—got sweat in my eyes." Simon glanced at Wade. "Rob and I worked a few cases in the New York area."

Wade hoped that was good. Knowing Simon, he wasn't sure. The man was known to speak his mind, uncaring of bruised egos.

"I've been busting my ass for weeks on this case and it seems Mr. Tremont has a pattern of marrying older women."

"That's not a crime," David spoke up.

"Are you gonna let me talk or you gonna keep interrupting?" David's lips tightened.

"Good." Simon shuffled through some papers. "Mr. Tremont has had four wives. Two are dead and one is in a health-care facility virtually a vegetable. All three women had car accidents. You see—" Simon leaned back "—that got me to thinking. What are the odds of three wives dying or almost dying in the same way? So I did some further checking on Glynis Lambert's car. It's been months and I figured it had been crushed by now. But it never hurts to check. The wrecker guy was really nervous at first and I knew he was hiding something so I kept pressuring him. Seems Mrs. Lambert drove a very nice Lexus and the wrecker guy had orders from Mr. Tremont to destroy the car. He even called a few times to make sure it was done. But the guy lied, hiding it out back hoping to make some money off of it."

He withdrew some photos from the briefcase and laid them in front of the agents. "I had an auto expert look at it and guess what he found?" He pointed to one photo. "That's the brake line and it's been tampered with. Very difficult to detect, but there's a slight crimping along the line causing the fluid to slowly leak out. And before you ask, the wreck didn't cause it. So boys, what we have here is a murder."

"God." Rob stood and raked a hand through his hair.

"And in case you need more convincing, Nigel Tremont is still married to his first wife, April. He failed to divorce her and they have a twelve-year-old son that Tremont consistently fails to pay child support for. He threatened to kill her if she ever told anyone that they were still married. That's another pattern for Tremont—manhandling and threatening women. Is that the type of man you want to have custody of three young children?"

David rose, a scowl on his face. "While this is interesting, Nigel Tremont is not the reason we're here. Callie Lambert is. We have to take her back and let the D.A. and courts decide her fate...and Nigel's."

"Kind of thought you boys would see it that way so I called the D.A. in New York and your superiors. I've faxed copies of all my findings so you might want to give them a call before you make any drastic decisions."

Rod shook his head. "Damn, Marchant, you're thorough."

"Yeah. Saved you boys a lot of work and I'll be sorely disappointed if that bastard's not put away."

Rod nodded. "But let's be clear on one thing. Callie Lambert is returning to New York and it will be in her best interest if the kids were here to return with her. Do you get my drift?" He looked directly at Wade.

"Rod, I think we all get what you're saying. Just wanted to level the playing field so she gets a fair shake," Simon replied.

"I'll make a call and get the details ironed out. And to prove to *y'all* that I'm a good ol' boy, I'm willing to forget all the sandbagging since we've been here."

"Thanks," Wade said as they walked out.

He immediately shook Simon's hand. "Thank you."

"Hell, Wade, you'd do the same for me." That was true.

Those bonds they'd formed in the trenches of Houston while being street cops had bound them for life.

"Still, you went above and beyond anything I expected. I'll never be able to repay you."

"Wait till you get my bill," Simon said with his dry wit. "Is there somewhere I can take a long nap?"

"Yes. Virgil," Wade shouted. Virgil appeared instantly. "Take Simon over to Callie's and tell Ethel I sent him. She'll even feed you, Simon."

"Sounds like heaven." Simon walked out with Virg, wiping his forehead with a handkerchief.

"I need to make some private phone calls," Gail said. "I have to talk to the D.A. in New York as soon as I can."

"You can have my office." Wade reached for his hat. "Just make sure there are no handcuffs in the deal. They're not handcuffing her and the kids stay with her."

"My sentiments exactly." Her eyes caught his. "Are you going to tell Callie? Or do you want me to?"

Wade knew she wasn't talking about the deal. She was talking about the fact that Nigel had killed Callie's mother.

"I'll tell her." He didn't want her to hear that from anyone else. As he walked to her cell, he searched for words and found there were none to make this easy.

He took a moment to call his father, then went into her cell. She was sitting on the cot as before and he sat by her, taking her hand. Slowly, he told her everything Simon had discovered. He didn't leave out a thing. Her face fell, then her tears evolved into anger.

"That bastard. That bastard," she cried.

Wade just held her.

"He murdered our mother and put us through hell."

"I know." He stroked her hair, his breath burning in his throat. "He'll be put away for a very long time."

She drew back, wiped her face with the back of her hands. "What happens to the kids?"

"Gail is on the phone with the D.A. in New York, trying to work out a deal." He tucked her hair behind her ear. "As soon as that's done, the agents will take you back to New York."

"So it's time?" Her voice cracked.

"Yes, it's time. I called Jock and he's bringing the kids in."

Her tear-filled eyes looked into his. "So this is goodbye?"

He nodded, unable to speak.

Her arms crept around his neck and they held on tight. "Thank you for everything."

He gently kissed a swollen cheek, then took her lips in a slow goodbye. "If you need me for anything, you call."

"I will," she breathed against his lips.

"Take care of yourself and those kids."

She nodded and he quickly left the cell before tears overtook him. They'd known this day had been coming, but neither were really prepared.

CALLIE DREW UP HER KNEES and wrapped her arms around them. So many emotions threatened to choke her, but she had to be strong for the kids. She wouldn't tell them about their mother just yet. It would be later when they were all strong enough to discuss what had happened.

She ran her hand along the cot, remembering the night she and Wade had stolen a time out of time. Sitting on the cot reminded her of all those good emotions—ones she'd never feel again.

Unable to stop them, more tears came. She cried for a mother she'd lost too quickly and needlessly. And she cried for the man she was leaving behind.

That done, she stood and dried her eyes. She was ready to face a future far away from Homestead, Texas.

Gail worked a deal with the D.A. The agents would bring Callie and the kids to New York without restraints and the kids would not be taken from her. In the morning, Callie would face a judge to decide her fate. But Gail assured Wade it was only procedure. He knew Gail would make sure Callie didn't spend any time in jail.

Jock called as they entered town and Wade brought Callie out. Rod was waiting with a car to take them to San Antonio for a flight. David had left with Nigel earlier.

When Wade opened the door, half the town was waiting outside on the lawn and across the street. They wanted to see what happened to Callie. She'd touched a lot of people in the short time she'd been here.

Jock slowly drove his truck behind Rod's car. The back door opened and three kids jumped out, running to Callie. She knelt and caught them close to her.

"Callie, Callie, Callie," they all cried, and she hugged and kissed them.

Adam drew away as he saw her face. "What happened?"

"I'll tell you later," she answered. "We have to go."

"Where we going?" Mary Beth asked.

"Home to New York."

Three faces fell. "We have to go," Callie said again. "The FBI agent is waiting."

The kids ran to Jock and Buddy, who were standing by the truck. They hugged and said goodbye.

"You come back soon," Jock said, his voice shaky.

"I promise." Adam kissed his palm and held it to his chest.

Callie hugged her father. "Goodbye, Buddy."

He blinked away a tear. "Now I've never been out of Texas or on a plane, but if you need me, I'll get on one of those big birds in a second."

"A visit would be nice."

"Miss Lambert," Rod called. "It's time to go."

The kids ran to Wade. He lifted Mary Beth in his arms, and Brit and Adam clung to his waist. He fought to breathe.

"Goodbye," he managed. "Take care of your big sister."

"I will." Tears trailed down Adam's cheeks.

"I love you," Mary Beth said, then whispered, "I'll leave Fred then we'll have to come back and get him."

"I'll take care of Fred." Wade tried to smile, but his face was frozen. They wouldn't be coming back for Fred.

"I love you, too." Brit held him tighter.

His heart melted and he didn't know how much longer he could keep this up. He knelt down to face them. "Love you guys, too. Be good for Callie."

One more fierce hug and they walked slowly to Callie, who was hugging Ethel, Odell, Wanda, Noah, Kristin, Kayla, Ethan and Miranda.

Callie glanced briefly at Wade before she joined the kids in the backseat. Gail was already in the front. The car slowly pulled away and the townspeople waved goodbye. His eyes stayed with the car until it rounded the courthouse. They were gone and his life would never be the same.

Not ever again.

CHAPTER TWENTY-ONE

THE NEXT MORNING CALLIE WENT before the judge with the kids clinging to her. She couldn't make them sit with her friend Beth. They'd decided if she was going to jail, they were going with her. But in light of the new evidence against Nigel, the judge dismissed the charges with a sharp reprimand, and awarded her full custody of the children and made her executor of their estate. It was over. The terrible nightmare was over.

Nigel went to jail with several charges against him. Callie left his fate in the hands of the court, grateful he was out of their lives.

They went out to eat to celebrate, but the kids were quiet. Callie was, too. The transition to their old life wasn't going to be easy. They'd left their hearts in Homestead. But as they'd proven when they'd gone to Texas, the kids adapted easily. Soon, they would fall back into the routine of their lives and their time in Homestead would be a distant memory.

For her, it would be more difficult. The memory of Wade would always be with her. But now she had to concentrate on the kids and their future.

WADE WALKED INTO THE LIBRARY for a meeting of the Home Free Committee. Everyone was present—Arlen, Frances, Ruth and Miranda.

"Sorry I'm late," he said slipping into his seat. He knew what the meeting was about—what to do with Callie's house.

"Everyone knows why we're here." Miranda started the meeting. "We have to make a decision about Callie's house."

Wade leaned forward. "We signed a year contract with her."

"But she broke it," Arlen pointed out.

"Not necessarily. Her father is running the café, keeping it open and taking care of the place."

"Who gave Buddy permission to do that?" Arlen asked.

"I did," Miranda said. "The café is good for Homestead and as long as we can keep it open, it benefits everyone."

"You people are missing the point here. The house is in good shape now and we could put it on the market and get a fair price. I could probably get a buyer within the month, and in my opinion that would benefit Homestead. Isn't that what we all want? The city could use the money."

"There's no place in the contract that stipulates the owner can't leave the property for a period of time." Miranda folded her hands across the contract. "We signed a contract with Callie and legally the house is hers. Her father is there taking care of things and that doesn't say to me that Callie has abandoned the house." She paused. "I vote to honor the contract."

"Everyone knows how I vote," Wade said.

Arlen slumped back in his chair. "The owner is not here. Do you people not understand that?"

"I think you're the one who doesn't understand," Wade snapped back.

"Why do these meetings have to be so stressful?" Frances asked in her perfect librarian voice.

"Because we all have different opinions," Wade told her. "That's just the way it is."

"Sadly, yes." Frances thought for a minute. "I vote to honor the contract."

Arlen snorted. "Well, Ruth, you don't get to be the deciding vote this time."

Wade pushed himself to his feet, needing to get away. He strolled quickly to the door.

"She's not coming back, Wade," Arlen shouted after him. "It's time you faced it."

Maybe it was. Maybe it was time to face a lot of things—just as soon as the pain stopped. And he didn't know if that was ever going to happen.

AUGUST WAS COMING TO A CLOSE and the kids were getting ready to go back to school. Callie was looking for work, but the kind of job she wanted wasn't available. Beth still worked at the old restaurant and told her the new chef was working out quite well and had no plans to leave. And Callie had a different kind of problem—she found Nigel had gone through a lot of the kids' trust funds and he'd sold the house in the Hamptons. She wasn't sure what he'd done with all the money, but now she desperately needed a job—a job where she could be at home at night for the kids. She not only needed to support them all, she also needed to replenish the money in the children's college funds.

During the day, she was restlessly searching for that perfect little restaurant that needed a daytime executive chef. But there wasn't one. She kept looking, though.

One day, she drove to New Jersey to thank Simon Marchant in person. She figured she owed him that much. They had a very good visit and she learned a lot more about Wade. He and Wade had gone to the police academy together and had also been street cops on the same beat. Simon said that Wade had saved his life once and there wasn't anything he wouldn't do for him.

Callie left, impressed but not surprised at what Wade had done for his friend. He'd risked a lot for her, too, and oh, how she missed him. The kids had talked to Wade, Jock and Buddy several times, but Callie hadn't talked to Wade. It would have been too painful.

The kids were upstairs and Callie sat in John's study, trying to figure out their finances. They'd have to sell the brownstone and move into something smaller. Everything overwhelmed her and despair wedged in her throat. She was unhappy and the kids weren't adjusting like she'd hoped.

What should I do?

She wanted to honor John's wishes. He'd been the only father she'd ever known and she loved him. A paperweight with Harvard on it caught her eye.

What should I do? I need a sign—one small sign.

She heard the kids coming down the stairs and wondered what they were up to. They marched into the study, holding hands.

"We want to have a meeting," Adam announced.

"Okay." Callie got up, came around the desk and sank to the floor. They gathered around her. "What's up?"

"We've been talking about Daddy."

"You have?" That surprised her. She was sure they'd been talking about the people in Homestead.

"Yes. Daddy and me talked a lot about the future. He wanted me to enjoy all the things he had as a boy and he wanted me to go to his alma mater. That was fine with me 'cause I wanted to be just like him."

Callie touched Adam's serious face. "I know, sweetie."

"But Daddy also told me if I decided to do something else, that he'd understand. He only wanted me to be happy."

"He told me that, too," Brit said.

"I don't remember," Mary Beth said, crawling into Callie's lap. "But I loved Daddy and he said I was his little princess and I was always happy. But I'm not happy now, Callie."

Callie kissed her cheek. "You're not?"

"No."

"Me, neither," Adam said.

"I'm certainly not." Brit made a face.

Callie knew where all this was leading. The sign she'd asked for had come.

"Your daddy is there," Adam went on. Callie had told them the story of Buddy and Glynis. "And you should be with him. Our mother was born there and we have roots there, too. When Mommy and Daddy were alive, our home was here. But they're gone and now our home is with Wade, Jock and Buddy and all our other friends."

Adam's words rang true, but she had to be strong. "I appreciate what you're saying and I know you miss everyone. I do, too, but we haven't given this enough time."

Three gloomy faces stared back at her.

"You always said we could discuss things and vote," Adam reminded her. "We'd have to be united or we'd be miserable."

Callie chewed on her lip. She hated it when they threw her words back at her. They were too young to make these kinds of decisions, but then she'd let them vote to run away. So now…

"We've changed, Callie. You have, too. And if we return to Homestead and I still want to go to Harvard when I graduate high school, I can apply. It would be a long way, but if Brit, Mary Beth or I really wanted to, we could. Of course, we wouldn't be able to go to Dad's private school, but I don't think he'd mind."

This kid was getting too smart and Callie felt a kink in her resolve. Going back to Homestead would certainly alleviate their financial problems. She had a job and a home there, but… She glanced at the family portrait on the wall of John, Glynis, Adam, Brit, Mary Beth and herself. They were all smiling and happy—a family, like John had wanted for his ideal world. Sometimes life wasn't ideal, though. Theirs certainly hadn't been. That family in the portrait was a loving memory—of the past.

John couldn't have known what would happen to them because of Nigel. So many things had happened to her, and to the children, that were beyond her control. It was time for new plans, a new future. It was clear now. They had a new family who'd been there for them when they'd badly needed someone. And she needed Wade more than she'd ever imagined.

She smiled at Adam. "How did you get to be so smart?"

He shrugged. "I don't know."

Brit raised her hand.

"What are you doing?" Callie asked

"Getting ready to vote."

"Oh."

"I vote we go home and marry Wade," Brit said quickly at her silence.

"Me, too," Adam said before she could get another word in.

Mary Beth raised both arms, then looped them around Callie's neck. "Let's go home, Callie. Fred misses me."

She gave the portrait one last glance. "I vote we go home, too."

"We're Texans," Adam shouted. "And we're going home."

Darn tootin' they were Texans. Callie knew that now. Once a Texan, always a Texan. They gave high fives, laughing and happy—the way they should be.

CALLIE'S CAFÉ WAS CLOSING for the night. It was Saturday and it had been a busy day. Jock and Buddy relaxed in the rockers, enjoying the warm breeze. Wade sat on the steps, his back against a pillar, watching the brilliant array of stars and wondering where Callie was tonight.

Wherever she was, he hoped she was happy. The publicity over her arrest hadn't hurt the Home Free Program. It was still going strong. People were coming just about every week. Greer Bell had been approved and was moving into the old Farley place. She'd been born in Homestead and was coming home to Loveless County with her nine-year-old daughter.

Outgoing Brit would have been a perfect playmate for her, but Brit wasn't here. Neither was Callie. Again, he wondered how long before the pain stopped.

"Ever been to New York?" Buddy asked.

"Nu-uh," Jock said.

"I was there once a long time ago," Wade replied. "Why?"

"I'm thinking of going to see Callie and the youngins. Never been on a plane, though, and that scares the crap out of me."

"You know, I might like to see New York," Jock said.

Was he serious? His father hated every place but Texas. The kids were just too big of a pull, though.

"Why don't we all go and surprise them?" Buddy suggested.

The offer was tempting. The thought of never seeing her again was about to kill him. So why couldn't he go? Virg could handle things around here for a few days. He'd see her face, be able to touch her, then maybe the pain wouldn't be so bad.

Ethel, Essie, Odell and Wanda came out the door. "There's a dance over at the VFW tonight, Jock. How about you and me go dancing?"

"Ethel, are you out of your mind? I haven't danced in years and dancing with you just might kill me."

Ethel laughed. "Oh, Jock. You're a devil with compliments."

"Hummph."

"How about you, Buddy?" Essie asked. "Care to go dancing?"

"Thanks for the offer, Essie, but I gave up dancing when I gave up drinking."

"Well, Sheriff, that leaves you." Essie zeroed in on him. "But with that hangdog expression, we wouldn't have any fun."

"Wanda and me are going," Odell said. "And no, Mama, you can't go with us."

"Your sister and me will find our own dates or just go by ourselves."

"Just don't expect me to take you home when you've had one too many."

"Now you listen here…"

A car drove up to the curb. "Ethel, looks like you have a late customer," Jock said.

"They can just go down to the Dairy Queen 'cause I'm through for the night."

Wade slowly stood as he saw the blond hair. *Callie.* Oh my God. It was Callie. Before he could move, three kids barreled out of the car. He met them halfway, gathering them into his arms.

"We're back. We're back," Brit shouted.

Wade just held them, kissing their warm cheeks.

Adam broke loose and ran to Jock, who'd come down the steps. Jock grabbed him and Adam buried his face in Jock's stomach. "I came back, Pop. Just like I promised."

"You sure did, boy, and I ain't never seen such a good sight." Jock's hands shook as he stroked Adam's hair.

Brit and Mary Beth raced to hug Jock, then Buddy. Rascal jumped up and down barking until Mary Beth hugged him. They danced up the steps to Ethel and the gang for more hugs.

"Wade, where's Fred?" Mary Beth called. "I have to tell him I'm back."

"He's on a table in the foyer."

Mary Beth charged into the house with Rascal on her

heels. In a second, she was back, dancing around as if hot coals were beneath her feet.

Wade's eyes were on Callie. Her hair was longer and hung loosely around her shoulders. Her blue eyes were misty and she was the most beautiful sight he'd ever seen.

He took a step toward her, but Buddy came around him and took his daughter in his arms.

"Ah, girl, it's good to have you home," Buddy said.

Callie kissed his cheek. "It's good to be home."

"I don't know why you're back, but I'm glad."

"We came back to marry Wade," Brit announced.

"Oh." The word slipped from Buddy's lips as he stared at Wade.

"Now that's about the best idea I've ever heard," Jock said. "Maybe we need to vote on it."

Brit shook her head. "No. We already voted." She placed her hands on her hips, her eyes pinning Wade. "So are you gonna marry us or not?"

"Yeah," Jock said. "We're waitin' for an answer."

Wade heard their mischievous voices, but his eyes and thoughts were on Callie. She was back. His world suddenly righted itself. She lifted an eyebrow and he realized she was waiting for an answer.

"Yes," he said in a hoarse voice. "Yes, yes, most definitely yes." He reached for her then and held her in his arms, needing to touch her. His lips found hers and they shared a long, deep kiss of love and hope.

The sound of clapping broke them apart, but he didn't let Callie go. He was never going to do that again.

"How would you kids like a ride to the ranch?" Jock said. "Give Callie and Wade some time alone."

"Yay. Yay." Brit caught Jock's hand. "How's Babe?"

"Gettin' fat."

Buddy picked up Mary Beth. "Think Rascal and me will go, too."

"Can we ride tonight?" Adam asked, taking Jock's other hand.

"Nu-uh. Remember I told you it's dangerous to ride at night. Could hurt the horse, could hurt yourself."

"I remember everything you told me."

"Good. 'Cause sometimes I forget and you might have to remind me."

"I will, Pop."

They waved bye as they went out the gate.

Callie and Wade walked hand in hand up the steps and Callie hugged her old friends.

Wanda held out her hand; a small diamond sparkled on her finger.

"Oh my, you're engaged. Congratulations." She hugged Odell and Wanda, so very happy for them.

"We're gonna have the biggest blowout this town's ever seen," Ethel said with pride.

"I'd rather have a small wedding," Wanda mumbled.

"My only son is having a big weddin'." Ethel's voice grew angry.

"Mama."

"Let's go." Essie came to the rescue. "These two lovebirds do not want to listen to the Stromiski family feud."

"See you on Monday," Ethel called as they left. "And, Callie, I haven't had a drag."

Callie gave her a thumbs-up sign.

She and Wade went inside smiling and she stopped for a moment, soaking up the ambience of this old house, from the hardwood floors to the antique light fixtures. This was home. This was where she belonged. Adam was so right.

Cupping her face, Wade kissed her long and deep. Ah, this was where she belonged most of all—in his arms—in his life.

"I missed you like hell," he whispered against her lips.

"Me, too," she murmured, stroking his shoulders.

"What made you change your mind?"

She told him about their financial situation. "But it wasn't just that. We were very unhappy and Adam pointed out that we've all changed, our lives have changed. So many things happened beyond our control and New York isn't home anymore. I finally realized that. Home is where the heart is and our hearts are here with the people we love. I know John would understand."

Wade tucked her hair behind her ears. "You have the most beautiful heart and I love you more than life itself."

She smiled. "I love you, too."

They kissed slowly, reverently, then Wade whispered, "First order of business is a marriage license and Noah can marry us by the end of the week."

"Sounds perfect." Her eyes sparkled, then a melancholy expression came over her face.

"What?" he asked.

"I always thought John would be the one to walk me down the aisle, but it seems so right that Buddy, my father, will be the one to give me away. When I first started this quest to keep the kids safe, I never dreamed I'd be rewarded in so many ways." She kissed him briefly. "I found my father, wonderful friends and the man of my dreams."

He took her hand and they made their way upstairs. They stopped on the landing for another lingering kiss, then she caressed his face. "Every night I tell the girls a story and they insisted on one on the plane."

"What was the story about?" He caught her fingers in his mouth.

Her eyes twinkled. "Once upon a time, there was a sheriff in a small town in Texas and he was very lonely. Then one day, a lady came from New York with three kids and a big secret. The sheriff noticed she was tense and defensive. But he became her friend, her lover and her soul mate. And they lived happily ever after in a blue house on Bluebonnet Street in Homestead, Texas."

He grinned. "A true tale if I ever heard one."

They shared a laugh as Wade led her into the bedroom. Callie knew she'd found true happiness and she was going to hold on for all it was worth.

If you enjoyed what you just read,
then we've got an offer you can't resist!

Take 2 bestselling love stories FREE!

Plus get a FREE surprise gift!

Clip this page and mail it to Harlequin Reader Service®

IN U.S.A.
3010 Walden Ave.
P.O. Box 1867
Buffalo, N.Y. 14240-1867

IN CANADA
P.O. Box 609
Fort Erie, Ontario
L2A 5X3

YES! Please send me 2 free Harlequin Superromance® novels and my free surprise gift. After receiving them, if I don't wish to receive anymore, I can return the shipping statement marked cancel. If I don't cancel, I will receive 6 brand-new novels every month, before they're available in stores. In the U.S.A., bill me at the bargain price of $4.69 plus 25¢ shipping and handling per book and applicable sales tax, if any*. In Canada, bill me at the bargain price of $5.24 plus 25¢ shipping and handling per book and applicable taxes**. That's the complete price, and a savings of at least 10% off the cover prices—what a great deal! I understand that accepting the 2 free books and gift places me under no obligation ever to buy any books. I can always return a shipment and cancel at any time. Even if I never buy another book from Harlequin, the 2 free books and gift are mine to keep forever.

135 HDN DZ7W
336 HDN DZ7X

Name	(PLEASE PRINT)
Address	Apt.#
City	State/Prov.	Zip/Postal Code

Not valid to current Harlequin Superromance® subscribers.

Want to try two free books from another series?
Call 1-800-873-8635 or visit www.morefreebooks.com.

* Terms and prices subject to change without notice. Sales tax applicable in N.Y.
** Canadian residents will be charged applicable provincial taxes and GST.
All orders subject to approval. Offer limited to one per household.
® are registered trademarks owned and used by the trademark owner or its licensee.

SUP04R

©2004 Harlequin Enterprises Limited

HARLEQUIN *Super Romance*

COLD CASES: L.A.
Giving up is not an option.

AND JUSTICE FOR ALL
by Linda Style

With three unsolved murders and only one suspect,
Detective Jordan St. James demands justice. He's
convinced the suspect, a notorious mob boss, also
killed his mother. What St. James doesn't know is
that he's putting his source, Laura Gianni—and
her daughter—in terrible danger.

On sale January 2006

Available wherever Harlequin books are sold.

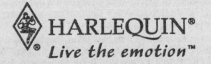

HARLEQUIN®
Live the emotion™

HSRAJFA0106

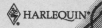

Kim

COMING NEXT MONTH

#1320 MORE TO TEXAS THAN COWBOYS • Roz Denny Fox
Home to Loveless County

Greer Bell is returning to Texas for the first time since she left as a pregnant teenager. She and her nine-year-old daughter are determined to make a success of their new dude ranch—and the last thing Greer needs is a romantic entanglement, even with the helpful and handsome Reverend Noah Kelley.

Home to Loveless County...because Texas is where the heart is.

#1321 NOT WITHOUT THE TRUTH • Kay David
The Operatives

Lauren Stanley is afraid of almost everything. Despite that, she goes to Peru to find a mysterious man named Armando Torres. It's the only way to discover the truth about her past. But before she can, an "accident" has her forgetting everything she once knew.

The Operatives—sometimes the most dangerous people you know are the only ones you can trust.

#1322 LONE STAR RISING • Darlene Graham
The Baby Diaries

Recently widowed, Robbie McBride Tellchick and her three young sons are starting over. Broke and pregnant, Robbie faces overwhelming odds as she tries to rebuild her life and gain financial independence. Firefighter Zack Trueblood wants to be by her side every step of the way, but how can Robbie let herself love this man when she's carrying someone else's child?

#1323 AND JUSTICE FOR ALL • Linda Style
Cold Cases: L.A.

With three unsolved murders and only one suspect, Detective Jordan St. James demands justice. He's convinced the suspect, a notorious mob boss, also killed his biological mother. What St. James doesn't know is that he's putting his source, single mother Laura Gianni—and her daughter—in terrible danger.

#1324 PARTY OF THREE • Joan Kilby
Single Father

Ben Gillard finally has a chance to build a real relationship with his twelve-year-old son, instead of being just a weekend dad. Unfortunately he and Danny can't seem to find any common ground. What a surprise it is that straitlaced, uptight Ally Cummings is the one to make their family of two into a party of three.

#1325 PAST LIES • Bobby Hutchinson

As soon as Alex makes peace with his birth father, long presumed dead after disappearing in the wilderness, he'll be leaving Alaska for good. Which means Ivy can't have a future with the man she's falling in love with. A man lost in grief...a man who doesn't even like to fly! To a pilot like Ivy, that should be reason enough to end it. So what's stopping her?